VIC VALENTINE:
LOUNGE LIZARD FOR HIRE

Will Viharo

THRILLVILLE PRESS

Seattle, WA

*To Scott,
cheers -
Will*

Front cover art by Matt Brown:
mattbrown22.myportfolio.com
Back cover art and design by Dyer Wilk:
aseasonofdusk.com
Formatting by Rik Hall – WildSeasFormatting.com

ISBN: 978-0-692-16485-3

First Printing
Printed in the United States of America

Published by Thrillville Press

www.thrillville.net

For the Love of My Life, Monica Cortes Viharo, PhD

AKA "The Tiki Goddess"

Chapter One
BORED AGAIN

Sometimes all you have to do to find something is stop looking for it, and let it find you. The proof of this theory was right there in front of me: a woman who looked like she could, would, and probably should kick my ass. And yet loved me anyway. Go figure. I didn't deserve her for so many reasons, not least of which was my fading zest for life, even with her improbable presence. She was a latecomer to my private party, if she came at all.

My sex drive was stuck in neutral, so it was time for me to switch gears. This despite being happily hitched, after decades of self-delusional detours down the rocky road of romance, to the dame that had been waiting at this destination all along, eager and willing to fulfill my deepest, darkest desires. She was so organically sensual it was like I conjured her up from the depths of an adolescent wet dream. But she was so much more than that. For one thing, she could cook. Best of all, perhaps, she was the nurturing maternal figure I'd never really had, with one mother of a figure to boot. Without her, I'd be just another lonely old man tripping over his own nose hairs.

The question now had become, was I still dreaming? Life is like that, at least for me. You never know if tangible consciousness is all it's cracked up to be, or if your nocturnal sojourns reveal the true nature of reality. But then one day your brain and body just quit working, both rotting in the dirt like so much forgotten fertilizer, and what's left of any true value? Love, that's what. Even if it doesn't last, either. Sometimes it just makes you *feel* immortal, and if you're really lucky, immoral, too.

It was hard for me to accept that I was now at the age where, if I simply dropped dead, people would no longer say, "He was so young," but "he wasn't that old." It was just a matter of time before they said, "I didn't even know he was still alive." If they said anything at all. Tomorrow will always come, even if my wife doesn't. We just won't always be here to see it. It's like I grew old suddenly, as opposed to gradually. What a gyp.

The average life span is broken up into four seasons: the first twenty years are spring, the second are summer, the third are fall, and the final twenty are winter. That's assuming you even make it to 80. By that metric, I was already deep into late autumn, past even the "September of My Years." More like October, around my favorite holiday, Halloween. All I had to look forward to after this phase was Christmas without resurrection. But that's seasonally correct, I guess. I love winter, and fall. I hate summer, though I love the song "Summer Wind." Spring is okay, especially here in Seattle, all the flowers 'n' cherry blossoms 'n' shit. Maybe I was born to be a late bloomer.

But what the hell do I know about anything? All I know is I don't really know anything for sure. Don't ask me to explain the mysteries of life, especially my own. It's all a dice roll in a dream to me.

I pondered all of this intellectually improvisational jazz as we sat at the bar of one of our favorite Seattle dinner spots, Vito's, over on First Hill, across from one of our favorite watering holes, the Fireside Room at the Hotel Sorrento. Mrs. Vic Valentine—formerly just plain Ava Margarita Esmeralda Valentina Valdez—just seemed too good to be true, as usual. Even her moniker was a mouthful of magic. Not only was she stunningly gorgeous (especially for a gal of her vintage), exceedingly intelligent, exceptionally talented, and best of all, totally devoted to a *schlep* like me, but she maintained a mysterious source of steady income that kept us both waist deep in mushroom pasta and Martinis, without either of us having to work for it. I was no longer a private eye, but then many would argue I'd never been one to begin with, and frankly, I have no hard evidence to the contrary. Plus I no longer had to walk dogs for a living, though I still took our pup Fido out for a poop 'n' pee several times a day. My old cat Doc, named after my dear departed best friend Curtis "Doc Schlock" Jackson, was now ours to share as our own adopted fur baby, too. No perfunctory procreation or baby-sitters required, so we were free to paint the Emerald City any damn color we pleased to suit our shifting moods. I had everything I ever wanted. And yet, I couldn't ditch the feeling that something was still missing. That would probably be my sanity. I didn't think anyone but me would miss that, anyway.

I couldn't shake this ominous premonition of impending change, which disrupted my well-earned late life sense of selfish complacency. The day had started out well enough, as all of my days have since meeting and marrying the love of my life. Actually, we first met a quarter of a century ago, even before I reunited with my first long lost love, Rose, down in San Francisco. That's another love story that is too violent for me, but maybe not for you, so Google it if you want to know more. Anyway, I met Val when I answered an ad to find her cat in my neighborhood. After locating her pussy, and then making a play for her, she told me she'd only fuck me once a certain orange-hued real estate reality star billionaire bullshitter became president of the United States. We both got way more than we ever bargained for. The whole damn world did.

But now something was slightly off, because for one thing, I was no longer turned on, and my wife had noticed. But it had nothing to do with her. Lately, I wouldn't or couldn't even fuck Lili Simmons' Amish *femme fatale* character from my favorite new show *Banshee* if she were spread eagle naked on my bed. Of course, I'll never be able to test that theory, which only made me that much crankier.

I blamed my current foul mood on the weather. Like I said, that morning was another in a series of perfect mornings, like waking up from one dream into another, right next to my nude, nubile goddess in our cozy little Ballard pad, along with Doc and Fido and no, we're not into bestiality. Not yet, anyway. The slutty Seattle skies were nice 'n' moist, as usual. But then the goddamn sun came out and ruined it, like a loud, brash, rude interloper intruding on a dark, private cocktail party. Sunshine always got me down, and not just figuratively. At least that's what I tried telling my skeptical wife, who sat there radiating raw sex with effortless grace as she sipped her Martini, the object of lust and envy within a visible radius, as always. She was too good for me, and I knew it. The question that always bothered was, did *she* know it? I didn't want to be the one to blow it for me. I figured she'd figure it out eventually. Until then, I'd try to enjoy my blissful windfall until it blew back in my face.

I wasn't always this lucky. Or this insecure. Life was a lot simpler, or at least less stressful, when I was a lone lover on the loose, bed-hopping with no strings attached, even as my loneliness threatened to bog me down in the depths of fatal depression. I just kept drinking my way out of that hole (and into others), but I was drowning in booze and bodily fluids.

Then magic struck, out of the proverbial blue, the seeds to my personal salvation sewn long before I even knew any fertile soil was out there. I thought I'd hit rock bottom early on in my so-called life and career, and so I just stayed there, crawling around for crumbs. Then I hit pay dirt, romance-wise, and I've been happy or at least quasi-content ever since, a sensation that was new and rather intimidating, given my history. Since I was already in my fifties, I had thought I'd die a geriatric gigolo, getting slapped in the rest home on a regular basis for pinching the nurses' asses. Instead, I now had my own private nurse, who took good care of me, body and soul.

Val, as I liked to call her—though she was accustomed to being addressed informally as Esmeralda or Esmy or Ava or even Maggie—didn't share my doubts about our future as a married couple. In fact, she exuded confidence, integrity and awareness of both her surroundings and internal state at all times. Of course, she had a PhD in psychology among her many attributes, so self-examination came easily for her. She came easily when she examined herself, too.

It took me a while to remember and realize that "Val" was what I used to call Rose when we were dating, since her real name was Valerie, long before she changed it. I'd always joked about us getting married and me having a wife named Valerie Valentine, or Val Valentine for short. I just dug the alliteration, plus I really did want to marry her, but she disappeared on me instead.

As it turned out, my real wife did turn out to be named Val Valentine. You just never know when intuition will pay off, even if it's a dividend you never imagined.

Anyway, when I told Val I was impotent because of the rare Seattle sunshine, she scoffed. "I know what's bothering you," she said. "You're bored. That's why you can't get it up anymore, or at least as often as I need you to."

"Hard to get it up when you're feeling down," I said. I was feeling too shitty to be witty.

"I thought you said you were happier than you've ever been?"

"I am. I just don't trust it. Plus that's a low bar."

"You need something to occupy your time other than worshipping me."

"Well, I guess, though that is my favorite pastime."

She nodded with grim resignation. "I'm the quintessential Madonna-whore, I suppose, both in one body. One reason I never settled down with one person. Until you."

"I was never really into Madonna, though 'Like a Virgin' gets stuck in my head sometimes."

She smiled. "You're so stupid and sweet. I love you, Vic."

"Why?"

"Why not?"

"Okay, by that logic, why not just fall in love with the bartender?"

"I make better drinks. And he's not my type."

"And I am?"

"Obviously." She flashed her cheap wedding ring, purchased at a kiosk in a Houston mall, just before we got hitched at city hall, with my surrogate family as witnesses. Soon after that they endured Hurricane Harvey. I swore there was no connection. Not sure they believed me.

"I wish we could do it right," I said. "I mean, formally. We can afford it now."

"Sure, but what's the point?"

"I dunno. The way we did it, it felt rushed."

"Well, I did need my citizenship papers."

"Exactly my point."

"Vic, you know I love you. I must. You're poor, older than me, and your cock is withering on the vine. Fortunately you're great at cunnilingus, which is probably why no one has chopped out your tongue by now. And you make me laugh, even if it's not on purpose. You're totally devoted to me. You're genuine, you're kind, you're loyal. You're my best friend. I could've found any sucker to get me a green card. But I chose you. In fact, we were destined to be together. We just had our own separate paths to follow first. But now here we are, at our final destination."

"You make it sound so fatal."

She huffed. "Lighten up. And find something to do with yourself, besides you know what. Maybe walk dogs again. For free. Just for the exercise, at least. It'll get you out of the house before I go out of my mind."

"You're getting sick of me, I knew it."

"No, Vic. I just hate watching you sitting around watching TV all day and night."

"I don't know. Maybe. I guess you're right. You know, I have thought about writing again."

"Really?"

"No." Of course, I'm writing this, but hardly anyone knows that, except for you. It's an exclusive club.

"Didn't think so. What are your other talents? Or just…talents."

"I have none. Except for eating pussy. I guess I'm getting full."

"You were a private investigator for over twenty years. Self-trained."

"It was just something to do, to kill time. And anyway, my main reason was to find love. Mission accomplished."

"So now you're just going to spend the rest of your days basking in my limelight?"

"That's a lot better than sunlight. Not as harsh or blinding."

"And yet you still can't see the obvious. Vic, you need to do something that fulfills your big, silly heart."

"I don't even know what fulfillment feels like. I was never fulfilled as a private eye. Now I'd have to join an agency, anyway. I don't work well with others. I dig my autonomy. Writing is a solo gig, but there's so much competitive content out there now, especially with self-publishing and all. Hard to stand out. Plus nobody really reads anymore, anyway. Not even me."

"That is true, sad to agree, though I read. But I'm an anomaly. Oh, come on. There must be something else you've always wanted to do."

Just then I hard Frank Sinatra singing "I'm Gonna Live Till I Die." Vito's was an old school Italian restaurant, much like the ones I ate in with my folks while growing up back in Brooklyn. Before my dirty cop dad got shot to death in an alley by my strung-out high school sweetheart, or my mother died in an insane asylum, or my older brother jumped off the bridge. Now it was just me. I'd made it this far. Partly due to the inspiration of Frank's voice, which was always there for me, singing my blues.

"I wish I could sing," I said after some contemplation, listening to The Voice.

"You can't?"

"Can't even pick up a tune much less carry it. I've just always idolized Sinatra."

"Well, *I* can sing."

"Of course you can."

"And dance."

"I know. You were in burlesque."

"I could do it again. I'm still in shape."

"You certainly are. But what about me?"

"You could emcee."

"Emcee?"

"Yes. An impresario is often someone that can't sing or dance themselves, so they make a career out of formally presenting the talents of others."

"Gee, that sounds fulfilling as hell."

"My point is, you could still sing. Even if you can't, really. It could be part of your stage schtick. You'd have the excuse, because I'd give it to you. Especially if I stripped while I sang. Or while you sang. Or both. People would be too distracted to notice you suck."

"That's always been my M.O. anyway. So, what, we'd be like an X-rated Sonny and Cher?"

She sighed. "I would prefer a blue Steve and Eydie, but all things considered, that's probably our most realistic aspiration, considering what you bring to the table. Or don't."

"True, I'm no Louis Prima. But can you sing like Keely Smith?"

"Nobody can."

"True. So what, then?"

"We could do some banter, a little comedy skit, and then I could do a really evocative striptease number. You could wear a smoking jacket and a fez to give the whole thing that old school appeal."

"Did somebody just cut the cheese? Really, a *fez*? Seriously? That is some cornball jazz."

"You *are* corny, Vic."

I nodded. She knew me too well already. "Well, my Fedora was my trademark till I lost it, though I'm no longer posing as a private eye out of an old movie, so maybe it's time I tried on a new hat, anyway."

"It could be your new trademark, something to draw attention, like a circus ringleader. And I'd be the one-woman circus. Just don't try to tame me."

"I'm more like a clown than a tigress tamer. In fact, funny you should say that because I saw this joker perform once wearing that same outfit, a fez and smoking jacket. Only he didn't exactly perform. He just hosted B movies with his sexy wife, who was called The Tiki Goddess."

"Oh. You mean Thrillville?"

"Yeah. How did you know?"

"I saw them when I was in Oakland once, ages ago. See what I mean? That show went on for years, and that guy didn't do *anything*."

"Except wear a fez."

"So why don't you steal his act? What's he going to do, sue you? Last I heard he was walking dogs, anyway."

"Really? Like me."

"Exactly. So if he can do your old gig, why can't you do his?"

"Hm. He's like my evil doppelgänger." I shrugged out of apathetic acquiescence. "It would be something to do, anyway. Vic Valentine. Lounge lizard for hire. I do like the sound of that. Especially if you say it in an Adam West voice."

"There you go! I'll pay for some business cards. We don't need money, so we could do it for free. And I can finance the whole thing. We just need to book some random practice gigs to get the ball rolling. They have a stage here, in fact."

I was into it, but I was on my third Martini. I'd recently switched from vodka to gin, and it was like liquid inspiration. "Who or where would be interested in this sort of shit? I don't think Vito's would book a striptease act."

"Maybe not, but there are plenty of other venues that would. We could play clubs or private parties or both."

"Huh. So…hm. What will we call our act?"

Val thought for a moment, her little brainstorm brewing. Then she said, "The Voodoo Valentine Show."

"I dig it. But why Voodoo?"

"Why not? It sounds mysterious and retro and vaguely sensual."

"Like you. We could even make 'That Ol' Black Magic' our signature song. I have to admit, I'm running out of roadblocks to this trip."

"Because you know I'm on the right path."

"You always are."

"That's why I love you, Vic. You're a smart man. Just let me do the driving."

As if on cue, Louis Prima was singing "Just a Gigolo," like an affirmative omen. Once again, Val had rescued me from the road to self-ruin. I handed her my virtual keys.

So anyway, that's how I ditched the P.I. pretense for good and became a professional lounge lizard. Well, semi-professional. Whatever I choose to do, I'm faking it, anyway. Except orgasms, those are always real, at least on my end. But in business, the trick was to fool the clients long enough to finish the job and get paid. The main difference was that now I had an enterprising ally and well-funded enabler. Doc was my ally back in my detective days. But this was my next phase, my new series, so I needed a new ethnic partner in crime, like Don Johnson going from *Miami Vice* to *Nash Bridges*. In fact, wow: he also swapped an African American (Philip Michael Thomas) for a Mexican (Cheech Marin). It was all connected somehow.

So why did I feel like she was slowly slipping away from me? This new lounge act could be the glue that kept us together, because we'd be a real team, with a mission, whatever that was.

But as we all know, you don't need a mission statement other than "mission accomplished" to justify it, at least in retrospect. And sooner or later, it's all reduced to retrospect, a mess of mangled memories, like so much splattered brain matter.

We went home after dinner and, still high on life and booze and the ambient second-hand pot smoke in the Seattle air, I showed Val some scenes from movies I thought she could emulate in our routine, like the nightclub burlesque act from *The H Man* (1959*)*, Debra Paget's sensuous ritualistic dance in *The Indian Tomb* (1959)*,* and of course the opening credits of *Faster Pussycat, Kill! Kill!* (1965).

"Vic, I know how to dance," she said. "Why are you showing me these ancient movies? I mean, these particular ones?"

"What did you expect, 'Dirty Dancing' or 'Flashdance'?"

"No, did *you?*"

"Well, I just want to make sure we're on the same page."

"At least we're in the same book." She smiled and kissed me, and I got a boner for the first time in a week. I couldn't even masturbate anymore, at least not on demand. It left me feeling both physically and spiritually drained, anyway, especially now that I had no excuse to indulge in self-gratification. Maybe it was old age creeping up on me, killing me softly with my dong. Plus the older you got, the better the odds the thing would just yank right off. I was also afraid of finding a bump or something. All I knew was the hourglass of my life was draining faster and faster, and I needed to make the most of it before the sand ran out. So I caressed the vivacious hour glass body beside me until Little Elvis made a comeback.

We made love. *Finally.* I shot my wimpy wad inside of her powerful pussy, and she came in tandem, or pretended to, anyway. And then even louder shots came flying through the window and shattered our carnal ecstasy.

Doc hid under the bed and Fido started barking. I felt like Michael Corleone in T*he Godfather, Part II* except, you know, I'm not.

"Who would want to kill me?" I said, cowering on the floor amid bullets and broken glass. "I haven't even started singing yet!"

"They're not after you," Val said with customary calm. "It's me."

"How do you know?"

"I saw them following me. They were even in that restaurant. Those two well-dressed Japanese men at the bar watching us."

"I didn't notice."

"That's why you're no longer a detective, dear. Anyway, that was probably just a warning, anyway."

"From who?"

"Yakuza."

Yakuza? I got hard again. I was a big fan of Yakuza movies. In fact we'd just watched Seijun Suzuki's *Youth of the Beast* (1963), *Tokyo Drifter* (1966), *Branded to Kill* (1967), and Takashi Miike's *Ichi the Killer* (2003), *Dead or*

Alive (1999), and *Gozu* (2003), all in one long night, like those old drive-in movie marathons on TV hosted by Joe Bob Briggs. Or I did, anyway. Val fell asleep after the first two, as usual. But then she didn't have to get her Yakuza action from DVD binges like some people.

My old, dead friend Curtis Jackson—"Doc"— introduced me to many, many classic cult movies when I lived in a studio apartment over his combo bar/video store The Drive-Inn, which became a burlesque club when our mutual good friend and occasional lover Monica Ivy—now living in Portland with her own new wife—took over after his premature passing, more than a decade ago. Then we each benefitted from Doc's secret will, investing our generous portions in our respective futures. That's what allowed me to settle in Seattle after fleeing here with a movie star that may or may not have been a serial murderer, even though he was eventually exonerated. I still wasn't sure. He had wanted to make a movie about my life before all that happened and put the kibosh on those plans. Then Mickey Rourke bought the option, and let it lapse. Just as well. I wasn't done living it yet. Hopefully.

"Why are the Yakuza after you?" I asked, another amazing question in a series of amazing questions I never thought I'd need to ask anyone, much less my wife.

"Well, both of us, now. It has to do with my past, Vic."

"Yeah, I figured."

"They want my money. They think I owe them."

"Why?" I could tell when she was lying, and she was lying, but I went along with it.

"Can we talk about this later? I want to fuck some more. I haven't come yet. And frankly, danger turns me on."

"You faked that orgasm? Shit, I knew it. Bullets tend to have the opposite affect on me, though."

"They're gone now. It was just a message, trust me." She stuck her tongue in my ear and grabbed my depleted cock and asked, "If I tell you why they want to kill me, will you fuck me some more?"

Little Elvis stirred. That twisted fucker was easily aroused by lurid tales of erotic debauchery, not threats of violence. "You got a deal. You sure they're gone now?"

"Yes. Otherwise we'd be dead already. They would've just kicked down the door and murdered us in our bed."

"God, I've seen and loved that exact kinda scene in so many movies."

"Life is not a movie, Vic."

"Rose used to say that to me."

"She was right."

"I'm still not convinced."

Oblivious to the chaos, Val stretched spread-eagle nude on our creaky old Murphy bed, her forty-something year old body as taut and curvy as a twenty year old's, at least from my admittedly subjective perspective. I ignored the wrinkles in her forehead, the slight sagging of her otherwise eye-popping breasts, the crow's feet when she smiled, because I'd learned to ignore my own vintage visage in the mirror, plus I hardly ever smiled, anyway. She reminded me a lot of my former lover Raven Rydell, who was also a burlesque dancer, at least until she hung herself with her own massive bra while awaiting trial for crimes she committed in belated response to her own vicious violation as a young girl. But that's another violent love story. Right now my love story was right in front of me, and I dug in.

While I ferociously fucked her voluptuous flesh, Val whispered a torrid tale of international laundered money operations, prostitution rackets, and dope rings in Tokyo, where she was raised by her adoptive family, who were in the military. Rose's father was in the military, too. Though I got the impression Val wasn't being totally honest with me. And she wasn't. It just wasn't adding up.

So she made up another fake background for my benefit: Her father was CIA, and so was her mother. They'd adopted her out of an orphanage in Mexico City, when they were "vacationing." Val was only eight years old. They took her back to Tokyo, where they were stationed indefinitely. Val grew up quickly, joined a street gang, learned martial arts, and got into a lot of trouble, eventually becoming a high-priced hooker for the Yakuza…

"*What*?" I said, my erection experiencing some deflection.

"Vic, they kidnapped my parents. I had to. I was forced into it. And then I killed a bunch of them and took some money and went back to Mexico. Then a bunch of other stuff happened and finally you and I reunited in Mexico City, where I was hiding out under the guise of a professional *lucha libre*. That's why I wore the mask in public all the time." I forgot to mention she was a pro wrestler when we met the second time, before she traded that ring for the one on her finger. And that wasn't all.

"You were also living with a woman," I reminded her. "Not that I'm complaining."

"You know I'm bi-sexual, Vic. I've been with *lots* of women. And men."

I shot my second wad of the evening. Val sighed and rolled over, unsatisfied. As usual.

"Well, I least I got it up," I said. "And I'm definitely not bored anymore."

"Well, good for you." She was softly sobbing.

"Just slow it down. Rushing interferes with my erection."

She didn't get it. Or maybe she did. I couldn't tell. She just kept sobbing.

"Aw, man, c'mon Val. Don't cry. Tell me some more stories. I'll get it up again, promise."

"Like what?"

"Like…*wait a minute.* Your folks, the ones that raised you, were United States citizens?"

"Yeah, so?"

"So you didn't need a green card when we got married!"

She wasn't expecting that, because she knew I was a lousy detective. She'd blown her own cover with that slip. You lie often enough, you'll trip over your own tongue. "No, actually, I didn't. Sorry, Vic."

"What? So why the big hurry?"

"Security."

"Val, I have no money."

"Emotional, not monetary. Obviously."

I sat back and took in this revelation. "Wow. Just...wow. You lied to me. More than once. About, like, important shit."

"I'm sorry, Vic."

"What else haven't you told me?"

"A *lot*. But most of it just isn't worth telling you, because it has nothing to do with us *now*. It's all in the past, so what difference does it make? At least now you know one truth that really matters: I married you strictly for love."

"You mean security."

"There's no better kind."

"You were on the run from the Yakuza even when you were living in Mexico, probably under an assumed identity, one of a Mexican national. Am I right?"

"Yes. I underestimated you, Vic. But I needed to keep moving around. I knew they were onto me in Mexico, because of my association with Hal, who was their business partner." More on Hal later, and no, she didn't meant the computer from *2001: A Space Odyssey*. If you read about my last missive, you'd know already. Of course, Val was already invalidating at least part of it, so it might as well be fiction, anyway.

"So now they finally caught up with you, here in Seattle, despite your cover as my wife."

"Yes. I'm afraid so, Vic. But that changes nothing between us. *Nothing.*"

"Well, I lost my boner again. Hope you're happy now." This was all happening so fast. And everything just accelerated from there. Hang on tight. "Tell me some other stories. Dirty ones, not necessarily true ones. I can't take any more true confessions today. Or ever."

"Is that what it takes, Vic? Are you really that sick? And you give me shit for changing a few details here and there?"

"I'm a pervert, but at least I'm not a liar."

"Okay, fine, you really want to know everything? How about *this*." Val got up and began performing some strange, ritualistic dance in the middle of the dark room, sidestepping shards of glass, as if in a trance. Doc was still hiding, and Fido was watching her curiously, head cocked to one side. My sailor statue, dubbed Ivar, was also watching, clapping along and even dancing a bit, even though he had one peg-leg. He was something else that had suddenly popped up during my mid-life crisis and refused to go away, like arthritis or warts.

Val began reciting some weird incantations in an eerie monotone, in Latin or maybe Esperanto, and writhing as if possessed. Then three horned, muscular, burgundy-skinned demonic man-beasts appeared, and took her, right there on the floor, with their enormous, wart-covered cocks. They bit into her flesh with their dripping fangs, and she bit them back, drawing blood, since she had sprouted fangs, too. Blood dripped down her neck and breasts, and the demons licked it off. She came several times as they entered her every orifice with ghoulish zeal. The ghastly yet salaciously seductive spectacle reminded me of a similar sequence in the 1981 erotic horror movie *Possession,* starring Isabelle Adjani as an emotionally disturbed woman having an affair with a slimy, reptilian entity. Anyway, I was both horrified and transfixed, not to mention insanely aroused. Inexplicably, I heard "Love Theme from Twin Peaks" as performed by Rat Rios on the *Twin Peaks* Tribute album

The Next Peak, Volume One playing from somewhere, either inside or outside my head, I couldn't tell anymore.

Obviously oblivious to my voyeuristic presence, they all had multiple orgasms, blood and semen spraying everywhere. Then a plume of blueish smoke or mist swirled around them, and they were just slithering shadows, illuminated by what seemed to be flashes of lightning from within the dark room, though I could hear a heavy downpour of rain outside as well. I heard my wife and the demons laughing and moaning and screeching with decadent delight. I just sat on the bed, masturbating, like old times. I was cured.

After all four of us lay back, exhausted, Fido licked up the blood and semen from the floor. Then puked it up. I passed out.

The next thing I knew the goddamn sunlight was streaming through the blinds. I looked over and noticed Val was there, sound asleep.

There was no blood or semen or glass on the floor, no evidence of the previous night's dangerous, hedonistic, supernatural escapades. I'd dreamed all of it. It was definitely time for me to go back to AA. Or stop watching gonzo horror movies late at night. Neither was a likely possibility,

With a stretch and a yawn, I snuggled up to my beautiful, blood-splattered bride, in all of her gruesome glory.

Those who have followed my series of chronicles have probably noticed that my subjective narratives indicate I am slowly—okay, rapidly—sliding into a state of dementia. I assure you this is not the case. I am not the proverbial "unreliable narrator." Even in a world of fake news in an increasingly surrealistic society, you can count on me to tell the truth. I mean, at least as I see it. However, I can't vouch for anyone else's corroboration of these events.

And sure, my last misadventure took both of us from Vancouver to Costa Rica, and in between I encountered flesh-eating zombies, by-products of a manufactured opioid epidemic, masterminded by a Bond villain, or equivalent thereof, named Hal Nickerson. (See? I told you I'd tell you.) Additionally, I kept seeing two bats on the ceiling when Val and her lover weren't around, two bats that would then disappear once their human equivalents re-entered the room, making me suspect, or rather hope, they were part of a global secret society of lesbian vampires. Plus a bunch of other stuff that makes no sense, at least in the conventional context of the world we all know, or once knew.

But then what *does* make sense by society's ever-shifting standards? Even excluding the bizarre nature of our politics and tribalistic nature of our culture these days (and always), what about Life itself? We're complex, sentient beings born into this complicated, temporal ball of mud and fire floating in a vast, apparently endless void, ever-so-briefly occupying these fragile little sacks of flesh, blood and shit that are built to fail, surrounded by a cacophony of conundrums we'll never solve, from the meaning of our brief existence to where that other sock went. Not to mention disease, war, racial strife, the mass consumption of other sentient beings for sustenance (Val and I recently went vegan as a matter of our own evolving empathy), pointless religious and political debates, traffic, pollution, sitcoms, you name it. None of it really makes any sense, at least via our limited perception, when you break it down, rather than taking it on faith that it all actually means something. To me, it's all a dream. Or a nightmare. In any case, as I grew older, I gradually accepted the elusive nature of this ephemeral existence in a realm of relative morality. So why *not* a demonic orgy in my living room? Who's to say that's outside the realm of possibility? I mean, crazier shit has definitely happened. Especially to me, and especially lately.

Fortunately, this really did seem to be a hallucination of the nocturnal variety, since there was no visible evidence of mischief and mayhem.

Then I noticed the fresh, deep red scratches up and down Val's back, and I got a chill down my mushy spine. I figured they were from me, inflicted unconsciously during our carnal wrestling match. I looked her over. Dried semen on both thighs. Also mine, I deduced. She was a heavy sleeper, and we'd just had sex, as I recalled, so I felt free to explore her unconscious body without getting #MeToo'd on Twitter. Plus I didn't have any social media accounts, anyway.

Then I saw the bite barks. Definitely not mine. They looked painful, inflicted by wild animals in the heat of passion.

Now wide awake, I jumped out of bed and pulled up the blinds. Someone had put some cardboard over the broken window panes. They'd just cleaned up the mess on the floor. Even the dog puke. Who did? Me? Val?

I looked over at Ivar on his pedestal in the corner. He winked.

#FuckMe.

Chapter Two
FASTER PUSSYCAT,
THRILL! THRILL!

I should warn you right now that you're going to hear the word "maybe" a lot in this narrative, because much of it is pure conjecture and subjective speculation. You're also going to hear repetition of theoretical hypotheses, none of which I can really vouch for, so you'll just have to deduce and decide for yourself what is what and which is which, and provide your own neat, tidy resolution to this existential mystery. Meaning you need to be your own damn detective in this maze-like mind-fuck most people call "Life." Don't look at me. I'm tired. And retired. I'll drop as many clues as I can along the way, though, like bread crumbs down a bottomless pit. Best I can offer. Good luck.

Anyway, back to it:

"We have to leave town for a couple of days," Val said as she made breakfast and coffee, wearing nothing but her silky black-and-silver Japanese robe, which now had assumed a sinister aura of impending doom.

"So we *were* attacked by gunfire last night," I said. "*Coitus interruptus* style."

"Yes. Sorry about that. I'll deal with it, don't worry."

"But you didn't conjure demons from hell for an orgy."

She laughed. "I keep telling you, Vic, you were having a nightmare."

"A tangible nightmare."

"Well, you're a sick bastard and a dirty old man. I knew what I was buying into when I signed up."

"But the scratches, the bite marks…"

She walked over and kissed me, her remarkably perky breasts protruding from the robe. I put my arm around her hour-glass waist and squeezed her round, juicy ass. My *Dream with Dean* LP was on the stereo, and Dino's effortlessly smooth crooning made everything seem copacetic. Apparently we'd finally had some decent marital sex, or martial sex, that is. The coffee smelt so damn good it would make Agent Dale Cooper cream his pants. Doc and Fido were happily lapping up healthy pet food, not bodily fluids from beyond. If it wasn't for the bullets, everything would be just peachy.

"So we're fleeing the Yakuza?" I said.

"Oh, hell, no," she said. "I can handle those clowns when the time comes. In fact, this is all connected. One solution for everything. We're going to Atlanta for our first gig."

"First gig? In Atlanta?" I really liked Donald Glover's TV series of the same name. Plus *The Walking Dead*.

"Yes. Well, practice gig, an audition, sort of. I used to dance at the Clermont Lounge there, many years ago. I still have connections."

"I know the place. Connections to what?"

"Private clientele who may be interested in what we have to offer, and may help me pay off the Yakuza, one way or another."

"What the hell does that mean?"

"The less you know, the better."

"That's always been my philosophy, yet one more reason I was a lousy detective."

"Follow my lead and don't ask questions. When the time comes, just stand on stage, act dumb and look pretty, like you always do. I'll do the rest."

"Like you always do. When did you set all this up?"

"Last night, after you fell asleep. I woke up early, restless, but then I didn't come four times like you did."

"So you cleaned up the mess."

"The glass? Yes. But there's plenty more to clean up out there in the world. It's my mess and I'll handle it. Sorry I got you into this, but relationships are always a package deal, right?"

"And what a package, baby." I looked over at Ivar, but he'd gone stone-faced again. Me, I was just stoned, I figured. Perpetually. High on life, all that jazz.

Though I hated leaving my city or neighborhood or even my house, especially now that I no longer had to work for a living, I was accustomed to these impulsive, impromptu trips, since Val had a seemingly open-ended travel expense account. Now, I knew that she had probably acquired this bottomless bank account via illegal means while dealing with dope dealers in Mexico and maybe even Japan, squirreling away ill-gotten gains via questionable ventures and avenues, but I never asked any questions. For one thing, she told me not to because she wouldn't answer them anyway, but really, I just didn't want to know. As long as the cash kept flowing my way, I was content. Plus she wasn't currently engaged in any antisocial activity. None that I knew about, anyway. Again, ignorance was bliss.

After a routine flight, we had dinner that night at a place in the Little Five Points district of Atlanta called The Vortex, a really cool, hip, popular joint with a cornucopia of kooky knickknacks lining the walls and ceiling beneath a giant skull with mesmerizing red eyes for a rooftop. That psycho-skull motif also served as the design of their signature tiki mug. It was dark and crowded, because not only was the offbeat ambience cozy, but the food and drinks were excellent. I'd been there once already, when a case took me here over a decade previously. In fact, I was on the trail of a woman that had also performed at the legendary Clermont Lounge, the most infamous strip joint in the South. I asked Val if she'd known her.

"Mona? Yes, we slept together once or twice."

"Hm. So did we."

"How was she?"

"Great! You?"

"Fantastic."

"Cool."

"I loved sucking her round, luscious nipples."

"So did I!"

"Wasn't her vagina exquisite tasting?"

"Yes, it was, as a matter of fact."

"Thanks for reminding me! I've been with so many women, and men, that sometimes they all blend together. Mona was special, though."

"Not as special as you."

"You're so sweet, Vic."

I smiled wanly. That was a particularly strange exchange, discussing a mutual past lover of the opposite sex with my wife. Well, my opposite, not hers.

We ordered the black bean burgers and the house cocktail, an exotic concoction called the Hip-Mo-Tizer, in the signature psycho-skull mug. It was like a combination goth/biker bar and pop culture museum. In fact, right next door was a massive emporium of nostalgic novelties called the Junkman's Daughter, which I planned to visit later.

To complete the perfection of the evening, Elvis was singing "King Creole" on the sound system. It was the remixed version from the Cirque du Soleil show called *Viva Elvis*.

"You know I call my pecker Little Elvis, right?" I told Val.

"Little being the operative word."

I shot her a mock-hurt glance, and she laughed, then kissed me. "It's the right size, I just wish he'd rise from the dead more often, though."

"Well, last night was his comeback concert, I hope."

"Me, too. Maybe he can have an encore tonight in our motel room." We were staying at some little hooker dive near the Clermont, even though we could afford much better accommodations, slumming it purely for the cheap thrill. It just felt like old times to me.

We drank our cocktails, laughed, listened to Elvis, and ordered refills waiting for our food to arrive. Our second drinks and burgers were served simultaneously.

"I gotta go take a leak," I said, my bladder at the bursting point after I took my first bite. "Little Elvis needs to throw up again."

"I thought that only happened when you jerked off."

"That too." I got up from my stool, as scatalogical as that may sound.

"I slept with Elvis once," she said matter-of-factly. "He *was* The King."

I sat back down on my stool, slowly, and said, "What? When you were what, ten? He died in Seventy-Seven!"

"I was younger than ten then. It was way after."

"After what? You fucked his corpse?"

"No, Vic. I'm not a necrophiliac. I've said too much already. Let's move on."

"I don't think so."

"Doesn't matter."

I remembered something just then. When I was much younger, during a case wherein I tracked down a Mob brat under the auspices of a huckster named Deacon Rivers who ran a compound for sexy young runaway orphans under the guise of an "Elvis church," someone kept leaving recordings of old 45 records on my answering machine, like "Cry Me a River" by Julie London. I called the mystery caller The Phone Phantom. After I reunited with Val, she admitted it had been her. Usually when I hit *69, it traced back to nowhere. But the one final time I tried, a voice that sounded a lot like The King answered, before fading away.

"You were at Graceland, with Elvis, in the Nineties?"

"I told you, I'm dropping this. How's your black bean burger? Mine is delicious!"

My head was spinning, and it wasn't all due to the strength of the Hip-Mo-Tizer. "Are you saying Elvis is still alive?"

"I'm saying it's time to stop asking questions again. Just enjoy it while it lasts, Vic."

"Our marriage?"

"Our lives." She kissed me, and I dropped it, like always.

Then I went to the bathroom, and naturally, Ivar was there, waiting for me. *Ahoy, motherfucker!* he said jovially.

"I know you're only a hallucination," I said. "But you didn't always talk."

What makes you think I'm not real? he asked.

"Because you're a statue that I left back in Seattle."

Am I? Perhaps I'm really a spirit of the sea.

"The only spirits that spawned you are getting pissed down this toilet right now." I unzipped and unloaded.

Ivar chuckled. *See you soon*, he said.

I turned to respond, but he was gone. Hell, maybe Ivar was The Phone Phantom, and Val was merely placating my curiosity. Or she was part of the conspiracy to fuck with my head.

I swear, this is all true. Well, it's what happened, anyway.

When I returned to the bar area, someone had taken my seat. It was a well-dressed Japanese gentleman. Val was conversing with him. In Japanese. That didn't surprise me. She could speak several languages fluently, while I could barely speak one, and it was my native tongue. She'd told me once that Spanish and Japanese had a lot of similar phonetics because of the common vowel sounds. Or something like that. I don't know. I'm still mastering English.

Politely yet impatiently, I stood idly by as they engaged in a lively conversation. Finally, the Japanese dude, who was quite handsome, looked at me, nodded with a smile, and left.

I resumed my seat and naturally asked, "Who the fuck was that? Yakuza?"

"No, but he knows they're trying to hit me."

"How do you know him?"

"Oh, that was my business contact. We have it all settled. Our first gig is booked back in Seattle."

"What? I don't even have my fez yet! And we need to rehearse!"

"We're about to. C'mon, eat and drink up. We're due at the Clermont in an hour for our show."

"What?"

No Junkman's Daughter for me. Damn it.

An hour later, we were waiting to go on stage at the Clermont. Instead of my usual sharkskin suit, along with my customary white shirt, and skinny black tie, I was wearing a bright green felt fez with a matching green smoking jacket, both of vintage value, that Val had packed in her suitcase without telling me, more psychological sabotage via subversive subterfuge. She wouldn't tell me where she bought them, either. As for her wardrobe, she had packed pasties, high-heeled pumps, and a G-string, more sartorial surprises. I made a mental note to rummage through our closet more often. God knows what other skeletons was hidden in there, perhaps literally. But again, maybe it was better kept a secret.

"I don't know what to do," I kept stammering as we waited in the wings for the current act to finish. It was some generic indie rock band with two near-naked female dancers sucking up the spotlight. Or something like that. I had trouble focusing at that point. I was in shock and suffering from stage fright. But when Val pulled off her dress and revealed her "outfit," my nerves gave way to lust.

When we were introduced by the announcer as "The Voodoo Valentine Show," Val literally shoved me out in front of her, ordering me to "be funny" and then she'd come out "when the time was right." Talk about throwing a baby into the pool and expecting it to swim. But as usual, I did as I was told.

The place was dark and noisy and I was immediately heckled. I heard someone call me a "Muslim terrorist," then realized it was probably the fez. I froze. People booed. I felt like a cross between Buddy Love in *The Nutty Professor* (the Jerry Lewis original) and The Green Hornet, though not nearly as slick as either. Just green as hell.

Finally, I managed to murmur, "Hey there, I'm Vic Valentine, Lounge Lizard for Hire."

"You're fired!" some asshole yelled. Everyone laughed. Everyone but me. Then a beer bottle was hurled just above my head, shattering on the wall behind me, but knocking my fez askew. More laughter. I wanted to die on that stage, for real.

"Um…well…uh…take my wife, please." Then I looked over at Val, waiting in the wings, and gave her a pleading puppy dog look. She relented and strutted out on stage in all her glory, just as a hidden D.J. took the cue and started playing "The Stripper" by David Rose over the sound system.

The crowd went wild. Val danced and shook her magnificent breasts, twirling those tassels for all they were worth, and apparently that was a lot. Impulsively inspired, I swung around the tassel on my fez in tandem. It was a hit. We left that night with a grand in cash. "I don't get it," I said in the Lyft car afterwards. "We didn't do anything. Well, I didn't. You did it all! But still, a thousand bucks?"

She literally shrugged it off. "It went okay. We still need to work on our banter, but that was just to get you used to a hostile audience, because there will be many, and I won't always be there to rescue you."

I wasn't sure what she meant by that, but she was totally naked beneath an overcoat after tossing her tassels and G-string into the voracious crowd, so I didn't care. The whole thing lasted maybe fifteen minutes, a whirlwind crash course in the business of a quick buck at the expense of my dignity. But I didn't think my dignity was worth the price of admission, much less a grand.

We spent a good deal of our profits on dinner and drinks at Trader Vic's downtown, one of only two left in the States, the other being the flagship in Emeryville, California, which I frequented often during my Bay Area days. Since the Atlanta air was typically moist and muggy, it was perfect Mai Tai weather, and I was in a tropical island mood. The exotic sound of Martin Denny performing "Jungle Madness" over the sound system augmented the already lushly lurid atmosphere. I got quickly soused and Val, who drank as much if not more than I did, didn't even seem fazed. The fact she was wearing nothing but an overcoat and pumps and I was still adorned with a fez and smoking jacket did seem to alarm the staff and patrons, but we ignored them. Our service was excellent, though.

Back at the hotel, we fucked like rabid rabbits. Val was so sweaty and hot I just couldn't get enough of her, licking her luscious flesh from head to toe. I came inside of and all over her, and she just wiped and licked it off, sucking me dry as well. We hadn't been this hardcore in months. Her plan to revive my zest was already working, even though I was a total flop as a lounge lizard. Who cared? I noticed Ivar in the corner watching us, but at least he didn't have any wood to yank. No horned, horny demons showed up this time, either. I still wondered about that Japanese dude back at The Vortex, if Val had ever fucked him, and his possible connection to the Yakuza hit back in Seattle, as well as our flash gig at the Clermont. Val wasn't talking. She was fucking, then sleeping, while I just lay there, wide awake, wearing nothing but argyle socks and my new green fez hat.

I removed it and looked at the label. "Made in Japan," it read.

The next morning we were on a plane to Las Vegas for our second sudden gig, at Frankie's Tiki Room. The desert air was hot and dry, quite a contrast from where we'd just been, but then whiplash changes of scenery were quickly becoming part of our regular lifestyle. I'd spent most of my time on this pathetic planet totally disoriented anyway. Normal orientation just wasn't in the cards for me.

I still had no idea who our agent was. God, maybe. So I asked Val.

"I am," Val insisted.

"You're God, or you're our agent?"

"Let's just say I know a lot of people in a lot of places. High places." She looked upward and pointed, smiling. I wasn't. She went on anyway. "Anyway, doesn't matter. Now this time, try to loosen up a bit. It's a small place, it won't be too crowded, so you won't have to be so nervous."

I just nodded and followed orders. Happy wife, happy life, all that jazz.

Tony Bennett was singing "With Plenty of Money and You" as we walked into the mini-oasis. The DJ switched over to Henry Mancini's "Lujon," one of my favorites, as we sat at the bar. I took that as a good sign, even though I didn't believe in signs. The place was beautifully decked out floor to ceiling, wall to wall with all things Polynesian pop.

That same Japanese dude I'd seen back at The Vortex was sitting in the corner with two extremely sexy Japanese babes, all dressed to the nines.

"Hey, there's your friend," I said to Val.

"No it's not," she said without even looking.

"Are you saying they all look alike to me?"

"No. I'm just saying he's not my friend. Just a business associate."

"What's his name."

"It's best you stay out of it, Vic. Trust me. Now what do you have planned for our show? We're on in five minutes."

"What? What the fuck am I, a master of improv? I have no fucking clue!"

"All right," she sighed. "I'll take care of it. Wait here."

She got up as our cocktail arrived. I started sipping my Navy Grog while Val changed in the bathroom. She came out wearing her pumps, her old *lucha* mask, and a leopard-pattern bikini, with a belly bracelet wrapped loosely around her curvaceous waist, instantly entrancing the small crowd assembled. Since I was still wearing my lounge lizard get-up, I got up to introduce her to the folks, who all seemed stunned into sexual submission. But Val and the music started without me, so I sat this one out. The DJ was now playing "That Ol' Black Magic" by Louis Prima and Keely Smith, the theme song I had suggested, so at least I felt like I was contributing something of value to the act. Val went from table to table, flirting with both men and women, twisting and twirling to the vintage Vegas beat. When she got to the Japanese dude, she froze. He put his arms around her waist and licked her belly button. I got a jealous boner.

Then suddenly, it was over, as soon as the music stopped.

"C'mon, we have to go," she said, grabbing me by the arm. I had barely started sipping my drink. We split without even paying for them. She threw on another overcoat that seemed to come out of nowhere, just like everything else. Then we grabbed a cab directly to the airport.

"How did I do?" I asked her.

"Sensational," she snapped. That's all I got out of her. She was locked inside her own head now. I couldn't reach her. I kept thinking of that Japanese guy licking her belly. I wanted to jerk off right there. Instead, she blew me, just to get it over with, smacking her lips with my semen. The cabbie pretended not to notice. He's been paid to look the other way, as the saying goes.

On the plane back to Seattle, I kept looking around for Japanese dudes, but only saw Ivar, perched on top of one of the seats, keeping a watchful eye on me. He winked. I didn't wink back. Other than Washington, the only state I wanted to be in was denial.

When we got back to our pad, Fido and Doc were missing, and the cute Rover sitter we'd hired was lying dead on the floor in a pool of blood.

"They must've thought it was," Val said, tearing up.

"They? Yakuza?"

"Probably. Though the fact her throat was slit makes me think it was the Cartel."

"*What?*"

"C'mon, we have to go. We have a gig at the Pink Door in an hour."

"Wait, Val. There's a dead body on our floor and our pets are gone. I don't think I can perform under these conditions."

"Since when do you perform? C'mon, let's go. Someone is on the way to clean all this up, and locate our pets."

"Who?"

"Shut up, we're in a hurry."

We went out, climbed into my Corvair, and headed to the Pink Door near Pike Place.

Normally the burlesque acts in this snazzy subterranean supper club did crazy things like erotic trapeze acts in the middle of the room while the patrons dined on fine Italian cuisine. Val had something else in mind, though. This time I did introduce her, since I was perpetually dressed to thrill these days. Val just got started, still wearing her pumps, mask, belly bracelet, and overcoat, which she decided to discard with a swirling flourish while deliriously dancing on the tables to the tune of Les Baxter's version of "Love Dance."

On the heels of that tune was another which I recognized or at least imagined to be the jazzy theme music for 1962's *Satan in High Heels*. By now Val was wearing nothing but her *lucha* mask and belly bracelet, having kicked off her shoes, too, and actually stepping in peoples' food. One guy grabbed the discarded pump that had landed on the plate in front of him and poured his Manhattan into it, then gulped it down. Val then whirled his way, and let him suck the marinara sauce off her red-painted toes before kicking him in the face, like Salma Hayek in *From Dusk Till Dawn*. Raven had reminded me of her, too. In fact, Raven looked and acted and danced so much like Val and vice versa that I actually started wondering if they were the same person, which would be impossible in anyone else's life but my own. But I was too distracted by the current scene of erotic chaos to give it any more thought, at least at that moment.

Again, watching Val do her thing to wild acclaim, I got a raging hard-on, which I tried to conceal from public view, but no one was looking at me, anyway. Some of the women began noticing that their dates were no longer noticing them, and cried out in protest, while most of the men seemed to be immersed in a hypnotic trance. Val just laughed like an evil vixen and kept table-hopping and boner-bopping. The scurrying staff was pretending to chase her so they could pretend to stop her, but truthfully, nobody wanted this show to end just yet. Except when we heard the sirens.

The cops arrived just as Val and I left. Nudie dancing was not allowed per the joint's liquor license. Val was only wearing her mask by now, having casually unhooked and flung her belly bracelet into the maddened crowd on the way out the door, like Elvis tossing a scarf into a mosh pit of wet panties. *Ladies and Gentlemen, Val has left the building*. Unsurprisingly, several cabs screeched to a halt to pick us up, crashing into each other. We jumped into one that wasn't impacted by the mashup, went back to our pad, which was was spic 'n' span. Our pets were there, too. It was like nothing had ever happened.

I was in a state of shock and awe. It was like she had stripped across the country in a single day, though per full disclosure, I can't be absolutely sure of the precise chronology. It was all a blur in my booze 'n' B movie-addled brain, where dreams and memories blended like a potent cerebral cocktail. I can't vouch for the veracity of these outrageous events, only their crystal clear existence in my murky consciousness.

At home in bed, I decided to consult my live-in expert on all things psycho. I hadn't told her my sailor statue had started talking to me. That might be a bridge too far over the edge of her cliff, and I already felt like I was constantly testing her patience as it was.

"Did I imagine all that?" I asked Val. "I mean, it all happened so fast. Of course, time goes by faster as you get older. So maybe it's just me."

"Shut up and fuck me, old man. No time or energy for your neuroses. I'm tired and I need some sleep." So much for in-depth counseling. Unless it was sexual therapy. Whatever works, I always say, even if it's temporary or delusional, like a band-aid on a tumor.

Wisely, I obliged her professional advice. She came, and so did I, but the latter goes without saying. I like saying it anyway.

Night fell, hard, like a piano on a pigeon. All was calm and peaceful yet vaguely unsettling, waiting for that other piano to drop.

Unable to sleep, I sat up chatting with my dead friend Doc, or his ghost, anyway. The cat I'd named after him just stared at us, while Fido cuddled with Val in our cozy little Murphy bed.

"I'm losing my mind, Doc." The cat meowed in response. "Not you, *him*," I said, pointing to the apparition leaning against the wall. Even in death, Doc looked cool. Not as black as he'd once been, being a spirit and all, but he looked around the same age as when he died, barely sixty, though I think he lied about his age in order to woo female customers at The Drive-Inn. Not that he needed to. Black don't crack.

"*No, Vic, you're just finally seeing reality for what it is, a subjective state of mind.*"

"But is any of this shit real?"

"*Only if you want it to be.*"

"I could be talking to myself right now. Or a cat."

"*Maybe. Don't ask me.*"

"I miss you, man. You always had time to talk me down from the ledge."

"*I'm right here, buddy. Always.*"

"So then…what happened to that sitter? Is she dead?"

"*I can't say. Call Rover and ask.*"

"Will do, first thing in the morning. What do you think of Val?"

"*I think you conjured her from your most far-out fantasies, Vic.*"

"So she isn't real, either?"

"*Vic, what difference does it make? Just dig it while it lasts. It's all a dream, anyway. Whether you're awake or asleep.*"

"How do I know where one ends, and the other begins?"

"*You can't. That's the point.*"

"I don't see it. The point, I mean. I see demons fucking my wife and a talking sailor statue, but I don't see the point."

"*And you see me, Vic. Have I ever lied to you?*"

"Not on purpose, as far as I know. But if you're really there, does the truth even matter?"

"Truth is relative to one's perception, Vic."

"What about Absolute Truth? Is there even such a thing?"

"You'll find out when you're dead, but then it won't matter."

"You're dead. Can you tell me?"

"No fair, Vic. You gotta find out the hard way, just like me."

"I always figured there was nothing, just eternal unconsciousness, which doesn't seem so bad, really. I mean, what difference does it make that's there nothing if you're not even aware of it?"

"Good question."

"What's a good answer?"

"Again, don't be in such a rush. Relax and enjoy the ride."

"Even if it's all in my head."

"Everyone sees the world from their own individual perspective, Vic. Like it's all a show just for them."

"Is it?"

"You tell me."

"If I knew, I wouldn't be asking a ghost."

"I bet the cat knows."

"But I don't speak his language."

"And yet he seems to understand you well enough."

"That's how cats get by, I guess. Playing dumb."

"Isn't that what you're doing?"

"I guess. Only I'm not playing."

"Go to sleep and dream, Vic. Then wake up and dream some more. Go on. Your wife needs you."

I nodded. "At least I'm not lonely anymore, Doc."

"See? Miracles can happen if you're patient, Vic. Keep the faith. Peace out, my man."

Then he was gone, like he was never there. That happens to all of us eventually.

The next morning I called Rover to inquire about the welfare of our sitter. They said they hadn't heard from her. I hung up hoping for the best.

"We got any gigs today?" I asked Val when she finally woke up. She slept in, and she's normally up at dawn, making phone calls and plans I'm only privy to when she feels like letting me in on the epic gag. I was putty in her hands. But what hands.

"We're taking some time off," Val said. "You need some practice."

"Yeah, no kidding. You were great, though. Except when you nearly got us busted for publicly exposing your bust. And bush."

"Sometimes I just need to amuse myself, Vic. Especially sexually, as of late. Plus that was part of the deal."

"What deal? With who?"

"Never mind, Vic. Just hold me and make love to me. That's your job from now on."

"I thought I was a lounge lizard for hire?"

"Yes, but you still work for me."

"Who do you work for?"

"No one."

"You sure?"

"That's the goal, anyway. Independence. Emancipation."

"From what? From *who*?"

"From everything, and everyone, Vic. Stick with me, and I'll set you free, too."

I lay down beside her and smelled the earthy sensuality of her warm flesh. "But maybe I like being a prisoner."

"You're mine, Vic. You belong to me. Forever."

I smiled and sighed and figured Doc was right. I was okay, Val was okay, the pets were okay. Everything was okay. Why fight Fate? Especially if it wasn't fighting back.

Fate is my pimp, anyway. And I'm its decrepit, senile whore.

Chapter Three
THE LADY IS A VAMP

I have a recurring dream where I'm forced to live in this cheap little hovel, like I did for most of my youthful adulthood, where a woman had recently committed suicide. She was beautiful but perpetually sad. She looked like a combination of Rose, Raven, and Val, but uniquely herself. A complete stranger. An amalgam of my female fantasies. While I'm lying in my cot she suddenly materializes with her back to me, then slowly turns to reveal her chalk white face framed by jet black hair, her dark eyes filled with tears, her ruby red lips quivering with anxiety. Something about her overwhelms me with both dread and longing. I started calling her The Phantom Lady, the title of a classic *film noir* from 1944. I am frightened and want to leave, but am compelled to stay with her. I know she's a ghost so it freaks me out, even as I'm filled with intense yearning, the kind I always felt as a young man in vain pursuit of a real relationship. I try to jump out the window to prove to myself it's only a dream and I'll wake up before I hit the ground, and be free. She dares me, and I decline. Finally we have intensely passionate sex, and then I fall in love with her. I never want to leave her.

That's when I always wake up.

In yet another frequent vision, I'm in the passenger seat of a dark blue 1963 Shelby Cobra. At the wheel is a young Diane Webber, born Marguerite Empey, a popular 1950s/60s model, dancer, and actress. She played a mermaid in both the 1962 film *Mermaids of Tiburon* and on "The Mermaid" episode on *Voyage to the Bottom of the Sea,* third season. Other than Bettie Page, I've always considered her my iconic feminine ideal, physically and spiritually speaking, and indeed, Rose, Raven and Val all reminded me of her in different ways. Rose resembled her the most, especially facially, while embodying what I perceived as Diane's rebellious independence, evident in her vintage photos. Raven had her same impossibly luscious, voluptuous figure. Val has her fierce, lusty spirit, seductively coquettish smile, and heart-penetrating bedroom eyes. Anyway, in the dream, Diane is driving through a strange, barren landscape under bright blue skies, furtively and flirtatiously glancing at me as she shifts gears, her brunette, slightly greasy, wavy long hair whipping in the breeze. Sometimes she's wearing a white halter top, black hot pants, and white, Nancy Sinatra-style boots. In others she's wearing a low-cut, purple suede top, hip-hugging jeans, and brown leather sandals. In all of them, "The Swingin' Creeper" by The Ventures is playing over a montage of us driving through this desolate desert, then later we're in lower Manhattan at twilight, it's late summer or early autumn with a cool evening breeze, the foliage is deep green amid the old buildings, the fading light shadowy and filled with secrets. We're waiting in line to see Godard's *Breathless* or Fellini's *La Dolce Vita*, then later we're having a late dinner at a candle-lit sidewalk cafe before hitting a bar or going out for coffee in the Village, because that's what sophisticated beatnik-types do. Diane is a professional nude model that poses for many local artists, but I don't mind, since she only has eyes for me. During the movie she licks and nibbles on my earlobe, then at dinner she kicks off her shoes and caresses my crotch with her toes. I look into her eyes and can't believe my good fortune. Then later we're in bed, she's on top of me, and as I cup her round, fleshy breasts in my hands, I suddenly wake up.

It took me a while to realize these weren't wet dreams of the nocturnal variety. They were daydreams. I wasn't asleep when they happened. I was wide awake. But the sensory realism of these dreams was so vivid I felt like I was reliving a memory from long ago, even though I was only a tyke in the 1960s. Still, I often escaped into these alternate realities, because they reminded me not only of being young, but enraptured in the first flush of romantic love. Much later, after my reunion with Rose, before I embarked on years of serialized sex, I realized this life-affirming gut-punch to the soul wasn't true love. It was simply delusional obsession, tinged with that desperation and insecurity that attend being enamored with the eternally elusive.

I miss it.

I realize most of you don't get my references. Few people do. They're even too arcane for Val most of the time. But that's aces with me. When it comes to contemporary pop culture and me, it's a terminal case of mutual apathy.

Sometimes I wonder why I keep surreptitiously issuing these underground chronicles of my life—especially now that they're increasingly incoherent and incredible— to you, my small but appreciative audience. To me, they feel like nothing more than sentimental slingshots into the vast, apathetic void. But that's all of our lives, really. So maybe I'm actually illuminating some valuable truth while being shamelessly self-indulgent at your expense.

But probably not. Sorry. I know you're probably just into it for the second hand sex. That's all right. So am I. But one thing I learned the hard way, as it were: there's no human desire more fickle and fleeting than lust. You could say the same thing about human existence, which is spawned by lust. It's all doubt about sex and death. One begets the other, inevitably.

Anyway, the next morning, I pulled out a couple of my Les Baxter LPs, *Jewels of the Sea* and *Sea of Dreams*, not only because I dug the music, but Diane Webber was the cover girl. I made no mention of the bats that kept popping up and disappearing, whether they were delusional projections or actual animals, nor did I remind Val of the rash of "vampire" attacks that plagued Seattle shortly after she moved in with me. The way I saw it, it didn't matter if she was a vampire or a witch or any other supernatural being. She liked me as I was, so I returned the favor. I was in no position to be choosey, especially at this late stage of a rigged game with fluid rules we all wind up losing, anyway.

Val was lost inside an inner netherworld as we went about our morning routine. I was feeling like a passenger on a plane with a preoccupied pilot.

"So was that my so-called lounge lizard career, flashing before my eyes?" I asked her, sipping coffee as I listened to the beautiful, slightly scratchy mood music from long ago.

"No, that was just to pay off some debts," Val said. "As well as a crash course in our new gig. You did fine."

"I didn't do anything."

"Exactly."

"So this is your show, really."

"Well, I'm the star attraction, of course. You're my, what did they call it back in the day? 'Lovely assistant.'"

"Thanks." That came out with more sarcasm than sincerity.

"Vic, I thought doing nothing was your ultimate career goal anyway?"

"It is. But we were talking about something to occupy not only my time, but my soul, which feels empty."

"So Love isn't fulfilling enough, Vic?"

"It suits that need, of course. I'm no longer lonely. But I am bored. One doesn't sate the other. It's like telling someone to just go to sleep when they're hungry, or eat a banana when they're tired. Different desires, different solutions."

"Trust me, Vic. With what's coming next, you won't be bored."

"What does that mean?"

"Well, that bullet through the window wasn't just a coincidence. It's connected to our new venture."

"Fucking critics jumped the gun as always. Tribalists."

"No, I mean my money, *our* money, is running out soon. I need to make more. Not just for us, but to pay my debts."

"To whom? Yakuza?"

"For one, yes. And others in Costa Rica, Mexico, Europe. See, Vic, when you married me, your married my past. And that's something we can no longer run away from, even here in idyllic Seattle."

"Shit. There always has to be a catch, doesn't there? Fucking Life. Anyway, so what am I to you now? Where do I fit into all this? I'm like, what. Your bodyguard? I don't even carry a gun anymore."

"More like I'm *your* bodyguard."

"Then what do you need me for?"

"Vic, your ignorance is only matched by your stupidity." She got up and kissed me, and Little Elvis fluttered. But then he slipped back into a comfortable coma once Val touched him. She sighed and I sat down and turned on the TV after turning off the stereo. I wasn't turned on, which turned Val off.

We had Netflix, something I eschewed for a long time before finally succumbing, because it was putting video stores out of business. But we still had Scarecrow Video here in Seattle, and I had my own collection of movies on Blu Ray and DVD. Though to be honest, I was getting way too lazy to get up and put it in, much like my sex life these days, so I preferred just streaming. Mostly we binged their original TV series. Anyway, we no longer had cable so I wasn't up on the local news anymore. I'd rather make my own news, anyway. Even if it was fake. That was very trendy these days.

So it was something of a shock when Val said to me, "Did you hear the killings have started again?"

I put *Riverdale* on pause, still keeping one eye on the hot Latina chick who played Veronica, the only reason I watched it, and said, "What killings? Who? Close to here?" I was always paranoid, but now it had become a chronic illness.

"The vampire killings." She stared off into space, as if contemplating something sad and gruesome.

"No. I didn't. How did you hear?"

"Word around town. Everyone is freaked out. Though I guess the Pacific Northwest is accustomed to serial killers by now. It's a historical haven for psychos. Ted Bundy and all."

"But they say he, or she, is a vampire."

"Yes, because their throats were torn and the victims drained of blood."

"You're still vegan, right?"

She looked at and smiled while stroking my face. "You poor little fool."

"As Ricky Nelson would say."

"What?"

"Never mind. Anyway, why are you bringing this up?"

"Just making conversation."

"Are we going out today, or just staying in?"

"Let's stay in. I'm exhausted."

"All right. Well, what about our next gig?"

"I'm working on it. Soon. Just sit tight."

"And wait for another bullet to shatter our window and my peace of mind?"

She just smiled and shook her head, sipped her coffee, then silently returned her gaze to something I couldn't see. I felt blind as a bat.

Val fell asleep with her head on my chest. She slept a lot for someone so active. I wondered if it was due to repressed depression. I also wondered if she was slipping out now and then to go slaughter innocent strangers in order to sate her thirst for human blood. But she wasn't strictly

44

nocturnal. She wasn't religious but she wasn't averse to theological iconography, particularly of the pagan cult variety. She seemed ageless as well. She reminded me a lot of actress Ingrid Pitt, star of Hammer's *The Vampire Lovers* (1970) and *Countless Dracula* (1971), among others. Even though she was Latina via Mexico, she had this earthy Eurotrash quality that really turned me on. At least cerebrally-speaking. Physically I just wasn't able to sync up to my own libido anymore, or so it seemed. Not often enough to suit her. Which meant I could lose her. Vampire or not, the stakes were high.

My life was getting so weird since I turned fifty that I wondered if I'd slipped into some sort of alternate dimension, but still retained memories of my other lives on parallel planes, like in comic books and science fiction, so all versions of me blended together into one surrealistic soup. I just went along with it, unsure whether I was living a dream or dreaming a life, only because I figured the only alternative was total lack of consciousness, i.e. death, and I just wasn't ready for that yet. So sleeping with the Undead worked just fine with me. Especially if I could also become an immortal bloodsucker via osmosis. Except for the bloodsucking part. That reminded me too much of my days stalking Flora at the blood bank down in San Francisco years ago. As for the vampire serial murders, I'd let Kolchak the Night Stalker take that job. I was retired. Even if I was living with the prime suspect, at least in my warped mind. Maybe Val was slowly draining my spirit, not just my fluids, or what was left of them. Maybe she secretly subsisted on souls and semen, like a cross between the cowboy mummy in 2002's *Bubba Ho-Tep* and the suburban sluts in 1973's *Invasion of the Bee Girls*. Yeah, didn't I wish.

But what scared me most: maybe I was finally burning out on my two favorite pastimes: sex and movies, which didn't leave me with much to do. I wasn't the sentimental sap I once was. As I get older, I want to make new memories, even if I won't have as much time left to remember them. Even if my new memories never actually happened. In the end, what the fuck difference does any of it make, anyway.

Val and I were hanging out down by Puget Sound near Pike Place, away from the marketplace and the crowds in a little secluded section of shore. It wasn't quite tourist season so my favorite city hadn't yet been invaded by suckers, truckers, and motherfuckers from beyond our beloved borders. Even though I was a transplant myself, I felt very protective of my adopted home. Also I just preferred my solitude. Except for Val.

As we lay there, I decided to play this guessing game, just to get her reaction.

"If you had to choose, would I be a vampire or a werewolf?"

She laughed but then said almost immediately, "Werewolf."

"Yeah? How come?"

"Because even with your old suits, you always look scruffy."

"So I don't clean up nice?"

"You do for a werewolf."

"What about you?

"Me?"

"Vampire or werewolf?"

"That's kind of a cut-and-dried way to divide the population, isn't it?"

"Just for fun. You know. Like are you an Elvis person or Beatles person. A Betty person or Veronica persona. A Ginger person or a Mary Anne person."

"A dumb person or a smart person."

"Well, we know which is which between us. Then there's the world according to Sinatra, divided into punks and bums."

"Really? I never heard that."

"I sorta made it up, but I think it's apropos of his worldview."

"Which am I?"

"Punk or bum?"

"Yes."

"Oh, you're definitely a punk. And I'm totally a bum."

"Oh, okay. Well, Frank was one of the smart ones."

"Cheers to that. But tell me. Back to today's divisive designation. You. Vampire or werewolf?"

She looked at me rather seriously, and said in a near whisper, "Vampire."

I felt a chill, which I attributed to the breeze wafting in off the water. "Yeah, I figured."

"Why?"

"You're so sexy. And mysterious."

"Werewolves can't be sexy and mysterious?"

"Not in the same way. Unless you're into bestiality. Or that naked chick seducing that dude by the campfire in 'The Howling.' You kind of remind me of her, anyway."

She rolled her eyes, then turned over on her belly, and I couldn't stop looking at her mesmerizing cleavage. She seemed to be contemplating something I'd never know about, as usual. It was as if she were gazing at an abstract painting while listening to improvisational jazz.

That's exactly how I was beginning to see my entire life.

Then she lightened up and we began designating passersby as either vampires or werewolves, based on their overall appearance and vibe, sartorially and physically. It turned out Seattle had a healthy mix of goths and growlers, no surprise.

So I was a werewolf. I know I was a teenage werewolf, *a la* Michael Landon. Now I was a middle-aged werewolf. And Val was my vampire bride. So what if she fed off the blood of innocent humans. At least she was vegan otherwise. I always liked animals more than people, anyway.

The gorgeous, gray clouds gradually gave way to the insidious glow of the evil orb which meant I had to seek shelter indoors. "Maybe I am a vampire after all," I said as we stood up and strolled back toward the market area, the Native American totems gleaming in the diabolical sunshine.

"That's just a myth," Val said.

"What? That I hate the sun?"

"That vampires do."

"How do you know?"

"I know a lot you don't know."

"Of course, that's presuming vampires are, y'know, like, real."

"They're as real as werewolves, Vic."

"And how real is that?"

She kissed me and said, "As real as you want them to be. It's all an illusion, anyway."

"Thanks for the confirmation."

We headed for Erik Hakkinen's swank new downtown bar, The Pink Lady, which occupied the space once claimed by one of the city's most infamous strip clubs, The Lusty Lady. The classy little joint was more than worthy of this legendary address. It was my favorite new regional watering hole besides Jason Alexander's Lovecraftian tiki oasis Devil's Reef, down in Tacoma. Anyway, Erik was there behind the bar and served us two perfect Manhattans as we continued our guessing game with our fellow imbibers. Kyu Sakamoto sang "Sukiyaki" over the sound system. Everything was copacetic.

Erik once worked at The Zig Zag Cafe, site of a particularly pivotal rendezvous with the late Raven Rydell. It was eerie sitting with my wife, who reminded me so much of Raven, at a different bar, not far from the Zig Zag, but with the same bartender. It almost felt like I was tempting fate. Fate doesn't like to be fucked with.

While pointing at patrons and saying either "werewolf" or "vampire," I noticed that Japanese dude from Atlanta and Vegas was sitting in the corner, with two different Japanese sirens at his side. Val pretended not to notice him as I said, "Vampire."

"Him?"

"Yeah, your pal that keeps popping up."

"He's not my friend, Vic."

"So why is he following us all over the country?"

"What are you talking about?"

"That's not the same guy we saw in Vegas and Atlanta?"

"Vic, you're just a fucking racist."

"Okay, I may be your basic Caucasian idiot, but I know that's the same guy we saw before. He even has the same shiny suit, which makes me envious, actually. He's straight out of an old Suzuki movie. He's got Yakuza written all over him. For all I know, he's the one who shot through our window the other night."

Val shrugged and said, "So what if it was? No one was hurt. Maybe it was just his way of letting me know he had his eye on us."

"Is that a new Japanese custom now? Like he couldn't just knock on the door or send flowers? God damn it, Val, stop playing with me. What's your connection to him?"

"If you're so sure of all this, Vic, why don't you go ask him yourself."

"I think I will." By then I was on my second Manhattan, and Erik didn't fool around with alcohol, so I was already feeling bolder than usual.

I stood up and walked over to him, interrupting his little powwow with the Japanese babes.

"Hey you, Johnny Sokko. Why did you try to kill us?"

His face froze for a moment, he looked over at Val, who was still at the bar, and then unleashed a torrent of expletives, or at least that's how I translated his obviously hostile response to my simple query.

Then he stopped, looked back at Val, gave her a quick nod, and quite abruptly everything got weird and dreamy again.

As if on cue, Val launched into another trance-like striptease dance as Les Baxter's "Papagayo" began playing out of seemingly nowhere. The blue mist that swirled around that imaginary orgy scene back in our pad appeared suddenly too, as if piped in via a Hollywood fog machine. Erik and the customers seemed to be hypnotized while Val began stripping off her clothes. I tried stopping her but I couldn't move. Literally. I was paralyzed with dread, as well as lust for my own wife. I wasn't alone in that department.

I turned to see the Japanese guy laughing and clapping. The two Japanese babes got up and began kissing and fondling me, giving me a massive erection. One blew me while the other kissed me. I came hard. Next thing I knew, I was making violent love with Val on the floor of the Pink Lady. Even the Lusty Lady would've blushed at this shameless sexhibition.

The small but enthusiastic audience stood around us, watching and drinking and drooling, as the exotic music kept playing. Now it was Arthur Lyman's "Taboo." Next thing I knew, all the men had turned into demons, and were madly fucking the willing women, including the Japanese guy and his two female companions. Then I noticed I'd grown canine fur, claws, and fangs, and Val, now completely nude, had razor sharp teeth as well, dripping blood down her chin, neck and breasts. My blood, apparently. She gnawed on her own wrist, partaking of her own essence, as she ferociously rode my lycanthropic loins, and I hungrily bit her bouncy boobs with animalistic fervor, raking the flesh off her back as I bucked 'n' fucked in a state of erotic ecstasy to the beat of the percussive, pervasive ambient music. The blue mist grew thicker and thicker until it was like everything vaporized, and then Val and I were sitting back at the bar, as if nothing had happened.

The Japanese guy and the two gals were gone, as if they went up smoke.

"What just happened?" I asked Val.

Erik put down our bar tab without saying a word, but winking at Val, who picked it up, as usual.

"We had a few drinks," Val said. "C'mon, let's go home. I'm tired and you're drunk."

So what else is fucking new.

Val passed out next to me in our Murphy bed while I randomly binged Netflix. I hardly ever dug into my precious DVD collection anymore. Like I said, I was just too lazy to get up and put it in. Or even lay down and put it in. Though to my recollection, Val and I had just had the best sex of our lives in front of a group of total strangers in a public venue.

She seemed not to recall that particular incident. Fine with me. I would recall it often.

Anyway, while I was sitting there, Doc, the cat, jumped up on the bed and began talking to me, in Doc's voice. Meaning Doc, my deceased human friend.

I looked around for Doc's familiar if disembodied visage, but no, it was just the cat. Apparently he'd been possessed by Doc's human spirit. Or I was possessed by Erik's spirits. Either way, I didn't want to be rude, so I engaged the cat in conversation. Our dog Fido sat cowering in a corner, glaring and growling at me for some reason.

So now you're a werewolf? Doc the cat said.

"Am I?"

I should know?

"Well, if my wife is a vampire, why can't I be a werewolf? Seems only fair. Especially if I'm just being delusional, anyway."

You've seen way too many movies, Vic. That's always been your problem. You can only view and relate to the world through a cinematic prism. I take some of the blame of that, force feeding you all that crap when you were at the bar in the Drive-Inn, bitching about your latest heartache before going upstairs to beat off to Bettie Page pictures.

"I jerked off to videos of her old loops, not just pictures."

Same deal. And look at you. You're still jerking off, even lying next to this fine, fine, fine mama. You're the one stuck in a loop! I think maybe you're just in love with yourself, Vic.

"I don't even know who I am anymore, Doc."

Me, either.

"Meaning you don't know who I am, or who you are?"

Oh, I know just who I am. Especially now.

"You mean a real pussy?" I made myself chuckle.

I don't find you funny, Vic. I find you sad. I find you very, very sad.

"Doc, how can you say that to me?"

Well, for one thing, you're talking to a cat.

"You started it!"

Vic, at some point, you need to take control of your own senses. That includes your brain, or what's left of it.

"Do you think I'm insane, Doc? Is that what you're saying?"

The whole world is nuts, Vic. I can't say I miss it. It's all relative. My main concern in your regard is that you're ceding dominion over your domain to this total stranger. And we both know how that always works out.

"This is different, Doc. She's my wife. I love her."

But does she love you?

"I guess. I mean, why else would she marry me?"

She needs you, at least for now.

"Well, I need her too."

For the same reason?

"I can only speak for myself. And for me, she's a cure for my loneliness."

And for her?

"You got me."

Exactly my point. That's what you need to determine, Vic. Before it's too late.

"Doc, I'm getting old. I'll be on your side of the fence before too long. Why rock the boat if the voyage is going so well?"

At least till you hit an iceberg. Like you always do. You could find an iceberg in a lava pit, Vic.

"Are you saying she's manipulating me, Doc?"

You tell me.

"But I'm the one asking the question!"

And only you can answer it, Vic.

"Well, I don't give a fuck, how's that?"

You say that now. But just wait.

"What do you suggest I do, Doc? File for divorce? I'd be out on the street!"

Vic, I'm not saying for sure she's bad news. But if she is a blood-sucking serial killer with ties to the Yakuza, I mean, is that really a firm foundation for a long-term relationship?

"Doc, can't you just tell me? Don't you see all from your celestial perspective?"

I don't see shit except what's right in front of me, Vic. Same as before. But from what's been happening in this world since I died, I'm kinda glad I'm not around anymore, except for your eyes only. The American dream is in for one rude awakening.

"Then you're still better off than me. All I see is a talking cat."

Look past the pussy, Vic. For once in your life. I miss you, but I don't want you hanging out over here with me any sooner than you have to. It's not that much fun.

"Really? The afterlife sucks?"

It's different for everyone, Vic. Same as life itself. It all depends on what you make of it. If you want to believe Val is the love of your love, or a vampire, or a gangster, or all three, fine. But then ask yourself: can you live with that constant sense of danger?

"Sounds like it's more exciting than what you got going on, Doc. Doc...? Doc!"

I felt Val's hand on my shoulder. She was sitting up with a worried expression on her sleepy face. "Vic, are you talking to the cat again?"

I looked at Doc, the cat, who was licking his own genitals, or the area where they once were. Then he looked at me, blinked, meowed, and hopped off the bed. Fido was still sticking to the shadows, as if I frightened him.

I couldn't blame him. Hell, I even frightened myself these days.

Chapter Four
WOLF IN CREEP'S CLOTHING

It was around this time I began to suspect I'm actually a fictional character, magically manifested via an unseen deity, pulling my strings and yanking my chain at will. As it were.

You know how you wake up from a strange dream and think, *What the hell was that about*? I've always wondered if that's what it's like after you die.

Only what if you don't wake up from this dream, *because it's not your dream*?

The older I got, the more I feared death, but oddly the less I cared about the afterlife, even as the momentum toward my own inevitable demise was picking up speed day by day, moment by moment, to the point where the notion of mortality was no longer an abstract concept, but a very tangible truth.

To be honest, I hoped there was no afterlife. I felt done, even though my bucket list was far from fulfillment. My bucket had a big hole in it, anyway. And all my dreams had already leaked out, long ago.

But if it all were a dream inside someone else's head, even my waking dreams belonged to someone else. If I am not the custodian of my own consciousness, then that relieves me of responsibility for my own fate. I can just relax and run out the clock, because it's not my clock to wind, or watch. I don't even know what fucking time it is anymore.

Naturally I asked my resident shrink what she thought of this theory. She didn't either confirm or deny it.

"If I'm just a fictional character in your fabricated universe, then I have no power over my destiny, either," she said.

"So why bother with ambition? Why should I be a lounge lizard?"

"Because your creator wants you to."

"Who is my creator?"

"That's the question we all ask ourselves. Maybe we're manifesting ourselves and we create our own consciousness, until we just run out of ideas. We simply write ourselves off."

"Or someone writes us out."

She nodded.

"So what's the distinction, if it's all merely a projection of someone's imagination?"

"Beats me," she said with a shrug. "I'm just humoring you, as usual. Otherwise you'd drive me crazy."

We were on our way to perform at a private party in Capitol Hill. It was a grand old mansion surrounded by other mansions, all ensconced in various shades of greenery. A place I would never afford to inhabit, only visit.

I was wearing my green fez and green smoking jacket, adding to the emerald ambience. It struck me that perhaps the person writing my story was someone I had met, or seen somewhere. Maybe the author has been making a cameo in his or her own movie, like Alfred Hitchcock. It could be anybody. Val. Doc (the cat or the ghost). Ivar. That other dude with the fez.

Or even you, my unseen friend.

Anyway, whoever was calling the shots had decided that Val and I would be performing at private parties around Seattle's high society circuit, billed as "The Voodoo Valentine Show." Of course, I had very little to do other than introduce my wife, who would then perform an exotic dance that would literally entrance the assembled audience, always performing to a classic lounge tune I would provide on a portable turntable, the records culled from my own vinyl vault. Val let me pick any tune I wanted, as long as it was old school lounge or exotica. Since that's pretty much the only type of music I owned, it didn't present a problem.

Sometimes I tried telling jokes during my brief part of the show, but they always bombed, or just fizzled out. Mostly they were gags I'd heard others tell in movies. Nothing original, much less amusing. Val told me to cut it out and just play off of her.

But this one gig turned out to be different, and a turning point for my participation in the proceedings.

This particular residence, belonging to the prestigious Marlow family, had a baby grand piano in the parlor. Val sprawled all over it during her dance routine, to the beat of Percy Faith's "Jungle Fantasy," winding up totally nude as usual, except for her belly bracelet and high heels. No ghouls or demons had crashed any of the parties lately, so things were going pretty smoothly. I was feeling more confident, if not competent, in my limited impresario role.

After Val's performance, which left everyone hot and bothered and thirsty for more cocktails, I sat down at the piano and began playing the Leonard Cohen song "Hallelujah" as she mingled with the rich folks. Then I began singing the lyrics, though more in the mode of the Jeff Buckley cover, which was my preference.

The next thing I knew, everyone had surrounded the piano, and when I finished, they rewarded me with an eruption of enthusiastic applause.

Here's the rub: though I loved that song, I had never bothered to memorize the lyrics. Moreover, I didn't know how to sing, much less play piano. I was totally tuneless and effectively tone deaf. And yet, I had just flawlessly executed a rather moving performance, if I do say so myself, corroborated by the crowd.

I felt as nakedly exposed as my stunning wife standing next to me, casually sipping her Martini as her breasts and bush got some air, though I was much more self-conscious. She was like an actress in an old Jess Franco flick, casually strolling completely nude throughout the entire dreamlike scenario. That's not a criticism, by the way.

With her encouragement, I launched into a totally different number, "Wild is the Wind," more the Nina Simone version than the David Bowie version. Val began slowly but sensually ululating to the tinkling keys as my voice kept expertly riding the scales like a seasoned sonic surfer.

We'd just accidentally hit on our actual act. I would provide the musical accompaniment from here on out, since I had magically acquired the necessary skills.

This is why I was convinced that I was no longer in charge of my own circumstances. They were being created for me. I was being written into corners, and all I had to do was write myself out.

If only real life were this easy.

But once you (or at least I) realized life wasn't real, there were no limitations. Simply acknowledging this fact emancipated me from the shackles of mundane, temporal existence. It was like you're dreaming you can fly, but you know you're dreaming, so rather than waking yourself up, you fight to stay asleep, so you can continue flying, even if the fear you're feeling is palpable. But that fear begins to gradually wane, too. Because even if you fall and die, it won't last, either. Because you'll either wake up, or stay asleep, flying forever.

Anyway, after that night, we couldn't keep up with the bookings in private wealthy homes all around the Puget Sound. Besides Tula's, we scored a semi-regular gig at The Triple Door downtown, starting out in the Musicquarium before our crowds grew too large and they moved us over to the main showroom. (Val kept her skimpy wardrobe intact during the public appearances, naturally). We even performed with El Vez a few times. The money came pouring in from everywhere. I didn't question it. No sign of the Japanese guy, either. Apparently Val's vision of my future had achieved maximum fruition. I felt more fulfilled than I'd ever had as a private eye. I was a true lounge lizard for hire, worth every cent.

At least until I woke up and smelled the swamp water.

The first sign we were sinking was when our gigs abruptly dried up. We had plenty of dough in the bank, so no immediate financial woes, but Val seemed worried, which naturally concerned me, too.

The second sign of trouble was when I stopped seeing Doc's ghost for a few days. That just didn't feel right, even if it did signal a return to relative normalcy. I even missed Ivar, who had also decided to just be a silent, immobile statue, as Nature intended.

It's like everything suddenly stopped, and then started again, but in slow motion, like we were underwater.

Finally, Val told me the "truth." The latest edition, anyway. It came out more like a report than a confession.

"Vic, you're still under the influence of opioids," she said without a trace of irony or even sympathy.

She was referring to the opioid-induced zombie epidemic instigated by the international criminal conglomerate based in Costa Rica, all conveyed in my previous chronicle. That's how we'd been reunited, when we both cracked the case, or at least slowed down their insidious operations. Apparently, according to my astute wife, I still had the hallucinogenic drugs in my system, despite the antidote, and they were seriously warping my perception of commonly accepted reality.

"So is my brain permanently damaged?"

"Yes, but no harm done, really. It was never quite right to begin with. If anything, the drugs have distilled your consciousness to its essence. Now you only see and feel what you want to see and feel."

"Does that include you?"

"No. I'm real. However, you are under my spell. I am a witch, Vic. And a vampire. Neither in the conventional sense. For one thing, I don't subsist on human blood. The person committing the killings around Seattle is not me, but someone from my past."

"A Yakuza vampire?'

"No, don't be silly."

"Oh, right. That would be silly. Unlike just a regular vampire."

"However, the incidents are related."

"What incidents?"

"The appearance of this killer, and the hitman that has been following us."

"How are they related?"

"Me. They're both after me."

"For what? I thought you were paying off the Yakuza with our gig money."

"I am, but that's not what this particular person wants from me. He's obsessed with me. So is the killer. Well, they're both killers. I've been involved with them before, and they can't seem to get over me. Now they want you dead. I'm sorry, Vic."

"Um, is this the drugs talking, or…?"

"No, Vic. It's me."

"My literally bewitching wife."

"Yes."

"So does this make me, like, Darrin to your Samantha? And if so, which Darrin?"

"It makes you, like, dead, unless I find a way to shake them."

"Can't we just kill them?"

"No. If either go missing, we'll bring the whole organization down on us."

"Organization?"

"Yakuza. Vampires. All of them. They're working together. I can't even tell them apart sometimes."

"Vampires are organized?"

"Loosely. Let's just say this one has friends in high places. Or low places, depending on your point of view."

"My point of view is rather blurry, since I'm obviously stoned or otherwise mentally incapacitated."

"Yes, and no."

"God, I hate that fucking non-committal answer. Pick a side."

I looked over at Ivar. He winked. Things were back to normal again.

That night, or maybe it was midday, hard to tell, since we always kept the blinds drawn, I had a dream I was a werewolf. At least I think it was a dream. Doc's ghost was with me as I stalked the dark shadows of Seattle by moonlight. But since Doc was often with me in paranormal form, that didn't help establish the veracity of the situation. I was bare except for a ragged pair of green pants, obviously a reference to the Marvel comic book *Werewolf by Night*, one of my youthful favorites.

"Doc, I'm a werewolf."

If you say so. Doc seemed unfazed, but then he was a ghost, so not easily impressed.

"Look at me. Fur. Fangs. I have a lust for blood, and I'm vegan."

That's very white of you.

"As opposed to Barry White of me? Whaddya want from me, I'm Caucasian. I have many flaws that aren't my fault. I'm just trying to restore some balance and justice to Nature by giving up pizza."

You just said you have a lust for blood, and I take it you don't mean V-8.

"I do, but…"

Just human blood, though, right?

"*Yes*. And flesh. I want *flesh*. But not dead flesh, like a zombie. *Live* flesh. *Female* flesh..." I could feel myself slobbering on my own fuzzy chest, like a dog salivating on a warm day during one of my old walks.

I noticed a lone feminine figure, wearing nothing but heels and an overcoat, coming out of a neon-lit nightclub in an eerily deserted downtown, like an Edward Hopper painting. Even from a dark distance, I could see she looked just like the pretty profile picture of the young Rover sitter we'd hired. The one who had been slaughtered, whose curvaceous body was never found after it mysteriously vanished from our Ballard apartment. Whose death was never reported to the proper authorities. I had assumed one of Val's many nefarious pals had disposed of the evidence, regardless of the perpetrator, who was perhaps me, even though I'd been out with Val when it happened, so I had an alibi. Or did I? Was this a suppressed memory of the actual murder, coming back to haunt me?

Compelled to solve this mystery by simply reenacting it, Doc and I followed her, though he was really just following me. Since I was in primitive beast mode, once I caught up to her I grabbed her and dragged her into a shadowy alley, despite the better angels battling it out with my inner demons. During our brief struggle we cast looming, ominous silhouettes on the moonlit wall, though everything seemed to be in black and white, like a scene from 1955's *Daughter of Horror*. I tore off her clothes, including the green Rover T-shirt she wore beneath the overcoat, growling and drooling. Instead of screaming, she seemed aroused by my primal aggressiveness. She assumed a submissive position, and we made mad love as Doc stood by, watching and shaking his head. The blue mist swirled around us as we grunted and rutted like canines in heat, the only color I could see in this chiaroscuro netherworld, my fur sticky with our mingled bodily fluids. I licked the wounds I inflicted upon her tender young flesh, and she giggled with delight.

After simultaneous screaming orgasms, the disheveled, scratched-up Rover sitter and I stood up and politely shook hands. I even apologized for startling her, and thanked her taking care of my pets, even though they too had temporarily vanished on her watch, though under the circumstances, I forgave her and promised to give her a 5-star review. She smiled, petted my furry face, kissed my cold nose, put on her high heels and what was left of her shredded clothes, and vanished in the blue mist like she was never there, because indeed, she was never heard from again, in any world, at least within my perimeters of perception.

I remember having vile dreams like this as a kid, when my hormones were raging out of control, and nocturnal emissions were my only release. At least until I learned to masturbate while awake to the voluptuous visions constantly floating around inside my head like mermaids in a fishbowl.

But I wasn't a kid anymore. I should've outgrown these demented sex fantasies post-pubescence, rather than justifying them with subjective moral relativity.

"I just cheated on my wife, Doc," I said. "And I committed rape, even though it was kind consensual, no? I mean, after I initiated it by force?"

Yes and no, he said.

"Goddamn it, Doc, not you too."

None of this is real, Vic, so it doesn't matter. You're not on trial here. Just enjoy the freedom to let your inhibitions and libido run wild, Vic. Most people would kill for that freedom. Literally. What's next?

He surprised me. "Why Doc, you voyeuristic creep!"

Vic, you know I've always lived vicariously through you, even if it's only your salacious subconscious. Now more than ever, of course, since I've become, shall we say, corporeally challenged.

"This just feels like one of my adolescent dreams."

As long nobody really gets hurt, what harm can it do? Same then, same now. As long as your dream life doesn't bleed into your real life, so to speak, all good. Sick, but harmless in the scheme of things.

"You don't think this reveals a repressed desire to defile innocent women as a power trip?"

Doc just laughed. *Vic, I've never known you to be anything but a pussy when it comes to pussy.*

"Good point." I decided to roll with it, but down a more innocuous path. "I want to sing in a nightclub like Frank Sinatra."

Okay, that might actually hurt people. Even if they are imaginary.

"Good. Then let's do it."

We went down to Tula's on Second Avenue, or at least its facsimile in my fantasy world. In the real world, it was one of my favorite spots. Val and I had spent many a dinner date there, listening to live jazz by folks like Dimitri Matheny. In fact, he was there when I walked in with Doc, playing his snazzy rendition of Angelo Badalamenti's "Audrey's Dance" from *Twin Peaks*. I was no longer a werewolf. I was back in my lounge lizard regalia, fur-free. I had literally shed my sinful skin and reinvented myself on the spot.

My pal Dmitri beckoned me onto the small stage. His quartet became my backup band. Nervously, I began singing "Angel Eyes," sounding just like Frank. Or a reasonable facsimile. Doc sat at the bar and watched with pride beaming from his milky white dead eyes.

That's when I noticed nobody else was there. And I woke up. Again. I think.

It was exactly like when you wake up from one dream into another, except now, the boundaries had blurred to the point where I didn't know which stage I was in at any given moment.

Val was making breakfast in the kitchen. I sat down after putting one of my exotica LPs on the stereo: *Voodoo!*, by Richard Hayman and his Orchestra.

I told her about my dream.

"Sounds like just another tired male rape fantasy to me," she said dryly. "No surprise, considering you get your rocks off imagining me getting gang-banged by monsters. Male insecurity masquerading as patriarchal domination. Common. And sad. But I'm used to it by now, so I forgive you, Vic. Just don't try to bring your fantasy life into our real lives, or I'll have to kick your ass."

"What the hell are you taking about, Val?"

"Isn't that what you told me the other night? You thought you saw me having sex with demons? And jerked off to it?"

"Yeah, but it seemed so real. That's why it was so disturbing."

"The only disturbing part was your enjoyment of it. As for whether it actually happned, don't be ridiculous. Everything, even dreams, seem real in the moment. That's the trick of God or whoever is conducting this tragicomic opera. It's part of the illusion, no matter how distorted your perception may be at any given moment, in any stage or stage of consciousness, self-medicated or otherwise."

"The narrator. Meaning my creator. The one I told you I can sense."

"And mine, too."

"Same one."

"Who knows?"

"Not Doc. I asked him. He doesn't know, or he just won't tell me. I get the idea he's holding out on me, though, possibly for his own amusement."

"Your imaginary dead friend, or our cat that only talks to you?"

"I think they're one and the same, actually. You think I'm nuts, don't you?"

"I think you're a dirty old man, Vic. Scratch that. I know. But again, I'm fine with it. You're harmless. Except maybe to yourself."

"So I've been told. But I'm not insane."

"I didn't say that. Sanity is relative. And dull."

"Madness runs in my family."

"It at least takes a stroll through most families, Vic."

"Are you really a witch and a vampire?"

"If you'd like to believe both or either, sure, why not? People believe whatever provides the simplest explanation and soothes their anxiety. Credibility is not a factor when it comes to blind faith."

"Why did you tell me you were a witch, then?"

"When did I tell you that? You must've been dreaming."

"You're fucking with my head."

"Well, you can fuck with my body, if you want, and we'll call it even."

I stared at her, a vision of astonishing beauty, waiting for her to dissolve and dissipate into thin air like all the superheroes at the end of *Avengers: Infinity War*. Sorry if I just blew it for you, though I'm sure they'll be fine in the sequel. Not that I personally care much. Full disclosure: I'd never actually seen it. The only comic book adaptation I really liked was the 1960s *Batman* series, since it didn't take itself so seriously, and I related to its absurdist worldview. But I'd read about all of these recent superhero blockbusters online. I always looked up spoilers to popular movies, just out of idle curiosity, since I avariciously devoured comics as a kid back in Brooklyn, though I preferred the ones with monsters, like *Tomb of Dracula* and *Tales of the Zombie*. I still never understood what the fuss was about. I guess I'd outgrown the little kid in me in lieu of more adult pursuits, chiefly sex. Movies provided an escape for me, perhaps even therapy, but I never got emotionally involved with them. It was all make believe, anyway. But people often reacted to imaginary events as if they were actual tragedies with real world consequences. I guess it made them feel more enjoyably alive, to virtually co-inhabit a fantasy world populated with ideal idols. This was why all of these first person action video games were so popular, I figured, though I'd never played one myself. The only game I ever played was air hockey, when I was a kid. After that, I was too busy playing with myself.

I put on one of my favorite albums, *Exotica*, by Ted Auletta and his Orchestra, as I made love to my wife, flashing back on my werewolf domination fantasy (which I preferred to "rape," naturally), and once we both climaxed, we drifted back to dreamland. It was beginning to feel more like a refuge than a revery.

Of course, it did seem odd that we were in each other's dreams all the time. At least I was no longer alone.

In this dream, I was a werewolf, but Val was walking me on a leash down the street, like I was a dog. My former occupation, though the roles had been reversed. Made sense to me as a metaphor.

It was only when I noticed that people were laughing at me and I wasn't actually covered in fur that I realized I wasn't really dreaming. I looked up at Val, who looked down at me and smiled.

"Just wanted to see how long it would take for you to catch on," she said slyly.

I stood up, completely naked and embarrassed.

"Come on back inside before the cops nail us," she said. We were only down the block on Ballard Avenue.

I ran upstairs ahead of her, but had to wait, since she had the keys. She took her time, of course. It was like those dreams where you're naked in public, except this time, I wasn't dreaming. I hate it when the wrong dreams come true.

"I've lost touch with reality," I said.

She poked me in my shivering, hairy ass. "No, you're real, all right, Vic. At least until you're not anymore."

"Why did you do that?"

"Payback for your sexist rape fantasy."

"But you weren't even in it!"

"That's another reason, asshole."

"Well, technically, it didn't actually happen, so why am I being punished for it?"

"How do you know it didn't? You thought you were dreaming just now, didn't you? And anyway, it's the thought that counts. Haven't you heard?"

Once inside, I threw on a robe, then sat on the bed and looked at Fido and Doc, who were staring back at me. They seemed to be laughing, too. Ivar just kept smiling. He always got a big kick out of me.

I lay in bed, eyes wide open, listening to my LP *The Rites of Diablo* by Johnny Richards. Val fell asleep next to me. I watched for bats to appear on the wall, but they stood me up. Because Val and her friend—possibly the vampire serial killer—were still in human form, of course.

Doc was standing in the corner, just looking at me. I didn't say anything. I waited to see if he'd disappear. He didn't.

I got up, got dressed, and went outside into the night. It was busy, probably a Friday or Saturday, Ballard bustling with business. I went into Hazlewood, one of my favorite spots, ordered a house specialty, something hard, and moped. At least the booze tasted and felt like the real deal, even if it wasn't. Johnny Jewel's "Windswept" was playing on the sound system.

That's when I sat down next to myself. I knew this would happen. When you spend too much time alone, you just wind up talking to yourself.

It wasn't me now, but me twenty or so years ago, when I was a private eye in San Francisco. I was amazed by what lousy shape I was in back then. My face was puffier, if smoother. I had the same hair, though it wasn't sprinkled with gray like now. Otherwise I was proudly recognizable.

Young Vic ordered a beer, which made me cringe. "Don't you have any pride, dude?" I asked him.

You kidding? You know better. We won't develop a sophisticated palette for booze for several years.

"Well, here's to our liver," I said, and we clinked glasses. The bartender didn't seem to notice I was talking to myself, or maybe she was used to it by now. It was Seattle, after all.

Glad we still have it, Young Vic said. *Our liver, that is. I wasn't a reliable custodian.*

"Neither am I, though I have learned to pace myself."

Did we ever wind up going to AA, like Doc always suggested?

"Yeah, eventually, off and on. It helped us achieve perspective. But I realized we're not a true alcoholic, because we can stop drinking anytime we want to."

Don't tell me: we just don't want to. Cheers.

We clinked glasses again.

So what else is new in our future? Young Vic asked me. *No spoilers, just generally speaking.*

"But we always liked spoilers."

Only for movies. This is real life.

"What's the difference?"

You got me. We're the wrong person to ask that question, aren't we?

"Well, okay, the main news is we finally got hitched."

Yeah? No kidding. Happily?

"So far. I think."

Uh, oh. Trouble in Paradise already?

"Nothing I can't handle."

So I guess we matured over time.

"Or just got more cynical and impervious to pain."

Young Vic nodded. *So tell me about her. The basics only.*

"She's a burlesque dancer, a masked wrestler, a professor, a witch, and a vampire. She can cook, too."

Wow! We lucked out. Does she dig us?

"Surprisingly, yes. Or so it seems. I keep looking for an ulterior motive."

Can't be for our money.

"We did make some after we sold The Drive-Inn."

You and Doc?

"Me and Monica."

"Why, where's Doc?"

I sighed. "Don't go there, man. Just enjoy his friendship. I still do."

Well, that's a big relief. You had me nervous there for a second. So we finally moved to Seattle.

"Yep."

How did that happen?

"Actually a case took us up here, and I stayed. A movie star accused of murder. He almost made a movie of our life, which would've changed everything. Instead, we're here."

Senseless in Seattle.

"Pretty much."

Young Vic nodded and gazed into his beer. *Figures. Never could catch a break. At least we finally found the love of our life, right?*

"Yes. Cheers." *Clink.*

You know what's weird? Young Vic said.

"We're talking to ourselves and nobody else can hear us?"

That. Plus neither of us thinks this is weird.

"Oh, we got over that. The hard way. It's *all* weird. No changing it. You wouldn't believe who's president now."

Of what?

"The United States, dumbfuck."

Oh. Well, nothing would surprise me in that regard.

"Trust me. You're in for a shock. Though we will personally benefit in an unexpected way that actually ties into our eventual nuptial bliss."

Okay. We never did really follow politics, anyway.

"But sometimes it follows us."

We were never good at following anyone, were we?

Still aren't. I'm retired from that racket, anyway. Our wife makes all the money. We no longer have to work."

Man, talk about a dream come true!

"Funny you should put it that way."

Why? You think we're dreaming now?

"One of us is, obviously."

So one of us is real, and one ain't?

"Or both."

Both real, or both not?

"Either or."

I hate those non-committal answers.

"Me, too."

We were quiet for a while. No one else was in the bar, except for the bartender, who was reading a fashion magazine, ignoring us.

So how is Monica? Young Vic asked me.

"She's good, actually. Also happily married."

Oh, cool. I'm glad. She deserves it. Lucky guy.

I let that pass and just nodded.

So, say one of us is in the other's dream, Young Vic said. *Which would you rather it be? Me or you?*

"Well, I think I'm happier than you ever hoped to be, but then again, you have youth on your side."

Yeah, but what good is youth without happiness?

"What good is happiness without youth?"

Better late than never, right?

"I guess. You have time on your side, too. But we wasted most it."

We were quiet again. It was like two old friends reuniting after a long time, excited at first, but then slowly realizing they no longer had anything in common anymore except memories.

I looked at Young Vic again. He was wearing the same sort of old sharkskin suit I had on, just a different color. His, or rather our, trademark Fedora was on the bar. He looked so sad. It made me feel better.

After a while we got bored with each other's company and I went home, only slightly soused by my standards, to find Val in bed with both the Japanese dude and the vampire dude that had been stalking Seattle. The Japanese dude was eating her out while the vampire dude bit and sucked her tits, blood dripping down her torso, her legs wrapped around that hungry Yakuza head, her pretty feet kicking the air, her toes splayed with tension before achieving release. She moaned with forbidden ecstasy as I fed Doc and Fido, poured myself a generous shot, and then turned on Netflix, casually jerking off to the savage sounds of paranormal pleasure emanating from the bedroom.

Young Vic sat next to me. He was also beating off. Doc sat in a chair, watching the TV, ignoring our little circle jerk, apparently invisible to my younger self, though I was being haunted by both at once now. Being full of vigor, Young Vic climaxed three times to my once, and I finished last.

I can see our marriage is a bit complicated, Young Vic said, nodding toward the bedroom as he wiped his hand on our sofa. I didn't say anything. Easily distracted, Young Vic seemed entranced by the anesthetic allure of Netflix, while I'd momentarily lost interest, still bummed about those two dudes fucking my wife, and her enjoying it so much, even if it was only a drunken, drug-induced delusion. Except I wasn't that drunk. Without thought I put on an episode of *Daredevil*. I'd already watched both seasons three times already. It dawned on me that the character of Elektra also had issues with the Yakuza. Maybe that's what was subconsciously fueling my perception of Val's sordid past, filling in gaps with shit I absorbed from TV, assuming she was either lying or I was hearing only what I wanted to hear. Both were socially acceptable behavioral norms these days, now that personally tailored distortion of reality had been normalized from the top down.

Young Vic, who had been naturally ignorant of the mind-numbing, sensory-overloading home entertainment revolutions around the corner from his era, was immediately enthralled by the gritty, violent, adult-oriented action on the tube. It was just like when we sat for hours at the bar in The Drive-Inn, watching Doc's cult movie collection on something called VHS.

Is this like regular cable?

"Sort of," I said. "It's called 'streaming.'"

Like stream of consciousness?

"I never thought of it that way, but yeah."

Hm.

We were never very savvy or even curious when it came to tech stuff, so he just let it drop and said, *I can't believe they made a 'Daredevil' series. Not a good one, anyway.*

"Also Luke Cage, The Punisher, Iron Fist, and Jessica Jones."

I never heard of that last one.

"Me either before the show, but she's hot."

Are these any good?

"Yeah. Better than the big screen Marvel movies, I think."

"What movies?"

"Spider-man, Captain America, Iron Man, Thor, Hulk, Avengers, all those guys we grew up with."

Are you serious? Wow!

"Doctor Strange, Ant-Man, and Black Panther, too."

Get the fuck outta here! Ant-Man!?

"And The Wasp, too. I know, who'da thunk, right? I forgot we were still into comics when we were your age.

73

That's when we still had some nostalgia left for our fucked-up childhood."

Oh, so we're so fucking mature now?

"No, just burnt out. Anyway, I've seen all these shows and most of the movies already. I'm over it."

Okay, I'll watch something else. I'm easy.

"I know. We always watched anything on a screen, just to distract us from the reality around us. Here's the remote. Just scroll around and pick something." I handed it to him, even though it was all sticky with our semen.

Any porn?

I sighed, saddened and sickened by how little we'd changed. I felt so old and tired, and almost dead.

After a while we fell asleep on the sofa. Or woke up. We just couldn't tell anymore. What's worse, we no longer cared. One way or another, it would all be over soon enough, at least for us. Speaking for myself, I would miss the music, but not the noise.

Chapter Five
FEVER SCHEME

Is something that's better than nothing really worth anything?

Since the borders between reality and fantasy, the real world and the reel world, had finally blurred then bled into one another, no semi-sentient experience of mine lasted, evaporating like exhaust fumes from a passing muscle car through my murky mental chambers. In this state of constant confusion, I was careful not to harm anyone else, even if I could do so with impunity, like The Punisher, because I was wary of any actual, tangible consequences. I tried to appreciate my current kaleidoscope of consciousness rather than control it, because for one thing, I could still feel everything happening to me, inside and out, which must've meant I wasn't dead yet. Just maybe trapped in a coma, like the last few seasons of *Archer,* or perhaps fully functional but locked inside my own head like the hoodie kid with big eyes on *Mr. Robot.*

In fact, I began theorizing that I was still back in the hospital bed after Tommy Dodge had nearly beaten me to death with a baseball bat upon finding me with his long lost love Rose, who was also my long lost love, only he didn't know that when he hired me to find her. I didn't know it, either. I wondered if the apparition of Doc was really a reflection of the real Doc, alive and well, sitting patiently by my side, waiting for me to wake up so we could get back to business as usual. That prospect really didn't seem so bad, even though I was mostly miserable in those days. It only seemed rosier in retrospect.

I pondered this as I sat listening to Elvis Presley singing "Danny Boy" after feeding Doc and Fido, not sure if they were merely furry fragments of my fuzzy imagination, but assuming they needed sustenance anyway.

I looked over at the Murphy bed, which was empty. Val was gone. Maybe for good. Maybe she was never there. Meantime, the kids had to eat.

I was softly crying in a fit of self-pity as I sat down with a bottle of Scotch at our red and silver 1950s kitchen table, across from Doc, the ghost, and Young Vic, status unknown. I kept wanting to ask if one could see the other, to at least confirm one of my mirages, but I didn't really want to know.

What's the matter? Doc asked me. Young Vic was staring at the TV with a quizzical look, trying to figure out if the Netflix reboot of *Lost in Space* had any callbacks to the original from our childhood.

"This song, at least this version, always gets to me," I said to Doc. "For some reason, it reminds me of all the pets I've lost over the years. I hope animals have souls. If they don't, neither do we."

Then what am I?

"Beats me."

You beat yourself five times a day, Vic.

"Not anymore. I'm too old, too tired. The mind is willing but the flesh is weak. Self-induced orgasms no longer relieve the stress, because for one thing, I'm no longer stressed. Just…"

What?

"I don't know. That's what's bugging me. I'm stuck in perpetual limbo between two worlds, maybe more, and I don't know which is which anymore."

Maybe there never was a real distinction, Vic. Could be this is an epiphany, not a psychotic break.

"Who said anything about a psychotic break?"

Your wife. Well, she inferred as much. I guess you don't remember that conversation.

"For all I know, she'a a projection of all my female fantasies into one idealized form, but not actual flesh and blood."

Can you touch her, feel her?

I looked around the sad, empty room. "Not at the moment."

She'll be back.

"When?"

When you need her most. Meantime, the show must go on.

"What fucking show?"

Life! We got a gig, Vic. Let's go. Bring your fez, smoking jacket, and musical chops. You'll need 'em.

"What about Val?"

I'm your new manager. And your old partner, remember?

I nodded. A sentimental shit parade was marching through my head. *Alone Again, Naturally. All By Myself.* God, I always hated those stupid, sappy fucking '70s songs growing up. But they were sometimes so apt, even still.

I remembered this old movie called *Blues Busters* (1950), starring The Bowery Boys. My brother and I would watch those movies every weekend back in Brooklyn. In this one, Sach (Huntz Hall) suddenly develops a beautiful singing voice after having his tonsils removed, so naturally Slip (Leo Grocery) scores him a gig at a nearby nightclub run by gangsters. Hilarious hi-jinks ensue, and naturally, Sach loses his talent and they lose the gig. Another dream of success dead. But it was fun while it lasted. I decided to adopt the ancient wisdom of The Bowery Boys and apply it to my immediate situation.

"We gotta go," I said to Young Vic, who barely acknowledged me.

We?

"Not you and me, I meant…it's just becoming a habit now. I mean just me. I'll be back."

OK, Terminator. I'll be around, wherever you go.

"That's like so not reassuring, but thanks for the thought."

Doc and I left, even though I had no idea where we were going. I never did, but I always trusted his compassionate compass. With his help, I was going to sing my way out of this midlife malaise, even if it was only to myself in the shower.

But as it turned out, I had a legit gig lined up at Tula's in Belltown, near the scene of my last crime against humanity. I wasn't sure how it had been arranged, but once Doc led me there, I was welcomed by the owner and a packed house. Since I showed up in my lounge lizard gear, I was ready to take the stage, where an unknown quartet of musicians—sax, piano, bass, drums—was already playing Dave Brubeck's "Take Five." Once I walked in, they switched to "Frankie Machine" from the soundtrack of *The Man With the Golden Arm* by Elmer Bernstein.

The audience greeted me with ecstatic applause as I grabbed the mike and leaned into it. After pointing then snapping at my backup band, whom I spontaneously introduced as "The Thrillers," I launched into a medley of some of Sinatra's biggest hits, coming out swinging with "Ol' MacDonald," "Come Fly With Me," and "I Believe," before blending some ballads: "All the Way," "One For My Baby," and "In the Wee Small Hours." The women were all sobbing, the men cringing with envy. I had them all in my hip pocket. One decked-out doll brought me a Martini, and I leaned over and thanked her with a kiss, Elvis-style, which ticked off her boyfriend, who came at me right there in front of everybody. But I socked him once in the kisser and he went down and didn't get up. Meantime, the crowd was clamoring for more so I accommodated them with more Sinatra standards, mixing in some Dean Martin and Bobby

Darin for good measure. I couldn't believe how well I sounded, the real deal. Doc sat at the bar smiling and bopping his head to my beat, raising a ghostly toast. My old friend Bud E. Luv, the Bay Area's reigning lounge singer, couldn't have done any better.

Later, everything slowed down and the sound suddenly got sucked out of the room. The Japanese stranger was sitting at the bar, with Val by his side. She was nuzzling his neck. On the other side was The Vampire, who looked a lot like Spider-man's nemesis Morbius from the Marvel Comics I read as a kid, only dressed in leather like a goth rocker. They were pointing and laughing at me. Then everyone else turned into skeletons and collapsed to the floor. I turned toward the band, and they all spontaneously combusted like the succession of doomed drummers from *This Is Spinal Tap*.

Then I was back in my pad. I was still wearing my lounge lizard gear, but Doc wasn't there. No sign of Young Vic, either. Ivar nodded toward the bedroom and winked. That's when I heard more groaning and moaning, and decided I'd had enough.

I kicked open the door and found Young Vic in bed with my wife, fucking her with all the ebullient energy I could no longer muster. She was so happy, so fulfilled, as my former self gave her the physical pleasure she craved, sating her every desire. I slumped to the corner and buried my head in my hands and sobbed, begging for it all to stop.

When I looked up, I was back at my old desk in my office/apartment above The Drive-Inn in San Francisco. I looked around and recognized all of my old stuff, including the autographed Mara Corday photo on my desk, my old heart-shaped dart board, my Bettie Page jerk-off poster, my cabinet of videotapes and DVDs, and my LP collection, most of which I still owned.

Cautiously I went downstairs and into The Drive-Inn. There was Doc, in the flesh, pouring shots and drinks for all the loners and losers that always frequented that glorious dive, where I fit right in. Monica Ivy was serving drinks too, wearing a mini-skirt and tight T-shirt, looking twenty years younger.

Because she was twenty years younger.

I saw my reflection in the mirror behind the bar. I was twenty years younger, too. I'd merged with my younger self, still conscious of the fact this was the past, not the present, but equipped with the powers of youth. I'd been reborn. Maybe this was my chance to start over, hit reset. But why would I want to do that? I was happy up in Seattle with my wonderful wife. That's all I'd ever wanted, wasn't it?

I sat at the bar and Doc greeted me like he always did. He was obviously not a phantom. I even reached out and grabbed his wrist when he set down my beer (this was before I got into mixed cocktails). It certainly felt corporeal.

Doc looked at me with those genuinely compassionate eyes, like he always did, even as a ghost. But somehow it felt more effective when surrounded by living skin.

"I love you, man," I said, tearing up. "I hope you know that."

"I love you too, my man."

"I know."

It was so wonderfully weird, I just went with it. Doc was disturbed by my emotionalism, though.

"You okay, Vic? You don't seem like your old self today."

"Funny you should put it that way. How can you tell?" I asked him, searching those familiar eyes for some glimmer of irony.

"I don't know. Ever since you got out of the hospital, you've been acting funny."

"Out of the hospital?"

"Okay, that right there is what I'm talking about."

"You mean Tommy Dodge?"

"Tommy Dodge? That guy is long gone, Vic. I mean, you know…the accident. You still don't remember?"

I felt like I was about to hyperventilate. I had finally, fatally lost it. If I ever had it.

"Well, maybe this will make you feel better." Doc popped out the disc of the movie that he'd been playing, the original feature film version of *Westworld*, and replaced it with something else. Val and I dug the new HBO series, even though it made no sense to me. But neither did anything else. At least it showed some tits.

The opening credits of the movie now playing on The Drive-Inn TV screen began to flash as Leonard Cohen sang "Everybody Knows." The flick's title was *Love Stories Are Too Violent For Me*. I'd never even heard of it. The movie, that is. I looked at Doc, who just smiled like he was the curator of my entire world, but didn't offer any further explanation, though that in itself was one possible theory among many. They were accumulating faster than I could keep up, like San Francisco parking tickets.

Now there was Christian Slater walking around snapping pictures of various places he'd like to take his latest crush if only she'd agree to go out with him. Then he pasted them into an album dubbed "The Date That Never Was," exactly like I once did. In the next scene he gave it to his friend Denise at the blood bank, who would then pass it on to a sexy, red-haired nurse named Flora, the object of his (my) unrequited affections. They even used the same names, including mine. The only difference was the setting: for whatever reason, instead of the Bay Area where it all actually happened, it had been filmed on location in Miami, Fort Lauderdale, and Key Largo.

I sat there silently, completely mesmerized, watching the entire Rose saga unfold before my eyes, but portrayed by various famous faces I won't name, because I don't want them to sue me. I'm only mentioning Christian Slater because I know from a reliable source he's a good guy. Doc was especially pleased with his character's casting.

Anyway, the film ran about an hour and a half. Most of the details were true. Even the dialogue was exactly how I'd remembered it. It was The Movie That Never Was, my life story on playback, flashing before my teary, weary eyes.

Except I also remembered everything that had happened to me in Seattle, and how I got there: on the run with a fugitive movie star named Charlie who was interested in making a movie out of my life. Let's just say it didn't work out as planned. Obviously. But then I decided to stay in Seattle, the city of my dreams, living off my piece of the inheritance Doc left Monica and me from the posthumous sale of The Drive-Inn. When those funds got low, I became a dog walker. Then Mickey Rourke optioned my life story. That didn't work out either. Then there was this lengthy series of murky memories involving spies, zombies, guns, exotic locales, drugs, and of course, loads of nasty sex with beautiful women.

Then I was back in Seattle, married to my dream girl in my dream city. Perhaps literally. And it wasn't Rose, since I hadn't seen her in many years, having completely lost touch with her after our final rendezvous down in New Orleans.

The movie ended with me, or rather Christian Slater playing me, back in the hospital following the Tommy Dodge incident, Doc and Monica by my side, or the actors portraying them, that is. Tom Waits' "Blue Valentine" played over the rolling final credits. After they were over, there was a teaser for the next movie, already entitled *Fate Is My Pimp*, with Vic Valentine, again portrayed by Christian Slater, tracking down a Mob brat to a sex cult run by an Elvis-obsessed nut who called himself Deacon Rivers.

That was one of my cases, too.

After it was over, Doc looked at me and said, "So? You remember now?"

I didn't know what to say. I was still waiting to wake up. I was becoming convinced this was just another opioid-induced delusion, though with much more realistic special effects. But other than the details I've described, there was nothing abnormal or suspicious about my immediate surroundings. No copulating demons or lecherous Yakuza hitmen or voluptuous vampire women, or me up on a stage singing like Sinatra, or turning into a werewolf, because that kind of shit was strictly make-believe-ville.

No, *this* was real. The rest had only been a dream. Apparently taking place after the "accident" Doc had cryptically referenced. An accident I couldn't recall, of course, but maybe selective amnesia just another lingering side-effect of this unknown trauma. Like when Sonny Crockett thought he was Sonny Burnett, his undercover drug dealer alias, and acted accordingly. Just like that.

So did this mean I wasn't actually a happily married middle-aged man living comfortably in Seattle now? For some reason, that depressed the hell out of me. But then I was always depressed, even when I had no reason to be. I'd seen shrinks and doctors and none could fix much less diagnose me. So I self-medicated with booze, movies, and sex.

Monica sidled up next to me at the bar. "Need some physical therapy tonight, Vic?"

I looked at her, marveling at her youth, though she was still beautiful even now, whenever that was, living with her wife down in Portland, or I guess that was *up* in Portland from this angle, back in the Future That Never Was.

As if operating per natural instinct, I nodded at Doc, who was just closing up shop for the night, then followed Monica back up to my room, where we made love. "Key Largo" by Sarah Vaughan was playing, but not out of thin air. Monica had put the record on just before we began making out, like old times. Old times that were inexplicably new again.

Afterwards, we lay in bed wondering why we just couldn't be a regular couple instead of fuck buddies, as we always wondered after mind-blowing sex. So I asked Monica, "Will you marry me?"

"Yes," she said without hesitation.

I looked at her, kissed her, felt her flesh, made love to her again because my body was healthy and strong and to confirm she wasn't a fuckable figment of my lurid, oversexed imagination.

"But only if you promise me something," she said after we'd finished again.

"Yes?"

"You won't cheat on me again."

"Again?"

"You know. The last time we tried this, we were engaged, and then you took up with that tramp from Mexico."

"Huh? Who?"

She sat up, exasperated, and put her bra back on, which is never a good sign. "Vic, I'm not doing this again. I'm sorry."

Stunned into silence, she left me alone in the dark, literally and figuratively.

In the shower, I tried to sing, but I couldn't carry a tune. Whatever this dimension I was trapped in now, my singing skills hadn't made the trip with me. That's okay. I never really wanted to be a lounge lizard anyway. I didn't even want to be a private eye, but now it seems I was anyway, against my will. I began feeling distressed, so I decided to walk it off.

As you would surmise, it was quite a shock to be in 1990s San Francisco again. I walked past things like newspaper stands and telephone booths and video stores. The good old days, at least by contemporary comparison—

from your perspective, that is. The fashions were all grungy—Seattle-style, ironically—except for the retro-hipsters like myself. Fortunately I hadn't altered my wardrobe since I was in my twenties, so the shiny but tattered vintage sharkskin suits and skinny ties in my closet didn't feel alien to me. I was always comfortable in my sartorial skin.

I wound up in my old cafe, Rendezvous, which had closed around the turn of the century, but that was before it turned back around again. Everything and everyone felt so present. There was no sense of dreaminess or disorientation. I was right where I was supposed to be. Whatever "accident" Doc was referring to had apparently resulted in a very, very long fever dream, and now I had finally snapped out of it.

Except I felt lonely as hell, as I did for most of my life. I wanted Val. But she was gone. She was never here, apparently.

Except, wait: I knew for a fact I had rescued her cat for her, before I even hooked back up with Rose, and made a play for her. If I could find her again, her younger self, I could maybe skip whatever alternate future was in store from this point and just go right to the one I really wanted. Val and I would get married and move to Seattle, *now*, and…then I would miss Doc, who in this point in time was still alive and well.

Maybe I could somehow get him to change some of his lifestyle habits so he wouldn't keel over from a heart attack way before his time, at least per average metrics. Then maybe I could convince him to move with Val and me to Seattle, and Monica too, and…

No, that wouldn't work. What would I do there? I had no idea what Val was doing during this period because she never told me. It was all part of her secretive past. For all I knew she was in Japan or Central America or Europe, doing whatever she did before we reunited in Mexico City two years ago, or twenty years from now, depending on which way you or I looked at it.

I strolled over to where she used to live, and knocked on the door.

Guess who answered.

The sight of her kicked me in the gut, because I mainly knew her as a knockout in her forties, not a hottie in her twenties, though she definitely lived up to that distant memory, which was no longer distant, nor just a memory.

"Remember me?" I said.

She stared at me long and hard, the accent on the latter, then said before slamming the door, "Remember what I said? Last I checked, a certain orange blowhard is not the president."

"I happen to know he will be, though," I said without a trace of humor.

She looked at me longer and harder, and Little Elvis reciprocated. She was wearing nothing but a robe, open to the waist. In fact, it was the same Japanese robe she wore around our home in Seattle, in the future. Or at least the one I had experienced, subconsciously or not.

Finally, she laughed and said, "I admire your persistence, um…what's your name again?"

"Valentine," I said with Sean Connery-level confidence. "Vic Valentine."

"I'm Esmeralda," she said as if to remind me. "And I haven't lost my pussy again, if that's what you're here for."

"No, I found that already," I said, thinking that *double entendre* was really played out.

"What do you want, then?"

"Just to talk."

"About what?"

"I don't even know where to start."

"You actually have something you need to say to me, a total stranger?"

"I do."

As if inviting in a pushy vacuum salesman, she waved me through the door. When I walked inside, Charlie Mingus's "Haitian Fight Song" was playing on LP. I noticed something else right away. It was a picture of Rose on the mantle.

I walked over to it, held the frame in my hands, and began shaking.

Val walked over behind me and said, "Do you know her?"

"Yes," I said in a whisper. "Do you?"

"Of course," she said. "She was my lover for many years."

"I need to sit down," I said.

"Sure, have a seat."

I backed up and plopped on a cushy couch, disturbing her sleeping cat, who hissed expletives and ran off. Where was the gratitude?

"You and Rose were lovers?" I said. "So were we."

"Yes, I know," she said. "She told me before she left town."

"She did?"

"When you were in the hospital, recovering."

"From Tommy?"

"Yes, so a while ago. I find it ironic, don't you?"

"Baby, my whole life is ironic. So I was in the hospital because of Tommy. Was that 'the accident'?"

"What accident?"

"The one Doc said."

"Who? You mean the doctor? In the hospital?"

"Never mind. Why did Rose tell you about us, you think? I mean, what was the point?"

"She wanted to unburden herself. Her guilt. About you, about Sammy, about everything."

"You knew Sammy?"

"I met him. She took him with her to New Orleans."

"How long ago was this?"

"You really don't remember, do you?"

"I'm a little mixed up lately. Sorry."

"Must be that mental meltdown."

"What mental meltdown?"

"How many have you had?"

"I don't know."

"Well, that's why they call it a mental meltdown."

My brain felt like a pinball machine about to tilt. "So is the Tommy Dodge incident, the 'accident,' and the 'meltdown' all the same thing?"

She looked at me like I was a crazy person, because I guess I was. "I have no idea what you're talking about. I only invited you in because she vouched for you, you know. But you can't stay long. I have a gig tonight at Bimbo's."

"Gig?"

"I'm a dancer."

"Oh, yeah, right."

"You knew that?"

"Just guessed, I guess."

"Well, Raven will be here soon, so you should go. I just wanted to prove something."

"What?"

"That Rose wasn't lying to me. She did that. A lot."

"Yeah, I know."

"I think she just enjoyed toying with people, even those she loved."

"Especially."

Val nodded. She seemed anxious, more so than me, for a change.

"Wait. Did you just say Raven?"

"Yes, why?"

"Raven Rydell?"

"Why, yes. She's my partner."

"On stage or off?"

"Both, as if it's any of your business. Don't tell me you know Raven, too?"

"Not yet."

"Excuse me?"

There was a knock at the door, and my stomach clenched, because I knew who it was. With a huff, Val walked over and let in my old love Raven, only she wasn't old, not as old as when I met her the first time, many years from now.

They kissed, which I admit strained Little Elvis's jumpsuit, but I was too preoccupied with the surreal situation to fully appreciate it. I filed it away for a beat-off image later, then Val introduced me to someone I'd already met and knew intimately, but who hadn't met me. Not lately, anyway.

No recognition flashed in Raven's gorgeous eyes when she shook my hand. I flashed on a vision of her hanging from her own bra in a Seattle jail cell, and my eyes welled with tears.

"Are you okay?" Raven asked me. Like Val, she was simply a younger version of her lovely self, the one I knew, or will know, depending on how long this dream lasted.

"I have to go," I said, feeling emotionally overwhelmed. "I'll be back. We'll all see each other again. Trust me."

I walked outside into the fog, which mirrored my inner state, all the way down to Market Street, where the grindhouses were still in operation. I bought a dirt cheap ticket at the Empire and sat through a triple bill of three of my all-time favorites: *The Howling, Re-Animator*, and the original *Dawn of the Dead*, long before the weak-ass remake, long before George A. Romero was himself undead. It was the movie my brother had watched just before he jumped off the bridge. I felt so sad and lonesome, I cried. I cry a lot when I'm alone.

The cavernous tomb was big and sticky and stinky like always, with drunks and junkies scattered here and there throughout the massive auditorium. I'd blown many a lonely afternoon here back then, or rather, now, and here I was, in the well-worn groove. Nothing ever changes, no matter which direction in time I travel.

This particular hallucination was even more vivid and durable than any of the others, at least so far. I mean, I was never a lounge singer or werewolf in real life, but I *was* a San Francisco private eye, so this fit within the scope of my known world. I'd already lived this life, so I knew it wasn't a fantasy, because it was a memory.

But memories are only dreams that can be recorded. Recorded.

Late that night I hopped a bus back to the Richmond, just realizing I had a car. My Corvair was parked behind The Drive-Inn, like it always had been. It was midnight. Doc was probably asleep, or maybe not. Monica was somewhere pissed off at me. Maybe she was screwing him again, just to get back at me. Again. Whatever. I needed to figure out which of these dimensions was the one that mattered, if any of them did. That's the one where I wanted to be, for better or worse.

The idea Val had once been lovers with two of my former lovers—in fact, my two greatest loves besides her—made perfect sense. The odds still seemed stacked against it, unless it was some sort of cosmic conspiracy to fuck with my head, something I always suspected, anyway. I was a pawn in someone else's game. I just needed to know whose dream I was inhabiting, and then we needed to have a serious conversation.

Inside my office, I put on Chet Baker singing "Let's Get Lost" while I sat at my desk, tossing darts at my heart-shaped dart board. Then I thought about that movie, *Love Stories Are Too Violent For Me*. This was before I had a computer, when the Internet was still young, so it wasn't like I could just Google it. If Doc already had it on DVD, that meant it came out in theaters a while ago. Apparently, it hadn't had much impact on my lifestyle.

Or had it?

One way to find out was to check out my bank account, something I normally avoided like dentist appointments, because I just didn't want to know. I called the automatic system. Whatever dividends I'd received were barely enough to cover my rent, though Doc would never just kick me out, so I wasn't worried about being homeless. I was broke, as usual. But Christian Slater or somebody must've paid for the rights to my story. Where did that money go?

Knowing myself as I do, I'd probably already blown it.

Then I noticed the red light flashing on my answering machine. My answering machine. Fortunately, I remembered how to play back messages.

Just one. Charlie Hayden's "Haunted Heart," in its entirety. I sat and listened to the whole thing, right up until it abruptly ended with a *click*.

The Phone Phantom was back. Only this time, I knew her true identity.

I wasn't sure what to do next, especially in a world I wasn't sure existed, so I decided to just go to bed and fall asleep after beating off to that image of Val kissing Raven. I put on another record, "Cristo Redentor" by Donald Byrd. If nothing else, this spooky shit required a suitable soundtrack, and this was an appropriately moody lullaby for the strange occasion of sleeping in my San Francisco bed again, inside a building that had already been torn down, owned by a guy who was dead.

Except my bed was already occupied when I got there. And it wasn't Monica.

It was Rose.

Chapter Six
LEWD AWAKENING

She was lying in my bed, nude, her legs open, studiously sucking on a pencil while reading a book called *Love Stories Are Too Violent For Me*. I couldn't see the author's name. It was blurred out, the way you can't really read words in a dream. If I were a true detective, that would've been my first clue I was trapped inside my own subconscious. But I think I've established by now I'm much more of an expert in misery than mystery.

I walked over and sat on the bed beside her, our gaze mutually locked. She had a slight smile on her beautiful face, which was the same age it would've been two decades before I left the Bay Area for Seattle. Our encounter in New Orleans may or may not have happened yet, per this timeline, so I didn't bring it up. I really couldn't think of anything to say. And I was a journalist when Rose and I first met. When she was still Valerie.

"*Val.*"

Since she was already nude, I went in for a kiss, uncertain of our dynamic at this point in an alternate past, but pretty confident I wouldn't be slapped for violating her boundaries, considering her position. I was wrong, of course. She pushed me away and held me at bay with her hand on my chest. I could see her, smell her, touch her, and almost taste her. If she wasn't real, then nobody and nothing ever was.

She was staring into my eyes with a mixture of restraint and resentment. "No, Vic. Not anymore."

"What do you mean? Why are you even here? Like *that*?"

"Because last night was a mistake. One of many. But the *last* one."

Obviously, I was missing something. "Last night? What happened last night?"

"Please stop, Vic. Faking amnesia, babbling about some alternate future, all this madness. It needs to stop. It's driving me away."

"Honestly, Val, I mean, Rose, I don't know what you're talking about."

In a huff, she got up and began getting dressed. As usual, she wore no underwear. She just slipped on a long, loose, low-cut peach-colored dress and some sandals. She definitely had the scent of recent sex. But I had no memory of it being with me. At least not this time.

"Please don't go," I said.

She turned and looked at me, leaned over and kissed me. "Vic, your ignorance is only matched by your stupidity," she said.

That's exactly what Val said to me. The other one, back in Seattle, twenty years from now, doing God knows what while I was stuck back here. I hoped someone was feeding our pets, at least.

"I'll be in touch," she said. "I have to go get Sammy."

Sammy. Her son. Father unknown, though there were multiple candidates, which was naturally a point of contention between us. I had wanted to be Sammy's surrogate dad, if that meant I could keep Rose in the bargain. Apparently that never happened, even in this universe. But we obviously had some kind of relationship, and it involved sex, so I didn't want to question it too much. As it was, I was afraid it would all collapse and evaporate, like that episode of *The X Files* where Mulder and Scully are buried unconscious underground with some hallucinogenic mushrooms, trapped inside their own visions.

I got up and approached her and she backed away like a scared puppy. "Vic, don't. I shouldn't have come here last night."

"I'm glad you did, even though I can't remember it."

"Not this again. You really need to stop drinking. I keep telling you that."

"And stop watching so many movies."

"Stop *living* so many movies, at least."

"Are you staying in town?"

She looked at me quizzically. "You really need to get some help, Vic. I can't expose Sammy to whatever your damage is. He needs a stable father figure, not a deranged pseudo-detective."

How many of me were there? I wondered to myself. But all I said was, "Please. I don't want to lose you again."

She sighed and relented. "Call me," she said. Apparently our timeworn bond was stronger than her contempt and disgust, but that's the secret to sustaining any successful relationship. At least one involving me.

She looked at me one last time with a wan smile of resignation, picked up her floppy purse and walked out of my office. I sat back at my desk. Ivar was sitting in the corner, smiling at me. Apparently he was following me across dimensions. Or else he'd always been with me, but I only recent gained the ability to see him.

I just shook my head and sighed, waiting for something to wake me out of this nightmare. I couldn't even remember making love to Rose the night before. But I did remember making love to her many, many other nights.

There was a knock on the door. Potential client? I was back on the beat, or so it seemed.

Standing at the door was a total stranger. He was dressed in black, even black shades. Black gloves, too.

"You Vic Valentine?"

"Yeah."

Then he pulled a pistol from inside his black jacket and shot me in the foot.

"Fuck!" I naturally exclaimed.

Then he was gone.

Bleeding profusely, I hopped back to my desk and sat down. A minute later Doc and Monica were there. They'd heard the shot, apparently.

"Vic, what the hell happened?" Doc asked as Monica gingerly inspected my gory shoe, which she then removed as I winced.

"You got me, Doc."

They took me to the hospital for treatment. It was beginning to feel like this dream had no end. And the pain felt as authentic as the pleasure.

"You have no idea who shot you?" Doc asked as we waited for the doctor to patch me up.

"Never saw him before in my life. He was dressed in black, head to toe."

"So it was either Tommy Lee Jones or Johnny Cash," Monica said dryly.

"Well, at least that narrows it down," I said.

Lying in the hospital bed, I felt dizzy. My vision blurred. But I was definitely sure my old flame Flora was my nurse. She leaned over me as she checked my vitals. I could smell her perfumed cleavage right in my face.

"Hi there," I said.

"Hi, Vic. I'd ask how you are, but I can see for myself."

"You still work at the blood bank?"

"Not any more."

"Still with that bum sax player?"

"None of your business, Vic. I think it's best we all move on, don't you? Anyway, the doctor will be here to see you in a moment."

She was all business, without even a hint of flirtation for old time's sake. The Date That Never Was stayed that way, even here and now, wherever and whenever that was.

I remembered we did get together for a consolation fuck/mutual pity party at some point, but maybe I had only dreamed that, too.

Flora had given me some sort of sedative via syringe, I assumed a painkiller. In any case, I began to blissfully drift away.

When I woke up, guess where I was.

Val was lying beside me. The one I was married to. I was back in Seattle. She was on her laptop, reading.

"Did you see this?"

"What?"

She turned the screen to face me as I groggily sat up. Oddly, my foot was sore. The one that had been shot in my dream of a memory I had forgotten, or maybe it was a memory of a dream. The headline of the story she showed me distracted me from any contemplation of that coincidence.

It read: "Vampire Serial Killer Identified."

There was a security camera photo of me. But not the current me. The old me. Rather, the young me. The one I just was a few minutes ago, or so it seemed.

"That's not me," I said.

"Not anymore," she said. "But I still need to hide you."

Hyperventilating, I shot up out of the bed and into the bathroom. Yup, that was my middle-aged kisser staring back at me, all right, creases and gray temples and all. I missed myself. That all-too-brief trip back to my youth reminded me of what it felt like to still have most of your life ahead of you, with the energy to live it. I went back into the bedroom and sat beside Val.

"None of this can really be happening," I said.

"I don't believe you're a killer, Vic," she said matter-of-factly. "Obviously you're being framed."

"Obviously. I'm more of a werewolf type, though. Vampires are too skinny."

She smiled and stroked my forehead. "Poor baby. You really need to stop drinking."

"And stop watching so many movies."

"Or living them."

A chill ran down my spine and into my balls.

"But I thought you said the vampire killer was your old boyfriend, back to torment you."

She gave me a quizzical look, the same one Rose gave me, often. "What are you talking about?"

I"Never mind."

She stroked my face and said sweetly, "Your ignorance is only matched by your stupidity, dear."

"So you've said. So you've both said."

"Both?"

I lay back on the pillow and stared at the ceiling, where a bat was perched on the overhead fan. I was going to ask Val if she saw it too, but was worried I'd further alienate her with my dementia. Maybe this bat was Rose.

It was best I kept all this to myself. Well, me, Doc, and Ivar, anyway.

I felt pain in my foot again. I had actually limped to and from the bathroom.

"My foot hurts," I said to Val.

"Must be that old wound you told me about," she said, surfing the Internet, seemingly unconcerned.

"What old wound?"

"Vic, c'mon. Remember? The one that acts up sometimes when it rains, which is often in Seattle. You told me one day in San Francisco you opened your office door and some stranger asked if you were you, then shot you in the foot and left. And you never found out who it was."

"That actually happened?"

"You tell me. I wasn't there."

But was I?

Then I remembered being in her apartment in San Francisco, the photo of Rose on her mantle, and Raven showing up and kissing her. I thought of a way to link the past and the present, the real and the imagined. "Do me a favor and Google, 'Love stories are too violent for me.'"

"Huh? What's that? A line from a movie?"

"That's exactly what I want to find out."

She shrugged and accommodated me. "Nothing popping up," she said, showing me the result on the screen as evidence.

"Oh, well," I said. "Nice while it lasted."

"Nice while what lasted?"

"The illusion of success."

"All success is an illusion, Vic, because all roads lead to failure. Of our organs if nothing else."

I scanned the apartment for any signs of Doc's ghost, but only saw Doc the cat, sleeping in a chair, Fido at the base, sleeping as well. I wondered what they were dreaming about.

Ivar was still right where he belonged. At least he knew where he belonged. I was the sailor lost at sea.

As I limped around our pad, it struck me that the dude who shot me way back when looked just like the vampire asshole that was nibbling Val's neck back at Tula's, and fucking her in our bed, tag-teamed with the Japanese dude, though of course I couldn't be sure any of that actually happened, either.

Then as we were having breakfast, I noticed the bite marks on her neck.

"Where did you get those?" I asked her.

"You gave me a hickey while we were having sex last night."

"We had sex last night?"

"Sorry it wasn't memorable for you."

"Did you enjoy it?"

"Yes, of course. More than you did, apparently."

"So it seems my impotence has been cured."

"Well, it's more sporadic now. I'll take what I can get."

"It will only get worse as I get older."

"That's why you have to keep in touch with your dreams, Vic."

"Dreams?"

"Aspirations, if not ambition. Look to the future, but don't forget the past."

"I'm losing any sense of distinction between the two. Some of my memories are of the future. Time is mashing up on me."

"What do you mean?"

"Nothing. I guess I drink too much."

"That's what I've been telling you."

"Yeah. Then again, what difference does it make whether I live or die, if it's all a dream, anyway?"

"Is that really how you see reality, Vic?"

"I don't see reality at all any more, Val."

"Do you think you need professional help?"

"Isn't that what I'm getting?"

"Someone more objective, I mean."

"No. I only want you, not a stranger."

"Lovers can be strangers, Vic."

"Dooby dooby doo."

"What?"

"Nothing. So I guess my lounge lizard career is kaput now?"

"Why do you say that?"

"Do you have any gigs lined up for us?"

"Yes, I do, as a matter of fact. But maybe you'd better lay low, since the police are looking for you."

"They could just knock on our door, especially since we hardly ever leave this joint."

"They came by and I told them you were out of town. San Francisco, to be exact. They'll be watching our place, so you're right, you just stay here, I'll go out and make the money and bring home the bacon."

"You mean tofu."

"Yes."

"How did they link me to these crimes?"

"Security footage which went viral."

"But that's obviously not me. Not now, anyway."

"Maybe you were wearing makeup to make yourself look younger?"

"Whose side are you on?"

"Well, I'm harboring a fugitive, so obviously yours."

"Val, why would I suddenly start killing people?"

"Because you're insane."

"Is that a statement or a question."

"Well, it does run in your family, right? Or limp, at least. Didn't you tell me your mother died in an asylum?"

"The Chipper Monks, in New York."

"Chipper Monks? There's no such place. That's a ridiculous name for an institution, anyway."

"True, but I was there. Maybe it's gone now. This was a while ago."

Val pulled out her cellphone and looked it up. Nothing.

"So I imagined that, too? This was over twenty years ago."

"Maybe you're just remembering it wrong. Unless something is documented, it's like it either never happened, or is forever left open to interpretation, surviving only as long as the minds that remember it. Of course, nowadays, everyone has recording devices like this one. And all the corporations monitor our every thought and action. So it seems like everything is being archived. But there's so much information being stored, it's a big cloud bubble bound to just burst one day. And who will even care? It's overwhelming."

I nodded. "I never really thought about it."

"Of course not. You're locked inside your own brain, Vic."

"And you're locked up in there with me."

"Maybe you're the one that is locked up with *me*."

No answers, just opinions and theories. This is why I stopped asking the hard questions long ago. I didn't even want to know the truth anymore, about anything, especially now that it had become so subjective.

I noticed the soundtrack to our breakfast: songs like "Black Magic Woman," "I Put a Spell On You," "Witchcraft," and "Superstition."

"Interesting mix," I said.

"Thanks. It's a CD compilation I made myself."

"Maybe you have me under your spell, Val."

She winked. "Or maybe I'm under yours."

I looked over at Ivar. He winked, too. Everyone was in on the epic gag. Even the cat winked at me.

Val said she was going out for groceries, and told me to stay put. I wanted to say if I wasn't there when she got back, Google me, but refrained. Instead I sat and watched my Blu Ray of *Wolf Guy*, a 1975 martial arts movie starring Sonny Chiba as a werewolf, sort of. It was painfully familiar.

Since Val hadn't returned by the time the movie ended, I started out on *The Bloodthirsty Trilogy*, which consisted of *Vampire Doll* (1970), *Lake of Dracula* (1971), and my favorite of the three, *Evil of Dracula* (1974). They were basically Toho's answer to Hammer's gothic horror flicks of that period.

When I finished up, Val still hadn't returned from her shopping sojourn. Since she often disappeared for hours or even days without notice or checking in, I wasn't too worried. But this time, something felt different.

While foraging in the cabinets for some food, Young Vic tapped me on the shoulder. He had blood dripping from his mouth, and his clothes were torn.

"Not you again," I said.

What, you thought you could lose me? I'm you! The better part of you, anyway.

"And so you're on a killing spree now, framing me?"

Kinda.

"May I ask why?"

Something to do. I'm bored. You're boring. Look at you. A fucking vegan. We became vegans? What kinda hippie shit is that? I mean, true, we never ate red meat, but c'mon, we live in Seattle, and no more fish? And what about pizza?

"They have vegan pizza now. Not as good, but decent. Also vegan burgers, hot dogs, steak, chicken, all that stuff."

Aw, fuck that! It's bad enough you like fake violence and fake sex in movies, but now fake meat too? What a pussy!

"We still draw the line at fake boobs."

You should maybe consider some silicone implants yourself, with those man-titties.

Self-consciously I looked down at my own chest, and jiggled it. Not too bad. Young Vic just laughed. It seemed everyone always gave me shit, and now I was finally giving myself shit. Made sense, in its own crazy way.

Hey, I liked those movies we were watching. Our collection has really grown, even if we haven't. I mean, as people and all.

"Stop haunting me. You're like that zombie ghost in 'An American Werewolf in London,' after he was killed by the werewolf."

Speaking of which, we're not a vampire. We're a werewolf.

"That's a grammatically incorrect statement."

But still true. As true as anything can be, that is.

"Impossible."

Really? Impossible. Everything seems impossible till it happens. Go back billions of years, the universe is just a bunch of dirt balls floating around in a vast, empty void, then boom! Suddenly on one little tiny speck of shit near one of millions of suns, a variety of gooey creatures pop up out of nowhere, in all shapes and sizes. Some claim dominion over others. Civilizations spring up. Religion is invented to explain everything, but it still doesn't make sense, people just pretend it does to keep from going crazy and just killing each other or themselves, which they do anyway. Sentient beings eat other sentient beings, so yeah, I get the vegan thing philosophically, but how can we give up pizza? I mean, none of it seems real. We're just here for a few moments in the endless span of time, and we act like it's a big deal, like it all means something. We don't matter, man. None of us do. Nothing does, because nothing lasts. And if it all eventually rots, what lasting purpose could it have? What do corporeal beings have that the phantoms of our dreams don't? Not longevity. And only temporal tangibility. So why can't we be a werewolf? Is that really any stranger than just being a talking, furless ape?

"Because 'we' can't be any one thing, plus 'we' can't exist in the same dimension at the same moment in time, because 'I' am the older version of 'you,' get it? And doesn't it make you wonder why nobody but me sees you?"

My victims see me. For a minute, anyway, before I rip their throats open.

"Because they're not real, either."

Then who are all these people getting killed out there?

"People get killed all the time. That doesn't mean we're the killers. It's just in us."

But rape is?

"We're not a rapist, either. That was just an aberration, not a manifestation."

You're floating down Denial again, man.

It would be ironic if I had become a cold-blooded serial killer during my recent blackouts, considering I wound up a local hero by busting one. In fact, I was even a suspect at one point. Still, I just couldn't believe I had it in me, even subconsciously. For one thing, I was too lazy to deal with all that drama. This whole thing was just another head trip, only it felt more like bumper cars inside my brain, going in circles. "You're fucking with me. Stop. *Stop*."

Young Vic was having too much fun at our expense, though, so he kept it up. *Hey man, by the way, I tried out our wife the other day. Nice going! She seemed to enjoy us, too. I just can't see what she sees in us.*

"Yeah, I noticed you helped yourself to my wife while I was out. Nice."

Our wife, you mean. Don't worry, she didn't know it was me. But I saw you watching us, so you know it was me. Well, us, but I was the one having all the fun while you just jerked off. That's a switch.

"Val's right. I'm clinically off my rocker. *Our* rocker."

Aw, c'mon, man, lighten up. We got a hot wife and we don't even have to work for a living anymore. Not that we ever did. This is the life, man.

"But it's not real. It can't be. It all has to end."

Yeah, no shit, Sherlock. You haven't figured that out yet? You don't need to be a detective to realize all consciousness, everything we perceive with our senses, is doomed to disintegrate into dust. Just dig it while you can, man. I wish I'd had as much sex as you are when we were my age. At least we stopped chasing romantic fantasies and realized sex is just sex, not the key to our happiness.

"Val makes me happy. I'm not alone anymore. Except when I am, like now."

Hey, what do you mean! We got each other, buddy! I'm not going anywhere. At least not without you. And vice versa.

"So it's like, sometimes I'm you again, and you're me, sort of swapping our proper places in time, is that what you're saying?"

Kinda. I mean, I fucked the shit out of Rose and Val just last night, simultaneously, and it was awesome!

"I don't remember any of that."

I need to have my own fun sometimes, man. I'm making up for lost time. It's like I put my old me on pause while my young me reaps the benefits of my stronger, healthier body. Well, more energetic, anyway.

"We're healthier now than ever, due to our lifestyle changes. And our marriage. Which may just be another illusion, but fuck it. We all want to live till we die, like Frank sang."

Exactly! Fuck it! Stop wasting time trying to find answers to questions everyone answers by just making shit up anyway! Life is a mystery nobody really wants to solve because the truth is probably too fucking depressing! None of anyone's explanations make total sense, but everyone takes that leap of faith just to get by till we all fucking die anyway! Right? Am I right? I wish we'd known this when we were still me and not you, all worn down and burnt out, you limp dick motherfucker!

"Maybe I'm already dead, and just haunting myself. Or I'm in a coma. Maybe everything that's happened to me since Tommy Dodge beat my brains out with a baseball bat has been nothing by a movie inside my head. Maybe they should just pull the plug already. Unless I'm just pulling my own."

There you go again, old man, trying to figure shit out. We're a lousy detective, remember? But we kick ass as a werewolf!

"Or a lounge singer."

Whatever! Remember when you were a kid, or we were, the sky was the limit. We imagined ourselves to be an astronaut, fireman, cowboy, gangster, samurai, Tarzan, Batman, Elvis, whatever shit we saw on TV. Then we wound up becoming a so-called private eye because why not? It was as arbitrary a choice as any. So now that our collective consciousness is waning fast, why not just go for it? Even if it's not real! Reality is relative, man! Live it up!

"By hunting and slaughtering innocent people. That doesn't sound like us, dude."

Aw, fuck 'em, man! Like you said, they're just paper dolls inside a fantasy we make up as we go! They exist merely for our pleasure! And we were always a misanthrope, anyway. What better way to pay back humanity for butchering animals for eons than to become an animal ourself, just like we wanted to be the first time we saw 'I Was a Teenage Werewolf' or read 'Werewolf by Night'? It's beautiful, man, because we can commit acts of total atrocity with complete impunity, just like these sleazebag politicians do in the real world!

"Since when do we idolize politicians?"

That's not my point and you know it. Unlike them, we possess empathy for all living things, except maybe the assholes. But our fantasy life knows no limits. That's healthy and natural. Or at least natural. Dig me?

I was wearing myself out with this inner monologue posing as dialogue, so I sat down on the couch, Doc the cat hopped up on my lap, Fido jumped beside me and licked my face. I buried my face in hands and cried.

Then I felt Val's soft fingers massaging my scalp. Only when I looked up, it wasn't Val. It was Rose. Here. In the Future That Never Was.

"I'm back, Vic. Like I said I'd be."

She leaned down to kiss me, and we made love. Not Young Vic and Young Rose. But Old Vic and Old Rose. She had aged since I'd seen her last, but then it had been twenty years, even though it only felt like twenty minutes.

Her body was still lean, but softer, her modestly sized, pointy breasts still supple, not sagging with age. Her black hair had streaks of gray, and her eyes, as intense as ever, were surrounded by crow's feet. But nothing diminished her beauty, not even the ravages of time itself. She reminded me of Val. Because she was Val.

We wound up in the bedroom, of course.

Afterward, she told me that Sammy had turned out to be a decent young man, though she wasn't sure where he was these days, since they'd lost touch.

"Aren't you worried about him?" I asked.

"No, he sometimes just disappears for weeks or months at a time, but he always contacts me, to let me know what he's up to."

"Did he go to college?"

"He dropped out to travel the world. He's a free spirit."

"Like his mother."

We kissed and made love again after she licked and sucked Little Elvis back into fighting shape and he assumed his kung fu stance, ready to rock. Doc and Fido seemed confused. Young Vic was nowhere in sight, and neither was Doc's ghost. Ivar was still smiling at me, but for once, it didn't creep me out. Maybe he was just happy for me.

I was coming inside of Val and kissing her neck as she came in tandem when I noticed her voice was different. I looked at her face and she was the other Val, my wife. Then she flipped me over and climbed on top of me, and rode me until she came again. I sucked her nipples and held her child-bearing hips—even if these particular hips had never spawned any more of our useless species—as she came again. Her face seemed to switch back to Rose's as she sobbed with pleasure. Or maybe it was pain. I couldn't distinguish those anymore, either. I was just grateful for any sensory perception, even if it was just sense memory, even if it was dream logic, even if I was already braindead and just didn't know it yet.

Chapter Seven
SIN ENEMA

If I had to sum up the essence of my existence in a single sensory manner, it would be sucking bourbon from the nipple of a female tit while a blues saxophone plays gently in the background. I feel totally ensconced in feminine flesh and cocktails, constantly, mentally when not physically. It's a very shallow, limited preoccupation, I admit. I used to explain my obsession with booze 'n' boobs as a side effect of never having been breastfed by my mother, which was complete bullshit. The truth is, I don't remember whether she ever breastfed me or not. And I never asked her, because that would've been, well, awkward. Plus she was already losing her mind, literally, as I entered the pubescent stage, and by the time I was a legal adult, she'd already been committed to an asylum, not long after my crooked cop father, her abusive husband, was gunned down in an alley by my high school sweetheart, Dolly Duncan Dunlap, the doper dentist's dame, with whom he was having an affair. At least that's what she told me. I think. That was a lot of mammaries 'n' Manhattans ago. Now I'm afraid I'm going to wind up just like my mother: insane, alone, and dead before my time.

These were my thoughts as I wandered throughout Seattle's famous "Underground City," a labyrinth of passageways buried beneath Pioneer Square. I took the formal tourist tour once, soon after moving here. Only right now, there was no tour guide. I was all alone. It was obviously after hours. I had no idea how I got here. I felt claustrophobic and trapped.

I looked down and noticed blood on my hands. Usually I had semen on my hands, and it was always my own. I hoped this was my own blood. But then I saw the body.

It was a pretty young woman with long black hair and ivory skin, half-nude and covered in claw marks. As I turned over her chalk white face with its dead eyes, I recognized her as a bartender I knew from No Bones Beach Club, a vegan tiki bar Val and I often frequented back in Ballard. I looked down and noticed I was only wearing pants. I realized how cold I was without my fur coat. Apparently I'd transformed back into a human after mauling this poor innocent person to death. She made really good drinks, too.

Believing or rather hoping this to be another in a series of unconnected hallucinatory nightmares induced by permanent brain damage from those opioids forced into my system during my Costa Rica adventure, or a spell cast on me by my witchy wife, or perhaps just an alcohol-fueled fever dream, I began banging my head against the stone wall. The tunnels were dimly lit by low lighting, and eerie shadows danced on the walls. One of them was Doc's ghost. He was just leaning there, looking at me.

Vic, you done fucked up again.

"Please tell me none of this is real, Doc."

I could, but then you'd have to accept I'm not real, either. Are you ready to let go now, Vic?

"Let go of what, Doc?"

The past, and the future. Both are gone, at least the ones you imagined.

"Are you saying I imagined my own past?"

Parts of it. I mean, if you're imagining this right now, the memory of it will mingle with your actual memories, and then what difference will it make? It all goes in the same cocktail mix.

"And the future I imagined?"

Present becomes past and future faster and faster as you age, Vic. Obviously you're not the person you thought you'd be at this point, am I right?

"I am happily married, at least. I'm not alone. That was always my biggest worry. That I'd wind up alone, like my mother."

I know, we talked about this frequently. Alone and crazy. And forgotten. Maybe you're just guilt-tripping yourself again, because you couldn't save her.

"I can't even save myself, Doc. Look at me. Look at her. You see her, right?"

I see only what you see, Vic. And it saddens me. Before I encouraged you because I thought if you indulged these twisted exploitation movie fantasies of yours, you'd finally outgrow them. But apparently not. Maybe you really are a demented piece of shit, beyond redemption.

"You really think so, Doc."

I don't really know, man. This is your journey, not mine. I'm already at my destination. I'm just tagging along for the ride, but not the whole way. I'm just a hitchhiker. You're in the driver's seat, Vic.

"So if you see what I see, sitting in the passenger seat, then you've seen my younger self around lately too, right?"

Sure.

"But he can't see you, it seems. Otherwise he would've commented on your ethereal, post-mortem presence by now."

No, he can't. Because you won't let him. You're hiding the truth from him, because you know how devastated he'd be to know our time together would wind up so short.

"I still feel alone sometimes, Doc. Even with Val."

Which one?

"Aw, man. You can see Rose, too, I take it."

I see all you see, Vic. I'm inside your head, remember?

"So is she real? Or just a phantom figure, like you?"

Vic, again, does it matter? Every single thing we perceive with our senses eventually and sometimes instantly dissolves into elusive mental images, anyway. Like me. Like you will, too.

"Maybe that's what's bugging me, Doc. I'm heading into the final stretch, and I know I'm going to lose the race already, so why even bother."

I hear you, man. When I think back on my life, I have so many regrets, but mostly for things I didn't do, rather than things I did do. You feel me?

"Yeah. Well, figuratively speaking, anyway."

So you ready to leave behind this werewolf nonsense and get back to business?

"Which is?"

Your call.

"Since when?"

Since always.

"We control our own destiny?"

No. Only how we perceive it.

"I don't get it."

You will. Now, you better get going before the cops show up.

"So that dead girl is real? And I killed her?"

Yes on one, doubtful on two.

"Doubtful?"

C'mon, Vic. You need to get cleaned up for your next gig, whatever that is.

These tunnels represented my own internal maze. Probably why I was lost in them. I had trouble navigating my way out. I kept bumping into things in the dark, and tripping. When it seemed I'd never find the exit, I began to panic. Doc was gone again. At that point I would've even greeted the company of my younger self with relief. At least I wouldn't die alone in the dark, like that poor girl.

Finally I just gave up and sat down, exhausted from stumbling around. Then I heard this clip-clopping sound.

There, coming down the tunnel towards me, carrying an old lantern, was my old pal Ivar, here to show me the way out. I hoped.

Without a word, I stood up and followed him as he winked at me, then turned back around, hobbling slowly forward, his little lantern barely illuminating our path.

The Underground City was built before the great Seattle Fire of some fucking year, I don't know, I'm not a history buff outside of B movies. Google it, if curious. I really only knew of it from *The Night Strangler* TV movie (1973). That's the scope of my historical curiosity and knowledge. Anyway, they rebuilt this section of the city on top of these old wooden buildings, or something. I don't know. Like I said, I took the tour once but didn't really pay attention to the spiel. The tour guide was this cute chick, and later I took her out for a drink and we balled. I mean, as far as I knew.

I do remember her saying something about how Seattle was once like ninety percent men and ten percent women, and all the women were hookers. Maybe I'm recalling that particular claim incorrectly, but some of it must be true, because it stuck with me. I realize how sexist that sounds, trust me. But it wasn't my fault. Plus I think the Madam in charge of the whore population went on to play a prominent role in establishing Seattle society, and founded a school or something. Not for prostitutes, either. I don't know or care. My own fading past was buried beneath the rubble of my decaying life, and I couldn't even confirm any of its historical accuracy, either.

Eventually, Ivar led me to an Exit sign and I found myself back at street level. It was very early morning, approaching dawn. I was miles from Ballard, and like I told you, only wearing tattered pants. But then no, I wasn't. I was also my trusty fez hat. My inner worlds were colliding.

This being Seattle, a half-naked old guy with bloody hands wearing a fez, especially at this time of the morning, didn't attract much attention from the few passersby heading to work, either by foot or public transit, but the I did catch the eye of a patrol car. I was put in the backseat and hauled off to jail.

For my one allowed phone call, I chose Val, of course. She came down and bailed me out. Ivar had bailed on me already and it seemed odd I wasn't questioned about the blood on my hands. But then I noticed it was gone. Maybe it had come off while I was groping around the walls of the dark tunnels.

In any case, the cops only charged me with public drunkenness, which was better than murder by lycanthropy, I supposed. But after they pulled my record and realized I was once Seattle's savior, they let me walk. After Val posted bail, of course. They needed her money for the policemen's ball, I guess.

Since I accidentally busted the serial killers corrupting their department and soiling their reputation, I was given a lot of passes by the local authorities. But I was getting the impression I was running out of mulligans at this point. Once that girl's body was discovered, they might start wondering why I was picked up in my state of mind and body not far from the crime scene. Then again, they knew I was nuts, anyway.

Still, as we drove home in my Corvair, which was sometimes there and sometimes wasn't, Val suggested we leave town for a while.

"Do you think I'm guilty?" I asked her.

"If I did, I wouldn't have bailed you out. Much less stay married to you."

"Are you just messing with my mind, Val?"

"Not unless you're messing with mine, Vic."

"What does that mean?"

"Think about it."

I did. Then I said, "Okay. What does that mean?"

"It'll come to you in time, Vic. The great mysteries always resolve themselves once you're dead."

That was no consolation, but I let it slide and let myself drift.

I woke up back in my San Francisco office. There was a copy of that day's *Chronicle* on my desk. It was 1998 again, woo hoo!

Just to make sure I was alone, I checked my bedroom. Nobody else there, except Ivar, of course.

While I was young again, I decided to make the most of it. I went downstairs and saw Doc, who was there serving drinks, in the flesh, as well as Monica. It was very reassuring, unreliable as it was. Then I went out into the foggy night to enjoy my reprieve from that other, shittier future reality.

Once outside, I remembered the headline from that newspaper I'd left on my desk: "Werewolf Killer Strikes Again."

I ran back up to my office and looked at the paper. Yup. I'd followed myself again. At least they didn't peg me as a vampire. That would be just plain inaccurate.

Sirens wailing outside my window chilled my blood. That's when Val walked in. Not Rose. The other one. My future wife. She was with Raven, my future dead ex-lover.

"Vic, we have to go, hurry," Val said.

Yes, it was exactly like that part in every action movie or TV show ever made, where someone is about to get shot, but just as the shooter is about to squeeze the trigger, someone else with a gun kicks in the door, emancipating the potential victim from imminent death. It's just one of those overused genre tropes. Anyway, they hustled me down the stairs and into a waiting taxi. Rose was waiting for us in the backseat.

"Vic, there's someone you need to meet," she said. "Don't talk. Listen."

All four of us went across the Bay Bridge to Oakland, to a place called The Parkway Speakeasy Theater. It was almost midnight, meaning Will the Thrill was about to take the stage.

The movie he was hosting was called *Love Stories Are Too Violent For Me*. It was on the marquee as we pulled up in front of the old theater, which had been renovated into a restaurant, with couches facing the big screen, both downstairs and up. It had a funky vibe, augmented by the scent of urine wafting from the men's bathroom into the lobby, where people were lined up to order pizza and beer.

As if in a trance, we sat down with our order number on a table between two sofas. Val and Raven took one, Rose and I the other.

Some Esquivel-type intro music played, ostensibly Will the Thrill's theme song. A gorgeous brunette called Monica "Tiki Goddess" took the stage first, snapping along to the jingly tune, and then Will the Thrill, wearing a green fez hat and vintage red smoking jacket, danced out of the wings.

Monica Tiki Goddess spun a big carnival wheel. People were granted prizes if their ticket numbers matched the numbers she claimed the Wheel had chosen once it stopped spinning. I saw zero correlation.

Then a burlesque act called The Twilight Vixen Revue performed onstage. Will the Thrill came out one more time and told some stupid jokes, then the movie started. Of course, I'd already seen it. In fact, I'd already lived it. Since this was a second run theater, it made sense it was already out on DVD. Though the fact it had been made at all defied reason, unless it was dream logic, in which case anything went.

After the movie, which Rose slept through, we hailed another cab and went out to a bar in nearby Albany called The Ivy Room. Will the Thrill and Monica Tiki Goddess greeted us when we walked in the door. It was a dark, cozy little joint, but I was just along for the ride.

I sat next to Will the Thrill, who was drinking a dirty Martini with three olives. I ordered the same. Monica Tiki Goddess took Rose, Val and Raven over to a corner table so Will the Thrill and I could talk. Apparently, he had something to tell me.

"I'm honored to meet you," he said. "Especially considering you're the subject of that movie, which is based on my book."

"No, it's based on my life," I said.

"Which I created."

"What're you, my stealth biographer? Or some kind of omnipotent goofball?"

"Only of your world. See, I only do this stupid show to promote the book. Now that it's a movie, at least in this alternate state of consciousness, I won't have to do it much longer. So thanks for that. Thanks for nothing, that is."

"Why are you thanking me? Thank Christian Slater."

"Well, he hasn't actually optioned it yet. Much less made it. In fact, he hasn't even read the book yet. None of this happening right now is actually happening, because much of it never happened. See, I created you, but the guy who created *me* is pulling the strings, or yanking our chains, to put it more accurately."

"That's what I said."

"I said it first."

"So you're saying you're on a mission from God."

"Hardly. He or she is probably just some jerk-off like you and me. He or she, though I think it's a he given my testosterone-driven tendencies, only controls what happens in *this* world. Not the real one. Presuming there is a real one. Though they're all real to those inhabiting them at any given time."

"So I keep hearing. You're telling me this isn't the real world. I mean, the *real* real one. You, me, the girls over there, none of us are real."

"Well, we are to each other, at least at the moment, and that's all that counts. In the moment."

"Thanks for confirming. The cops are after me in this world. *And* my other one. In fact, I seem to be screwed across multiple dimensions."

"Yeah, that's how it goes, pally. You can't escape your ultimate fate. All parallel lanes lead to the same destination, which is preordained or maybe not, I don't know. Anyway, fuck it. Live it up while you can. Or while you're allowed to. How's your drink?"

"It's okay. Doc makes 'em better."

"Over at The Drive-Inn."

"Yeah. You been there?"

"Only in my head. Because I created it."

"What are you saying? When I go back home, it won't be there?"

"For you it will be there, sure. For me, no. But I don't care. I hate leaving my house anyway, even to do this stupid show. Once those checks start rolling in, Monica and I are probably moving to Seattle. First we're getting married, though. Probably at the Cal-Neva in North Tahoe."

"Frank's old joint."

"Yep. We're both fans of Sinatra. All three of us, I should say."

"Maybe Sinatra is calling the shots for the guy calling our shots."

"Maybe. He doesn't know what the hell's going on any more than we do. The chain of command seems infinite, so there is no ultimate authority, just trickle down cause and effect, without any ultimate purpose."

"That's depressing."

"If you think about it. You think too much, that's your problem."

"But isn't that your fault?"

"Yeah. You do my thinking for me. Thanks for that."

"Can't you provide me with some answers, then?"

"Sure, but they'd only be made up anyway, so what's the point? Plus the fun is in the search for answers. Once you find them, you're dead."

"Why?"

"Because that's the only way to really, really know anything."

"And by then, it doesn't matter anymore."

"Exactly! Now you're getting it, pally."

"Stop calling me pally."

"Rat Pack lingo is part of my stupid schtick, sorry. Hey, speaking of which, did you hear they're planning to remake 'Ocean's Eleven'?"

"Yeah, they did that already. Or rather, they will."

"I'm going to boycott it."

"You do that. But just so you know, there will also be an Ocean's Twelve, Thirteen, and Eight."

"Yeah, I know."

"You can see the future?"

"Only yours. I know what you know, but you don't know everything I know."

"That's not fair."

"Nope. Welcome to my fucking world."

"No thanks. I got too many of my own." I looked over at the ladies, all laughing and having a great old time. "That Tiki Goddess is pretty hot."

"They all are."

"But you didn't just make up Monica."

"Didn't I? How do you know?"

"You know, I have my own Monica."

"I know. I gave her to you. But that was before I even met my Monica, so no relation. Just a coincidence."

"So there is no such thing as Fate? It's all a dice roll?"

"How the fuck should I know? I'm just some clown in a fez hat hosting crappy old movies."

"And I'm just a fictional character."

"We all are. Eventually." He then pulled out a business card and handed it to me. It read: *Will the Thrill: Lounge Lizard For Hire,* like he was the puny white guy version of Luke Cage: Hero for Hire. But then what did that make me? He read my mind, because he probably wrote it. "Coincidence? You tell me."

"I can't, because you won't let me know anything."

"Now you feel *my* pain. Which is why you even exist. I gotta put it someplace, right? So thanks again. *Pally.*"

We clinked glasses and said, "Cheers," simultaneously.

Just then a cute little blonde dude plopped down on the counter. Yes, on the counter. And when I say little, I mean fucking *little*. He was only about a foot tall, though that was just a guess since it's not like I pulled some measuring tape out of my utility belt. He just smiled and waved at me.

"Who the hell is that?" I naturally asked.

"Oh, that's my other creation. His name is Chumpy Walnut."

"Really? Funny, I've used that name as an alias. It just popped into my head one day."

"I know, because I popped it in there."

"Aw, shit. Why?"

"Just to give the little guy some more exposure."

"Exposure to what?"

"The world. He was supposed to be my Holden Caulfield, and his life story my 'Catcher in the Rye.' But it didn't pan out."

"At least it didn't become your 'Confederacy of Dunces.'"

"Yeah, I'm not the suicidal type, unfortunately. Anyway, what's the point of success if you're not here to enjoy it?"

"I agree. Sorry. I guess if you're right, and you created me, I let you down, too, then."

"That's why I have to do *this*," Will the Thrill said with a nod, pointing with contempt at his fez hat on the bar. "You came along much later. I made up Chumpy when I was a kid. At first he was just a cartoon talking walnut. It was going to be a comic strip. But I figured I wasn't a good enough artist, so I made him the human protagonist of a novel, which remains unpublished."

"That's a shame."

"Yep." Will the Thrill ordered two more dirty Martinis.

"Make it three," said Chumpy Walnut.

The bartender served up three Martinis. Chumpy's glass was half his size, so he just slurped from it like it was a horse trough filled with gin.

Yes, I realize how crazy this sounds. I also admit that whenever a story gets crazy, one of the characters is obligated to say, "this is crazy." And then the crazy shit happens anyway, just to move the story forward. It's kind of like sinning all week, then making it all okay by going to Sunday confession, *a la* washing down M&Ms with a V-8. Then Monday you start the cycle all over again, since if you acknowledge you're a sinner, you can keep sinning, and even enjoying it. In my case, merely admitting this is all crazy doesn't always cleanse the sins of lazy storytelling.

Except this *is* my confession. To you. I don't expect or even desire absolution. I just need to get all of this off my chest. I know this doesn't make sense in your world. It doesn't make sense in mine either. At least not the one I remember. I'm just learning we don't live in the same world. You just visit me sometimes. Thanks for that. Makes me feel a little less alone and isolated from society. Even though I hate people and don't want to socialize, anyway. This barrier between us is the only thing keeping me from hating you. And probably vice versa.

I know I masturbate too much. But everyone does in one form or another. Social media is nothing but mass emotional masturbation. Celebrity is self-worshipping masturbation, often a circle jerk, like the Academy Awards. Hell, even this book is mental masturbation. I mean, why should anyone give a fuck what I think or feel? Sure, it's all relatable as part of "the human condition," but what distinguishes my life or justifies my public venting of my many problems and frustrations and sexual fantasies?

Nothing. Absolutely nothing. It just makes me feel good, or at least better, for a minute, anyway. It doesn't matter to me how you feel about it. That's the very definition of masturbation. It's not just me, though. Humanity is an entire civilization of jerk-offs. Whether spewing semen or sermons, it's all just a way to blow off some steam.

Anyway, Chumpy Walnut, Will the Thrill and I sat there sipping our Martinis, which felt and tasted real even if they weren't. Chumpy held and ate his three olives with both hands, like they were melons on a skewer. Will the Thrill didn't seem too thrilled. Neither was I. I was just waiting for something to happen that would help explain all this. I just wanted to wake up already. But first I had to actually pass out. So I kept drinking. My vision blurred. But Chumpy Walnut was still there, unconscious on the bar. I envied him. I wondered if he dreamed of a different life somewhere and sometime else, too, where he was the giant, and everyone else was miniaturized.

I studied Will the Thrill's face. He looked a bit like me, actually, but puffier, with rosier cheeks. Beneath the free-wheeling facade, he seemed rather sad, even with his gorgeous wife. Like me. It was like we both felt undeserving of this one piece of luck in our lousy lives. He was my doppelgänger in an odd, inexplicable way. I even related to little Chumpy Walnut, also feeling like a small man in a big world. But then so did most people, I imagined.

While I was imagining stuff, I decided to conjure up a third Martini, hoping this one would finally knock me out, and I'd wake up someplace else in time and space, just for the hell of it. I slurped it down in two gulps and finally the Ivy Room swirled around me and my head hit the bar with a thud.

An indeterminate amount of time passed before I finally opened my eyes again. I was back in my office above the Drive-Inn. It was quiet and no lights were on, night having fallen like my head on that bar back at the Ivy Room. I went into the bedroom. Nobody there but Ivar. I thought about what Will the Thrill told me, that he was my creator and curator, but he himself was being manipulated by an unseen puppeteer. And yet, I felt like I had complete free will, as it were. So I decided to exercise it, just to see how far I could take it before Will the Thrill pulled me back into his auspices. But last I'd seen him, he was also unconscious. So maybe I had a chance to sneak away.

I walked out of my Richmond District studio and straight into my apartment back in Ballard. Before closing the door behind me, I turned to see if my office was still there. It was. I was literally stepping from one dimension into another, consciously and visibly. The barriers had fallen. My self-awareness had resulted in willful time travel, even if I was stuck in a loop like the final scenes of *The Time Travelers* (1964). God, I always loved that movie, and hardly anyone knows about it nowadays. It's become lost in time itself, but lives forever inside my dreamworld, as long as that lasted.

Inside my Seattle apartment in the future, which became the present as soon as I stepped inside and closed the door behind me, Ivar was there, but no one else. Not even the cat or dog, much less my wife. Like my office back in 1998 San Francisco, which I'd just left, my current Seattle pad was likewise eerily deserted.

I looked outside the window. I thought about just jumping out head first onto the sidewalk, exploding every world inside my head, and ending this multi-leveled nightmare once and for all. Though I've never contemplated suicide, I know what it's like to feel dead inside. I've bottomed out many times before, but life was always too precious to me to just end it, even when it sucked. Plus I was curious to know what happened next, like in a movie with an indeterminate running time.

I thought of Val, my wife, who was now missing, and evidently took our pets with her. Maybe she was never there. Or she was back in San Francisco, twenty years ago, long before we reunited and wed. If we ever had. Without her, I really had no more will to survive. The randomness of my existence was exhausting. And I couldn't shake the sensation that I was locked inside my own head, while my body wasted away, somewhere in time. Maybe even beneath the ground.

But fuck it. I went downstairs and into the bleak, black night that seemed as vast and empty as a bottomless pit.

At least it was still Ballard, not the Richmond District, maintaining some circumstantial consistency. But nobody was in sight. Maybe it was just the middle of the night. I went outside to see. The streets were illuminated by a full moon. It was howling time.

Except I wasn't a werewolf. I was just me, wandering around aimlessly. As if by animal instinct, I wound up back at No Bones Beach Club, on 17th, right off Market. Even though it was the middle of the night and no one was around, the lights were on, so I walked in the open door, expecting to be greeted as *persona non grata*, considering I may have murdered one of their best bartenders while under the influence of the full moon.

On the TV, *Horror of Party Beach* (1964) was playing, one of my old favorites. I felt like I was back at The Drive-Inn. The pretty, previously slaughtered bartender was there, all right, though alive and well in all her goth girl glory, sans any scratches or other remnants of her violent death. Since I didn't want to make either of us uncomfortable, I didn't mention our previous encounter. Her healthy presence confirmed it really had been only a nightmare, anyway, meaning mine, not hers. I was beyond relieved.

I looked around the empty bar and said, "I'm surprised you keep such late hours. But I guess animal-loving tweakers get urges for buffalo cauliflower wings at all hours here in Seattle."

She just smiled and didn't say anything. Even though I hadn't ordered yet, she was already making me a cocktail. She set it down in front of me. I looked inside the tiki mug. The contents made it resemble a small bucket of blood, garnished with mint.

"What's this?" I asked.

"Taste it," she said. That's when I noticed she had razor sharp vampire teeth. "We call it a 'Humanhattan.'"

Aw, shit, here we go again, I thought. At least she was the one with the fangs this time.

In the spirit of the surreal moment, I complied, because when confronted with insanity, it was best to just remain as calm as possible. The concoction she gave me tasted like bourbon, thankfully, mixed with some other tangy ingredients, including passionfruit. So I kept drinking. The vampire bartender disappeared into the kitchen and returned with a plate of hot food. It looked like a human heart.

"Um…I eat here because I'm vegan," I said politely.

"That means you don't eat *animal* flesh," she smiled. "Neither do I. Trust me. You'll like it. It's very fresh."

I felt like I was in an Italian cannibal movie directed by Ken Russell. "Is it made out of tofu?"

She smiled. Then she lifted her shirt, revealing her ivory breasts, which looked like two scoops of soy ice cream with cherries on top. "No, and neither are these. Would you like to feast on my living flesh?"

Little Elvis stirred, which meant I was either still alive, or about to have one of my adolescent wet dreams. I felt sorry for the nurse that had to clean me up during my epic coma, if that were the case. I must've been squirting sperm in my hospital gown like a busted pipe through a rotting wall.

Anyway, I walked behind the bar and embraced her. The vampire bartender chick bit my neck as I bit into her breasts. I felt the hair tingling on my arm, and realized it was fur. I was a werewolf again, fucking a nubile vampire in a vegan tiki bar. Whether this was a dream or an illusion or a fantasy, I liked it. I didn't know whether someone else was making this up for me, or I was making it all up as I went, but it didn't matter. Nothing did. This was my belated epiphany.

We fucked like wild animals in heat on the dirty floor. It was a while before I realized I was covered in fluids, not all my own. It was a mix of blood and booze dripping from the bar, from the ceiling, and oozing from the floor. I was licking and sucking blood and bourbon from the vegan vampire's juicy nipples. She in turn was draining my essence from both my jugular and my cock. I was delirious with pleasure and pain, the two building blocks of existence on this plane, or all planes, apparently.

Then this particular plane encountered some turbulence and went into a nosedive. I felt like I was drowning in flesh and blood. I was suffocating. I stood up, gasping for air. The vegan vampire just laughed.

Then I noticed Ivar, Chumpy Walnut, and Will the Thrill were all at the bar, laughing along with her. Slipping on the gore on the floor, I staggered outside and was confronted with flashing lights and cops with their guns drawn, yelling at me to get on my knees with my hands behind my head. I can't count how many times I've had these same dreams, where I'm a fugitive from the law for a crime I didn't mean to commit.

Reality had finally caught up with me. Maybe it would tell me where I was.

Chapter Eight
DREAM FATE

I've always found it odd that life goes by so fast, even though we're all dying slowly from the moment we're born.

I thought back on the episode of this show called *Parts Unknown* that was about Seattle. The host, Anthony Bourdain, had recently hung himself in his hotel room. I didn't watch his show regularly, but Val did. I happened to catch the Seattle episode with her. I was intrigued by the places he chose to visit, particularly one of my favorites, the Shanghai Room over in Greenwood. Val and I often drank there after dinner at the adjacent North Star Diner. There was a scene toward the end of the program where Bourdain was sitting alone at the bar, drinking. He looked so sad. In retrospect, it seemed portentous, as if he were contemplating taking his life at that very moment, his existential angst, despite all of his fame and fortune, now captured on film for posterity.

A lot of people hang themselves in their jail cells. So I was on suicide watch as I sat in mine at the Seattle downtown precinct. I was back on the official cop shit list, despite my history as a local hero in that one case. Actually, Raven did most of the work. I just happened to get most of the credit. As you know, she hung herself in her jail cell with her own bra. Bourdain used the belt of his bathrobe, reportedly. They had taken my belt when they booked me for multiple murders. It was all so ironic, and as usual, the irony was on me.

Also in that episode, Bourdain seemed obsessed with the fact so many serial killers thrived in the Pacific Northwest. Now I was one of them, apparently. The fact that

I'd helped bring one down, however accidentally or incidentally, no longer mattered. I'd betrayed the trust of the police and the people. I was a monster.

But hey, I always loved monsters, at least in the movies. Initially the reports were that the killings were done vampire-style, but that was upgraded to werewolf-style when the victims had their entrails devoured. After being sexually violated. As usual in our patriarchal society, women were the victims of these heinous crimes. Now all women probably hated me. Except for the freaks that wrote fan letters to psychos, offering conjugal visits. But most women hated me before this, anyway. I always hated myself, too, so at least we had that much in common.

I'd been in several jail cells over the years. I knew the nauseating smells and sense of isolation and futility all too well. I often suffered those same sensations on the outside, too, so I was used to them.

While staring into space, contemplating my predicament, I noticed a couple of words on the wall, carved inside a crudely constructed heart. It read quite plainly: "I'm sorry Vic."

I recoiled as if I went to pet a raccoon and instead got a wicked whiff of ripe roadkill. Could it be I was in the same cell where Raven hung herself? And how would she know I'd ever read this? I mean, I am a fuckup by nature, so the odds of me winding up in a Seattle jail cell were at least as high as when I wound up in various Bay Area jail cells, for sundry reasons. But how could she know I'd wind up in *this* one?

Okay, maybe this missive from beyond wasn't from her, and was meant for another Vic. More likely, she just wanted to leave this sentiment behind even if only strangers and the cosmos would actually ever see it. But I did see it. It reached me, like a note in a bottle flung into a stormy sea from a desert island. I got her message, and I wept. I'm a big baby. A skinny cat running across an empty field can make me bawl. This time, though, my tears were more than warranted. Raven was communicating me to me in her hour of lonely dread. I was the person she reached out to. And in a way, I'd put her here. I didn't think I could live with myself anymore, in any version, whether young or old. My stomach churned like sour butter before wrapping itself into tight little knots like a neurotic octopus. I vomited my stress and grief all over the floor, making my smelly little cell even stinkier. I didn't care anymore. About anything. I wanted to end it all and go apologize to Raven in person, whether up above or down below or somewhere in between, since I was the chief offender in our case, not her. Not really. She committed the crime but I deserved to do the time, if for no other reason than it would be the gentlemanly thing to do, after her life was destroyed by the oppressive patriarchy. Okay, I'm more or less channeling my feminist wife right now, but that doesn't make my socially conscious sentiments any less sincere.

I looked up and noticed Doc, Ivar, Young Vic, and Chumpy Walnut standing around me in a circle, looking quite concerned. No sign of Will the Thrill, but that was probably because he still actually existed somewhere outside my own tormented head. Or I just existed in his, and he was tormenting *me* just to blow off some steam. In either case, at least I wasn't all alone, like Raven was in her final moments. Unless she hallucinated, too. I'll never know unless and until I hook up with her someplace beyond the borders of anyone's fevered imagination, even God's.

Meantime, I had company to entertain. "Hey, guys. Even if you're not really there, good to see you. Even if some of you can't see each other."

We just don't want you to surrender, Doc said. *Your life is still worth living. Trust me. I know*.

"I love life, Doc. But it's obviously unrequited."

That never stopped you before, he said.

"But Life is so cruel and unfair about it. At least I got sex from women before they dumped me."

And love, too.

"They still dumped me."

Maybe you should take some responsibility for that, instead of playing victim all the damn time like a little bitch.

"My fuckin' name is short for Victim, Doc."

Vic stands for Victor, too.

"Yeah, yeah, yeah…"

I looked over and saw Raven, or at least her shapely spirit. She was stark naked and stunning. Also, she had tucked Chumpy Walnut between her ample cleavage, where he clung like an infant seeking nourishment. In fact, he began breastfeeding from her enormous mammaries, which was an unsettling yet oddly moving sight. Young Vic saw her too, and immediately pulled out his putz and began masturbating. I sighed loudly. Ivar just laughed and laughed and laughed some more.

"Raven, I got your message," I said, ignoring everyone else.

I knew you would, she said with a smile, cradling a thirsty Chumpy to her leaky bosom.

"I'm the one that is so, so sorry," I said, just noticing the dark purple bruises around her neck.

Young Vic shot his wad all over her tits, face and Chumpy Walnut, spouting like a busted fire hydrant. It was extremely embarrassing, since he was more or less acting on my behalf, or rather ours, because I was him and he was me, as much as we didn't want to admit it.

"Jesus Fucking Christ, dude, have some dignity and show a little respect," I said to my younger self. "Fuckin' pervert."

You should talk, Young Vic said with contempt, scrubbing his hands clean on his virtual pants.

Raven simply wiped the eroticized ectoplasm off of her spectral body and face, licking her fingers clean. *I remember that taste*, she said. She even licked some glop off poor Chumpy Walnut, who looked quite frightened and confused by this vulgar display, though he seemed to enjoy the feel of Raven's tongue on his gooey scalp as he continued suckling milky sustenance from her cum-drenched boobs. I couldn't blame him. Lucky little guy.

It was freaky, to say the least. I even got a boner, leaking a bit through my trousers. Young Vic noticed, shaking his head in disgust.

Fuckin' hypocrite, he said. *How do you even live with yourself? I can barely live with you! Much less myself!* We just hated each other so much, at least in that moment, probably because our selfish indecency had been so flagrantly exposed. Fortunately, we had a friendly audience.

It seemed like Young Vic still couldn't see Doc, or else they would've interacted, I figured. Doc sure saw him, because he shared both my disgust and my lack of surprise at my own disgraceful, degenerate conduct, especially in the presence of a lady, albeit a naked bombshell without any apparent inhibitions. When it came to my type in women, I've always preferred bombshells to firecrackers. Subtlety just ain't my style.

I knew Raven wasn't really there, except as an apparition, but it was sweet to see her again, and in such a serene state, too. She was very maternal as she stroked Chumpy's little head while he guzzled and gorged on her ethereal essence, looking at me as if I were the father.

Then she put Chumpy down gently and walked over to me, pushed me back on my cot, and climbed on top of me. *Live for my sake, Vic*, she whispered in my ear as she nuzzled it. Next thing I knew we were fucking like old times. She even began pounding me in the face and head like she always did when aroused and achieving orgasm, at least while she was alive. Sucking her large, erect nipples, which felt a bit creepy considering little Chumpy's innocent little mouth had just been there, I came in tandem, squirting all up inside of her curvaceous and seemingly corporeal body. Whoever was calling these shots, as it were, sure had their creative juices flowing. Like all over the joint.

Quite abruptly, our *coitus* was rudely interrupted by loud, frequent bursts of gunfire. Then all of the lights went out. I heard people screaming as if bones were being broken. It was like *The Punisher* meets *Assault on Precinct 13* (the original version from 1976, of course; fuck the remake). I even had John Carpenter's iconic theme music playing in my head for ambient effect. I thought maybe this was just part of the dream, so I went along with it. Sex and violence had always been fine with me as long as they didn't actually hurt anybody. That's why I loved the vicarious thrill of cinema so much.

No, it wasn't The Punisher, but close enough: it was my gal pal Val, along with that annoyingly ubiquitous Japanese dude, now in a designated sidekick role. Both were dressed in black like ninjas, except Val also wore her *lucha* mask. She was magnificent. I never liked people much, even imaginary ones. But Val was a major exception to my otherwise zero-tolerance policy.

To her world-weary, gorgeous eyes, when she showed up I was just lying there alone in my cell with my own sticky dick in my hand. She didn't seem at all fazed, but then she knew me all too well. I was merely living up, or down, to her usual expectations. "Vic, would you please stop jerking off for a few seconds so we can get you out of here, deal?"

Val had obviously taken the keys from one of the guards, which she'd used to unlock my cell. I looked around. My invisible friends had vanished again, replaced by either actual beings or simply more reflective shadows from the recesses of my brain. In any case, while I was still desperately pulling up my pants, Val grabbed me by the arm and then karate-kicked and chopped our way out of the precinct. The gunshots were only from the cops, on the defense. The Japanese dude had a sword, which he used judiciously, so nobody got killed, just strategically sliced. It was quite a show.

Next thing I knew we were in my Corvair, and Val was at the wheel, heading toward the 5 at full speed, which wasn't that fast in my old clunker, but fast enough to elude capture, even with what seemed like zillions of sirens wailing behind us. She turned off on the 520, then merged onto the 405, then swerved onto the 90, obviously headed toward Snoqualmie/North Bend, with a vengeance. It was pitch black and quiet outside.

An owl hooted in the trees above us as we stopped and got out of the car somewhere in the middle of the forest, not far from Snoqualmie Falls, which made soothing sounds in the disquieting darkness. We all climbed out of the car and just stood there, listening, hearing nothing but that lone owl, which augmented the eeriness, but also relieved us of any pending fear of capture. We were all alone out here in the dark woods. For now.

I half expected Val to take me through some red curtains into The Black Lodge. Instead, she held and kissed me while her ninja pal just stood there, like a robotic henchman.

"You keep saving me," I said.

"You keep needing saving," she said. "Come with me."

She took my by the hand and led me deeper into the forest, leaving the Japanese dude behind, which was a relief. I just didn't trust that guy. For one thing, I was still unsure exactly how he was connected to Val's past and present, and for another, he hardly ever talked. It was almost like he was an incomplete creation, not quite fleshed out, a convenient semi-sentient mannequin whose presence was only required to sustain forward momentum in a randomly concocted chronicle of fabricated events.

In a clearing illuminated by rays of moonlight streaming through celestial cotton patches of slow moving cumulus clouds, Val stripped out of her ninja outfit, having already discarded the *lucha* mask. As usual, she wore no underwear. I took off my wrinkled sharkskin suit and we made love, because why not?

See, whenever watching any TV show or movie in any genre from any era, I always thought, "An explicit sex scene or the guy turning into a werewolf or the chick revealing she's a lesbian vampire or a sudden zombie apocalypse would really spice this up." And so I'm doing the same in my own life, because who's gonna stop me?

So we fucked and then I turned into a werewolf and Val sprouted vampire fangs and we clawed and bit each other in the moonlight.

It dawned on me I wasn't free, but trapped in a loop that would always end the same way. Just like all lives on all levels of consciousness. No matter who you are or where you start out, you always wind up the same way: dead. There's no escaping fate. There's no eluding the Grim Reaper, no matter what guise it chooses, whether cancer or cops.

So when the moon rays were blended with flashing red lights, I wasn't at all surprised. I looked down desperately at Val as a bunch of cops with guns drawn, along with an entire SWAT team armed with much more lethal assault weapons, completely surrounded us. Val got up, stark naked since that's how she rolled best, and began to fight back with fangs, feet and fists. She took down a few of the cops before they unleashed a barrage of bullets and tore her beautiful body into bloody bits of undead meat.

Still in werewolf form, I fought back with lycanthropic fury, but was quickly overwhelmed by the sheer force of numbers. I was beaten with billy clubs into submission, like a rabid dog or any random black male, until I changed back into a plain old lounge lizard for hire, now off the market for good. I wondered why they hadn't just killed me, but that was probably because they didn't have silver bullets, so they didn't bother to try.

I sobbed as they cuffed my hands behind me then threw me in the back of a cop car. The Japanese dude was nowhere in sight during this whole violent scene. At least until I noticed he was at the wheel of the cop car. He smiled with sinister satisfaction as he sped off, sirens wailing. He wasn't even dressed like a cop. Apparently he had just taken out the one that had been driving this particular vehicle. Oddly, Phil Collins was singing "In the Air Tonight" over the police radio.

Noticing I was sitting behind the cage separating us, naked and dazed, the Japanese guy took the opportunity to formally introduce himself. "My name is Hayata," he said.

"What? You mean like the guy who turns into Ultra Man?" I said, momentarily distracted from the seriousness of the situation, nostalgically referencing a vintage Japanese TV series I loved as a kid.

"Yes, exactly," Hayata said. "And this is Morbius."

I looked over at the passenger seat and there he was, Val's sanguinary pal. "You mean like the Living Vampire that fights Spidey," I said.

"Actually, I'm named after the scientist stranded on Forbidden Planet," Morbius said without turning back to look at me. His voice was low and deep and chilling.

"You mean the guy that created Robby the Robot?" I said.

"Yes."

"But he wasn't a vampire."

"The monster from the Id, which he summoned, was a *psychic* vampire," Morbius said. "And that's what I am. A monster from the Id. *Your* Id, to be specific."

"But then why are you mixing up references?" I said.

"So we don't get sued by Marvel Comics," Morbius said. "Or MGM. We're taking artistic license by altering the source material just enough to avoid litigation for copyright infringement."

I nodded. Made sense. As much as anything did.

Godley and Creme were singing "Cry" over the police radio.

"Is this like an oldies station?" I asked.

"Just songs featured in the television series 'Miami Vice,'" Hayata said. "It's a select mix."

"Pandora?"

"You mean the box? Yes, it's open now. It was never really closed."

"No, I meant…never mind."

I sat there in silence as we drove through the forest, which seemed endless. Moody Jan Hammer synth music played as we continued down the lost highway, with some Angelo Badalamenti mixed in for good measure.

At one point we were parallel with a train, which seemed reassuringly quaint given the bizarre circumstances, until I noticed that the rotting revenants of the Knight Templar from Amando de Ossorio's 1972 zombie classic *Tombs of the Blind Dead* (the first of four films in the series) were deliberately making their way through each car, murdering and maiming the screaming passengers. Additionally, the really bad pop-rock band from the cheesy but fun 1985 horror anthology flick *Night Train to Terror* played and danced to the grating tune "Everybody But You" in the cab car, oblivious to the mayhem.

Finally, our own car came to a stop in front of an apparently deserted motel with no lights on except the neon sign, which beamed in bright purple and green electric letters, "Motel Capri." Hayata and Morbius got out and then Hayata opened the door for me. I climbed out, Morbius broke my cuffs off, and then I was led into one of the wood-paneled rooms, where Val was waiting for me, along with Raven. They were both naked, making steamy love as a scratchy LP of the funky soundtrack to Jess Franco's 1971 erotic horror cult classic *Vampiros Lesbos* played on a turntable sitting atop the dresser.

Hayata and Morbius closed the door behind me, and I was left alone with the ladies, who didn't seem to notice my presence. I didn't need Val to explain to me how she'd survived that barrage of bullets, since she was an immortal member of the undead, and nothing could kill her but my imagination, which was the only world I knew anymore. And I wasn't even sure it was my imagination, or Will the Thrill's. Or someone else's. Maybe yours.

Regardless, there was no denying I saw Robby the Robot standing guard in the corner, his lights and bells and whistles flashing and buzzing like crazy as he witnessed the unbridled debauchery. It reminded me of the dream sequence from Albert Zugsmith's *Sex Kittens Go to College* (1960) starring Mamie Van Doren, where an anonymous burlesque stripper ululates provocatively, stimulating both an overheated robot and a frantic monkey, though this kinky interlude was cut from the domestic release. Of course, Doc had a bootleg VHS of the European version with the nude scene intact, so I knew it well.

On the dresser was a brochure for a joint called L'Hotel du Frisson. French, I took it. But the sign out front said Motel Capri. Maybe the place was under new management. Or else the old owners left behind the original marketing materials. Then it hit me: someone calling himself "The Mantis Man" had once called me from a joint called L'Hotel du Frisson, asking for my help. I did a little research for him, but I turned him down when he wanted to make a whole case out of it, because he sounded too weird, plus I'm lazy. Didn't matter. Either way, this was a cozy if spooky little dump, the kind I knew intimately from my many youthful days of solitary suffering.

Since I was already naked and had a raging boner, I jerked off until I creamed all over Val and Raven, just like my younger self had done back in the jail cell, which now seemed so far away and long ago now, like it had never happened. They licked my cum off of each other, then asked me to join them. We had a mad *ménage à trois* as *Love Stories Are Too Violent For Me* played silently on the crappy motel TV, which was so old it actually had an antenna. The reception was lousy. The picture was fuzzy and kept rolling, plus like I said the sound was off since the stereo was on, but since I'd already seen it twice, and lived it once (at least), I didn't mind. Besides, I was too busy making sweet love with my lesbian vampire friends, who sucked every fluid out of every orifice I had before I finally fainted from exhaustion and depletion.

When I opened my eyes, Doc and Monica were standing there, looking down at me. Both were younger, and Doc's beautiful black flesh looked fresh and healthy and vibrant, so I realized I was back in 1990s San Francisco again, just like that.

"Vic, you okay?" Doc asked me with genuine concern. Monica looked worried, too. Me, I was way too disoriented to accurately assess my own well being. "We've been here for days and nights, waiting for you to come out of it. It was touch and go there for a while, but now that your eyes are finally open, there's light at the end of this long-ass tunnel."

"Do you see us, Vic?" Monica asked. "I mean, clearly. How's your vision? You took some pretty hard shots to the head. The doctors were worried it might affect brain function and senses."

"More than usual, that is," Doc said with a wink and a smile.

"Um...I guess I'm...all right. Just a little woozy. You're not blurry or anything, and yeah, I recognize you, but...what the...where the hell am I?" I also wondered "who" and "when" but I didn't want to overload them with questions right away.

"San Francisco General," Monica said. "You've been out of it for days."

"Daze..." I mumbled in response, spelling it differently to myself.

I tried sitting up, but I hurt all over, and lay back down as Doc and Monica soothed me. I was back in the hospital after Tommy Dodge had cleaned my proverbial clock with his baseball bat. This meant Rose was already gone, down in New Orleans, and Doc had a goodbye note from her, as well as a heart-shaped dart board.

Except I saw that Rose was in the room, too. So were Val and Raven. It was like the fucking final scene of *The Wizard of Oz.*

I began to put the jigsaw pieces of my broken memories and splintered dreams together. It was possible I did know Val and Raven from this place and period, since they both lived in the Bay Area at the same time I did, and in fact I first met Val in San Francisco, before my reunion with Rose. Could it be my battered brain mashed-up these memories into a futuristic fantasy that had me marrying the girl of my dreams, literally, in a different city, one I had always wanted to visit or even inhabit, due to its rainy reputation? And then blended into that were images of all the B movies I'd absorbed over the years? And then while under this comatose spell I skipped around in time, reuniting with Rose, maybe even wrongly imagining her leaving town for New Orleans, when in fact she had stuck around and waited for me to wake up, so we could be together? And the rest of it was just an epic revery?

Or was everything I'd experienced recently, including this very moment, simply a result of the toxins still coursing through my system due to the experimental, mind-altering opioids and drugs I'd been exposed to down in Costa Rica? But then again...

Had I ever actually *been* to Costa Rica? "Hal" could've been short for "hallucination," after all. I recalled it all in

such lurid detail, however. Was it simply an amalgam of all
the jungle/Tarzan movies I'd seen? The old TV series
Tarzan starring Ron Ely was set in Africa, but filmed in
Mexico and Central America. As a kid I'd loved that show,
so maybe that was the source of this perverted playback.
The Costa Rica trip did seem excessively cinematic in
flashback, or maybe flash-forward. In any case, it remained
a vivid vision.

In fact, all of the imagery on both sides of my eyeballs
was now merging and manifesting into a randomly
morphing mirage, whiplashing between the past, present,
and possibly future, between the corporeal and the
concocted, the celestial and the celluloid, projecting both
possibilities and probabilities based on the people and
places in my life so far.

Paranoid, I scanned the room for any evidence of my
old nemesis Ivar, just to verify my self-diagnosis. His abrupt
arrival in my life signaled the beginning of this
hallucinogenic nightmare parade, though my alcoholic
blackouts, peaking during a case in Chicago in 2005, were
also signs I was mentally unfit for duty. *Any* duty. But
mostly the duty of daily life in this world. Ivar's sudden
appearances were concurrent with my arrival in Seattle, the
Emerald City, maybe in more ways than one.

I felt a pang in my stomach when I realized Ivar was
gone or at least not around at the moment. Perhaps he had
only been a sardonic specter from my subconscious all
along. That made me sad, even though I was now
surrounded by my true loved ones, not talking sailor statues,
all alive and well, seemingly, and I was young again, too, if
still recuperating from my bout with Tommy's bat.

If this was the *real* reality, I'd take it. It was like I was
Tony Soprano, awaking from one of his famous dream
sequences, and...

Wait a minute. That show didn't even come on cable
until 1999, six years after my episode with Rose and

Tommy. How would I even know about it if I were still alive in that time and place, and the rest was just a dream?

I looked over at the bed beside mine. There was Chumpy Walnut, wrapped in bandages like a miniature mummy, recovering from his own traumatic incident, a gunfight with gangsters that resulted in a burning cabin. By his side were two hoboes that resembled Abbott and Costello, a beautiful burlesque dancer, and an old black guy dressed like a janitor who reminded me a lot of Doc. Shit, maybe my whole life was just the dream in Chumpy Walnut's head as he lay there unconscious. If so, I really wished he'd wake up already. I was tired of living his dream.

Nirvana's "Heart-Shaped Box" was playing over the sound system. At least that song was from the same exact period I was supposedly in right now. I noticed Will the Thrill's fez hat was sitting on my bedside table, next to the heart-shaped dart board, like Santa's cane left by the fireplace at the end of *Miracle on 34th Street.*

Merry Fucking Christmas.

Chapter Nine
BUZZ CHILL

My perimeters of perception as well as my sensory surroundings were either rapidly expanding or slowly contracting, depending on how you looked at it. Or rather, how I looked it. I'd learned to keep an open mind, but it's not like it was my choice. It obviously had a revolving door.

Years ago, I began receiving letters from the inmate of a Florida prison. Her name was Helen Black. This was before I met Val for the first time or hooked back up with Rose, when I was still considering becoming a private eye. I didn't even know how she got my address, but she attached some photos of her, or allegedly her, wearing nothing but a bikini or a halter top and cut-off shorts with high heels, along with lurid descriptions of her many illegal, amoral exploits, all of which fueled my fantasies. She wrote about setting up guys to get hit by the Mob, shootouts in the Everglades, and other torrid tales of true crime that only deepened my unhealthy long distance obsession with this total stranger. Her flirtatious missives soon devolved into explicit erotica and then outright offers to come visit me when she got out. This actually terrified me, given her record, at least how she described it, so I started sending her letters back, unopened, writing "Return to Sender, Address Unknown" on the envelopes, Elvis-style.

For a long time after that, I was afraid she'd show up at my doorstep, ready to kill me for cutting her off. Hopefully she'd violently violate me first, though. This strange, sexually stimulating exchange was the fodder for many a masturbatory marathon in lonely days to come, so to speak. I never really got her out of my head, even though we'd never met.

So do those fantasies count as memories, since they mingle with elements of reality? I mean, she really did exist, outside of my imagination. Our erotic encounters were detailed in our letters. We may as well have fucked. And I didn't wind up like one of her Mob hits as a result.

One day I read about a woman jumping off the Golden Gate Bridge, identified as one Helen Black of Miami, Florida. The photo published in the *Chronicle* matched the ones she had sent me from prison. Had she come to find me then beat me up, kill me, fuck me, or all three? I'll never know. But the fact we shared that geographical proximity for whatever reason only served to preserve my infatuation with a very charming and dangerous sociopath. I was so lonely back then, I would've willingly died in the loving arms of a woman, any woman. Even a dead one.

As time went on I learned to stop giving a fuck, becoming a *menefreghista* as the Mob referred to the King of Cool, Dean Martin. Apathy turned out to be a big turn-on for a lot of women, ironically enough, at least those that sought no attachments, and in fact went out of their way to avoid them. My descent into sexual addiction was a byproduct of my loneliness, not a cure. But it sure took my mind off myself, even though I continued to masturbate on a regular basis, often thinking about my copious copulation for inspiration.

I think my psychotic break with what you would call reality began before Costa Rica or even Chicago. My regular escapes into the world of *outre* cinema, often accompanied by excessive alcohol consumption, usually down at The Drive-Inn—Doc called himself my "enabler"—began warping my cerebral synapses, to the point where I saw my life and the world in general as one long movie, with me as the star. The script was improvised, and I wasn't allowed to see anything more than the sides I was given on a daily basis. I assumed the director was David Lynch, but now it was becoming apparent how ridiculous that theory was. Will the Thrill was my self-appointed producer, director, and scriptwriter, at least according to him, even though he felt like he was also starring in a movie with no cameras or crew to guide him. Where did it end, or begin? Who, if anyone, was the Ultimate Visionary in charge of all of these intersecting spectacles designed for the amusement of no one, including the participants?

You got me. But Will the Thrill was a start, since he claimed to be my creator, however improbable that was, even amid all this other wild shit. While I was still in 1990s San Francisco, I decided to track him down for more answers. The secret to my existence was buried somewhere beneath that green fez. I hoped.

The latest problem, I realized, was that this was still 1993, and Will the Thrill wouldn't start hosting Thrillville for another four years or so. The Parkway Theater over in Oakland was shuttered, in between incarnations as a neighborhood grindhouse theater and a gang-banger nightclub. The upshot was I had no idea where to find him.

So I figured out a way for him to find me.

I placed a strategically composed personal ad in the paper: "Bettie Page Lookalike Looking For Love. Prefer Someone Poor, Short, Slightly Overweight, Lives in the East Bay, Likes Tikis and Fez Hats and B Movies." Basically, it was the precisely worded come-on I would've answered myself, since he and I shared so many sensibilities, which only served to support his otherwise incredulous explanation for all this.

My phone rang the next day. In fact, it seemed to become "the next day" literally overnight, except it went by in the blink of an eye.

Anyway, while on the phone—a landline, which still put me in the early 1990s—Will the Thrill, though he wasn't quite a Thrill just yet in the orderly scheme of things, gave me directions to a place called Forbidden Island Tiki Lounge over in Alameda. He didn't even seem upset I'd fooled him, as if he were expecting me. His rendezvous designation didn't make sense to me, either, since I knew from future experience that place was still a dive bar and wouldn't be converted to its future exotic glory for well over a decade from where I was literally sitting. But I went along with it because at this point I had nothing to lose, not even my mind.

I headed down Geary all the way through downtown, onto the Bay Bridge, the 880 then exited into the Webster Tube. I got a funny feeling after I emerged on the other side. The tranquil island of Alameda was much like I'd remembered it, which didn't gel with my present reality, since back in 1993, I had no memories of Alameda. I didn't make it over there till after the turn of the century.

When the soft sunlight hit my hands once out of the tunnel, I noticed the liver spots. Then I checked my face in the mirror. My temples were gray, crows' footprints all around my eyes. I was old again. Another time jump, but within the same general space. I just went with it, because I had no choice. I kept driving, recognizing most of the island, which had become a boom town once the locals had been priced out of San Francisco and Oakland. I hung a left on Lincoln and then pulled into the lot behind Forbidden Island, which was up and running.

Once inside the dark, cozy joint dense with retro-tropical decor, I said hello to my friends and frequent patrons Scott and Jenn, sitting at the bar as always, as well as the owner, Michael, who was taking care of business as usual. Everyone seemed happy to me, not questioning what the hell I was doing there after all this time. But then I figured out we were functioning on different schedules simultaneously, so by their watches, I was right where I was supposed to be.

I ordered my usual drink, aptly called a "Vic Valentine," from my favorite bartender, Becca, and was promptly served by my favorite waitress, Lee, out in the back patio. Damn, they were both so hot. I looked at my watch. Same batshit time, same batshit channel. Will the Thrill was late, but I had a feeling he'd show up eventually.

Upon taking a seat in a bamboo chair, I was greeted by the decapitated head of Hal Nickerson, the international business mogul who was the mastermind behind the mutated opioid epidemic that was turning its users into flesh-eating zombies. The last time I'd seen Hal, his bloody body was dumped in the back of a jeep, then driven off deep into the jungles of Costa Rica by his henchman, Brett. I assumed Hal had met the same fate as many who crossed the Cartel down there would, namely dismemberment, followed by gratuitous exhibition of their remains in order to send a message to both authorities and the population at large not to mess with them. Usually this came in the form of heads on a stick, or a corpse dangling from a rope in full public view, like in *Sicario*.

Apparently, I was at least partly right. Either that, or I was mixing him up with somebody else's dead head I saw down there. In any case, regardless of his actual fate, Hal's messily removed head was currently situated atop a tiki torch behind Forbidden Island. He just winked at me and smiled. Naturally none of the other aloha-shirted hipsters around me seemed to notice, which was just as well, though I would've welcomed their confirmation of the circumstances.

While I had Hal's attention, however fanciful, I decided to ask him if I was under the influence of his diabolical drugs, even now.Especially now, in fact.

As he was in actual life, Hal was very friendly and accommodating. You'd never guess his nice guy exterior masked such a devious fiend bent on world domination. He was always quite polite, even as a talking head:

Well, for one thing, Vic, we haven't officially met yet. You haven't even moved to Seattle, much less traveled to Costa Rica. But of course, being a disembodied spirit, I'm speaking from the benefit of both hindsight and foresight. So yes, perhaps. I can't say for sure. I mean, you are talking to a dead severed head, are you not? That would most likely qualify you for the loony bin, by conventional standards. So you're definitely hallucinating, but whether it's permanent and progressive damage done to your sensory perception by my hand, wherever that is, I really can't say for sure. I'm just a talking head, after all. But now that I think of it, since I still have a brain attached to a stick if not to a stem, it may just be your wife. She's into all that Mexican folklore, witchcraft and demons and such. Could be she just put a curse on you. I wouldn't put it past her.

"Or a combination of both supernatural and chemical elements," I said. "Could be I'm under her spell, Screamin' Jay Hawkins-style."

You're still better off than I am, Vic. The rest of me is hanging off an overpass somewhere. So I really don't want to hear your complaints, asshole.

I nodded in agreement. Hal was right. I was relatively healthy, physically intact if not mentally sound, but of the two, I already had my preference. I pondered the various possibilities of my situation, both causes and ramifications, as I continued sipping my deliciously intoxicating "Vic Valentine," figuring since I was already stoned I might as well add in some choice bourbon and the other secret ingredients concocted by other favorite bartender, Susan, in honor of the fact I once frequented the joint so much.

"Thing is, my life started getting weird before I even met you," I said to Hal's head. "So I don't think I can retroactively blame it all on the drugs you pumped into me."

You mean you remember things getting strange before we met. That doesn't mean they did. It just means your recollection has become as warped as your immediate cognizance.

"So you mean I'm just remembering shit that never happened?"

Maybe. Or maybe they happened, but not in the same exact manner in which you recall them. Since you're the only one who made a public record of these events, there's no one around to either undermine or authenticate your account. And given the nature of the narrative thus far, your credibility is dubious, to say the least.

I was going to forcefully if emptily respond to that charge when Hal spit up and dribbled some gore down his chin. It was quite disgusting. I was glad no one else there could see it, at least as far as I could tell. I was wrong. One other person noticed.

"Yuck," said Will the Thrill, just making his brash entrance, wearing the obligatory aloha shirt, taking off his customary green fez, setting it atop Hal's head, then sitting down at our table nonchalantly. He took off his shades, look us both over, and chuckled. "Man, you guys are fucked up."

I noticed he had also ordered the "Vic Valentine," which was one of the most popular house drinks, after all. It was damn good. Here's the secret recipe:

"Vic Valentine"
2 oz Bourbon
1 oz Lemon Juice
1/2 oz Cinnamon Vanilla Syrup
1/2 oz Cherry Heering
1/4 oz Luxardo Maraschino Liqueur
2 Dashes of Angostura
Shake and strain over fresh ice garnish with a cherry

"Cheers," Will the Thrill said to Hal and me, as he and I clinked glasses. "Hey Hal, should I get you a straw?" Will the Thrill asked the bloody head, who did not respond and did not seem amused by the fez resting atop his rotting cranium.

"Kinda reminds me of 'Re-animator,'" I said. "Especially that one scene with Barbara Crampton."

"Of course it does," Will the Thrill said. "That's what made me think of it."

"Think of what?"

He nodded toward Hal's head. "That, what else?"

"So everything going on here right now is all inside my head? Or his?"

"Neither. Mine." Will the Thrill tapped his temple.

"Oh, really? I'm supposed to just believe that? I came here for some hard answers to harder questions, man. Lay it on me, but be straight. I won't believe just anything you tell me, though."

He shrugged. "Believe what you want, man. That's everyone else does. Even me. I have no idea who is making me do the things I do to you, so don't blame me. I'm just following my instincts and impulses, believing they're all entirely my own autonomous decisions. Like you, I imagine."

"I do."

"I know, because I'm the one that imagined it for you."

"Imagined what?"

"All of this. All of that. Everything you've ever perceived. All of your dreams, desires, doubts, memories, fantasies. Most of them are mine. But not all of them. There is a deliberate line drawn between my consciousness and yours, so you have your own unique identity, and I maintain mine. Though mine is merely a product of someone else's imagination. And so it goes."

"Vonnegut."

"Yep."

"I read all of his books."

"Well, I read them first."

"Don't be childish."

"I can't help it. It's how I'm made."

"You just keep repeating the same bullshit everyone else does."

"Who?"

"Val. Rose. Doc. Or Doc's ghost, but even Doc the cat. And Hal's head. They keep giving me these same theories, basically variations of what you're saying."

"That's because I'm the one always actually saying it all to you, Vic. Don't you get that yet?"

"Okay, so which is it?"

"Which is what?"

"Is it the opioids, too much booze, black magic, a psychotic break, or what?"

"Yeah, all those, probably. Or none of them. Whatever works best for you. Just pick one. That's what I do. And you can always change your mind, too, as more is revealed. That's how it works, Vic. For everyone. You, me, Hal, everyone sitting around us right here, everyone on Earth, everyone who ever lived or will live. It's just a guessing game. You're provided clues here and there, but they're meant to be subjectively interpreted. Or maybe not. Could be it's all random. I can't tell you because I don't know myself. I mean, I'm putting thoughts in your head and words in your mouth, but who's putting them in mine to put in yours?"

"That sounds nasty."

"It is. Someone is pulling a train on us, Vic. You're just the caboose. Sorry."

"Even what you just said, I've heard before. I've said it myself. Everything is stuck in the same cycle. And I keep arriving back at the same place: nowhere, with no answers."

"That's my point, Vic. Just pick one and stick with it. The point of repetition is to eventually make it credible, even if it isn't really true. To wear down your resistance to the point where you'll accept any explanation just so you can relax without worrying about the actual truth, which you'll never know, anyway."

I sat back and sighed. Apparently I was just wasting my time here, even though I didn't know which time it was at any given moment, since it kept changing. Hal rolled his eyes at me, as if completely bored and revolted by this whole exchange. I didn't think he was buying any of this crap, either. But then he was in no position to second guess anything.

"Here's a theory for *you*," I said to Will the Thrill, deciding to flip the script on him. "To me, *you're* merely some shit I made up. You're just this crazy-ass clown I saw once up in Seattle, with your sexy wife, and what she sees in you, I'll never know."

"Neither do I, frankly. But whoever is in charge of her life circumstances, and mine, knows everything, and whoever it is ain't telling. The ones in charge never tell us shit. They just keep us guessing. I suppose for their own amusement."

He was right about one thing. "I just want to give up and believe you."

"Good choice. At least I get you laid."

"Thanks for the newly acquired singing voice, too, if that came from you. That's always been a dream of mine."

"I know. Not mine, though. I made that one up just for you."

"So I'm like a replicant, and you're just implanting thoughts into my head, like 'Blade Runner,' and now as a sentient being I'm beginning to question my own existence, what's real and what isn't, is that what you're saying?"

"Exactly the metaphor I would've used. In fact, I did use it. Just now."

"Fuck me."

"In a way, we fuck ourselves constantly. All that mental and emotional masturbation. But you jerk-off way, way more than I ever did, anyway."

"Why is that? It's compulsive. I just can't help it."

"Yeah, I know. It's disgusting."

"Don't you beat your meat just as much as I do?"

"No way, man. You're a fuckin' juggernaut. But not your fault, so don't sweat it."

"Why make me be and do these things if you couldn't or wouldn't?"

"Because I'm real, Vic. Like in the accepted, old-fashioned, traditional sense. See?" He pinched himself. "Flesh and blood. I mean the organic kind. Go ahead, pinch yourself, but trust me, you could disappear at any moment. As could I. But at least I *know* I'm real, at least temporarily, while you keep questioning your very existence. Who but a fictional character has the time or energy to sit around jerking off all day, both mentally and physically? But it's not all bad, Vic. You've also fucked way, way more women than I ever have, at least virtually speaking, fulfilling all my young bachelor fantasies, and then some. In a way, I've sublimated my darker desires into your story, even though I'm picking low-hanging forbidden fruit."

"I got your low-hangin' forbidden fruit right here, man."

"C'mon. Where's the gratitude? You should feel lucky, Vic."

"Gratitude? You call this pathetic life of mine fucking lucky? Johnny Depp is lucky. I'm a fucking failure and loser, no matter how much I get laid, which is only a transitory distraction from despair at best. And on top of that, you're telling me none of it actually happened, anyway."

"Then that should make you feel better! Right?"

"I've been miserable most of my life, or what you're calling a life, however fabricated on the fly, so thanks for that, asshole."

"Hey, I've enjoyed it, at least. The gratuitous sex, anyway. You have more orgasms than any actual male could ever have. I should've made you a porn star. You even have a porn star name!"

"So I've heard. Thanks."

"You're welcome. But hey, look at it this way, Vic. We're *both* happily married now, so there's that. Except I've been married and off the market much longer than you, whereas I gave you a lengthy bachelorhood for us both to enjoy."

I nodded. Maybe he had a point, after all. "Well, Vic is short for Vicarious."

I was panicking, because the crazy stuff he was laying on me was actually starting to make some sense. In fact, I couldn't come up with any rational alternative explanation. This was all I had. And it sucked. It sucked harder than a whore on her last fix. It sucked harder than a barnacle on a boat. It sucked harder than these stupid metaphors Will the Thrill keeps putting inside my head.

But no. I rejected this reality, or this version of it, anyway, which was apparently my prerogative, because I couldn't accept it without blowing my brains out, and also just to spite Will the Thrill. Even if he was the only one who could supply me the gun, and make me pull the trigger. I was determined to defy the destiny he had in store for me. I already knew it up to a point.

So now that I was back here in the Bay Area, and hadn't left for Seattle yet, I planned to either stay indefinitely, or move even sooner to Seattle, but without Charlie and all that mess. I would start by avoiding Bimbo's nightclub over in North Beach, where the first burlesque murder happened, the catalyst for everything that drove us north. And since I knew who Charlie was, if I saw him at The Drive-Inn, where we first met while he was shooting a movie up the street, I'd go out of my way to avoid him.

I was taking charge of my own life, for the first time ever.

"Which is exactly what I want you to think," Will the Thrill called after me as I peeled out of the back lot in my Corvair, headed back toward San Francisco with a renewed sense of purpose.

Since it was 2014 again, or thereabouts, there was such a thing as the Internet. I didn't own a computer, so I went to a local internet cafe (yes, I just spelled the word "internet" with both a lower and upper case 'I' since the controversy rages on among grammar cops) and started Googling myself. I know that sounds nasty, especially in a public setting, but I get the idea most people do it, at least secretly.

Anyway, the first article that popped up when I typed in my name wasn't about excessive masturbation or B movie binge-watching or gratuitous cocktail consumption or anything else anyone would think of when my names pops up, if it ever does, but instead it was an academic piece published on a site I'd never heard of, much less visited. I am not scientific by nature. More intuitive, i.e. I just wing it.

Since for some reason this article came up first under an online search for myself, I started reading and was immediately lost in the dense academic verbiage, though it still spoke to me on some level, even if I didn't quite understand the language. The main topic was about a condition called "dissociative identity disorder," or DID for short. Basically, multiple personalities, which could be a hereditary gift from my mother. While the bulk of the piece might as well have been hieroglyphics in a pyramid scheme as far as I was concerned, I related to its overall premise. From what I could glean, I was a prime candidate for this DID thing. I seemed to suffer all the specified symptoms. Of course, psychos can't really diagnose themselves, which is part of their mental issue, though I'm sure a lot of people spend a lot of time online trying to find out what's wrong with them so they won't have to actually go see a doctor, either confirming or discounting the worst case scenario so they can get some sleep without worrying about that blue bump on their leg or the pink elephant in the room.

So the question now was: DID I, Or DIDn't I? Was it me, or was it Memorex?

Seeking more practical answers to my condition, I scrolled around the article, excited by the prospect of enlightenment while navigating around hyperlinked high-falutin' terms like "cosmopsychism" and "constitutive panpsychism" and other intellectual jism.

One term I did sort of grasp, mainly because it didn't have an "-ism" attached, was something called "the hard problem of consciousness," a phrase that seems to sum up everyone's existence, from human beings fighting traffic on down to worms digging their way through the dirt, but is specifically designated as such per the all-knowing Internet:

The hard problem of consciousness (Chalmers 1995) is the problem of explaining the relationship between physical phenomena, such as brain processes, and experience (i.e., phenomenal consciousness, or mental states/events with phenomenal qualities or qualia). Why are physical processes ever accompanied by experience? And why does a given physical process generate the specific experience it does—why an experience of red rather than green, for example?

Fuck if I knew.

Some stuff I read seemed to suggest that all functionality, self-awareness, and sensory experience take place across the entire spectrum of species and sentient (and even non-sentient or semi-sentient) beings, right down to the microscopic level, known and unknown, across the entire galaxy and beyond, i.e. shit you and me can't even see.

As I understood it, there is one big universal consciousness to which we all have random, individualized access, not limited to our personalized prisms, but subject to our unique, apparently fluid, and even interchangeable perception of our immediate surroundings and circumstances, whether tangible or intangible, all mere fragments of one infinite Truth. Which means we're only allowed to know what we are allowed to know via our restricted scope, which unfortunately seemed to support Will the Thrill's thesis.

However, I also stumbled upon this contrasting philosophical theory called "idealism," which is hereby defined verbatim per my heavily caffeinated research:

Idealism is the metaphysical and epistemological doctrine that ideas or thoughts make up fundamental reality. Essentially, it is any philosophy which argues that the only thing actually knowable is consciousness (or the contents of consciousness), whereas we never can be sure that matter or anything in the outside world really exists. Thus, the only real things are mental entities, not physical things (which exist only in the sense that they are perceived).

Idealism is a form of Monism (as opposed to Dualism or Pluralism), and stands in direct contrast to other Monist beliefs such as Physicalism and Materialism (which hold that the only thing that can be truly proven to exist is physical matter). It is also contrasted with Realism (which holds that things have an absolute existence prior to, and independent of, our knowledge or perceptions).

Makes sense in the context of what I've been relating to you, right? Yeah, me either.

OK, fuck all this, I have no idea what the hell I'm talking about and neither do you. I'm merely trying to translate this crap I read to you, filtered though my uneducated and substance-abusive brain, so make of it what you will, which is exactly what I did. In any case, the subjectively distilled gist of it was enough for me to realize that Will the Thrill was full of shit, which probably didn't require an expert opinion anyway. Unlike that poseur, whoever wrote this philosophical mumbo-jumbo seemed to know what they were talking about, and so did I: They were talking about *me*. I admit that sounds both incredibly paranoid and self-aggrandizing, but for all I know, I'm just a dream inside *your* head, so maybe it's all your fault, anyway.

Or maybe you're just a dream in *mine*. Chew on that for a while, sucker.

Anyway, assuming I was finally onto something semi-substantial, I scrolled up to the names of the authors. Never heard of them and they didn't sound like people I'd associate with, even in a dissociative state of mind. Then I noticed the publication date at the top of the article: sometime in the futuristic year of 2018.

But then designating "now" was no longer any more meaningful to my consciousness than "me." I had lost all sense of identity and place in the multiple realms of sentient, sensory experience, just drifting in and out of memories and fantasies, all blended into one expressionistic (or impressionistic, whatever) painting. I felt like *The Incredible Shrinking Man* at the very end of the movie, dissolving into the cosmos with a blissful feeling of resignation and relief.

Of course, Hal's head suddenly appearing didn't either confirm nor debunk my new pet theory, which I adopted anyway, if only because it was so lonely and sad. Like me. There was a chance I was still suffering the lingering and possible fatal effects of those opioids from my Costa Rica adventure, or that my wife Val was indeed a supernatural bitch messing with my head for her own diabolical reasons, maybe just amusement. But this psychological explanation was the most comforting, even if I had no way of curing it, not on my own, anyway. Even if my wife was a Mexican witch, *la bruja*, she also had a PhD in Psychology (I think), which made her more than just a witch, but a witch doctor. Maybe she could help me, after all, even if she was the one behind all of this.

Identifying the problem is the first step toward solving it. Right? Just say "right" and shut up and let me tell this my way.

This self-realization gave me a miraculous sense of power. I no longer felt constrained by the whims of my alleged creator, since I literally had his number now. Maybe he had no idea who was surreptitiously guiding his existence, but if Will the Thrill was right, he'd blown his own cover, and I now knew exactly who my puppeteer was. Whether this was a cosmic epiphany or twist of fate no longer mattered. I finally solved the greatest mystery of all: Life itself. My own, anyway. You're on your own.

And as per my usual M.O., I'd cracked the case totally by accident.

Chapter Ten
SEATTLE SLEAZE

The infamous "Seattle Freeze" never fazed me. That phrase basically refers to the idea most people in this town seem very friendly on the surface, as long as you don't invite yourself over for dinner or anything cozy and intimate like that, maintaining a healthy distance despite the bullshit niceties. I've always been the same exact way, and I wasn't even a native, so I immediately fit right in.

It was good to be home again, at least my most recent one, the one where I felt most comfortable, even if it was where I was the oldest iteration of myself, at least so far. I loved Seattle. I loved my Ballard neighborhood. I loved my witch doctor wife. I loved my pets. I loved the rain. I loved it all. The trick now was holding onto it without slipping back into alternate realities that were either unreal or undead. Or both.

Despite what Will the Thrill or Hal's head tried to make me think, the truth of it was, my life didn't start getting truly surreal until I arrived in Seattle with Charlie a few years ago, and Ivar the sailor statue started popping up here and there throughout our escapades, unexpected and unexplained. I assumed at first he was a prank, maybe by Monica, but she denied it and had no reason to lie to me. But as his appearances in sundry places only became more frequent, I began to seriously question my sanity. In fact, I was my own lead suspect in the serial killer case I was on, or rather, slipped on. This was all long before I met Hal and then the drugs and the zombies and Costa Rica happened. And before I reunited with Val in Mexico City, however contrived that reunion may have been.

Once she was in my life, I decided to just accept the increasing irrationality of my daily existence. But now it had reached a fever dream pitch, and other than Will the Thrill and Hal's head, only one person was in a reasonable position to explain it to me: Ivar himself. Since he had begun walking and talking not long ago, I assumed he'd be up for the conversation.

So imagine my surprise when he just stared back at me, silent and stone-faced, like a, well, like a statue.

"Why are you talking to that creepy sailor dude?" Val asked me as she came out of the bathroom with a towel around her wet, wonderful body.

"He started it!" I said.

Accustomed to my boyish babbling by now, Val shrugged, and got dressed. She put on a tight red bikini-body suit, exactly the type worn by Vampirella in that iconic six-foot poster painted by Jose Gonzalez that adorned my wall in the '70s, including the trademark knee-high black boots.

Then she stood in front of me, extended an arm, and a bat flew to her fingertips. She stood and posed exactly like the poster. And froze that way.

I walked over and touched her. She didn't move, blink, or otherwise acknowledge my presence, just standing there with that sensuous smirk on her face. She was identical to the poster painting.

While I was staring at her in awe, she seemed to flatten out into a single dimension until she merged with the wall behind her. I went to touch her flesh, but instead felt paper. She'd turned into the poster from my old room. In fact, it was a bit frayed and yellow at the edges, showing some signs of wear and tear. Like me.

But where was Val?

I kept feeling up the poster in a state of panicky perversion, attempting to find a portal into the dimension where my wife had suddenly vanished. Gently, I removed the poster and began pounding on the wall behind it. It was solid. She was just gone.

Desperate for answers, I looked back at Ivar, who was still giving me the silent treatment. I picked him up and shook him violently, as if trying to break him down during an interrogation. Nothing. He was just a statue. My vampire wife was just a poster.

And I was just a lounge lizard for hire. Right.

I looked out my window, half-expecting to see *Saturday Night Fever*-era Brooklyn. But I was still in Seattle. It all looked disturbingly normal.

I didn't know what to do, so I pulled out my Blu Ray box set of *Miami Vice* and started binging.

Day turned to night, night turned to day. Every now and then I'd get up, grab some random food from the fridge, or make myself a drink, without ever pausing the player since I'd seen every episode a hundred times.

The food in the fridge was all leftovers, cooked by my wife, not a Vampirella poster. I kept looking over at Ivar, waiting for him to blink or wink. Nothing.

No Doc. No Young Vic. No Chumpy Walnut. No Will the Thrill. Just me, Crockett, and Tubbs. Just like old times. How very sad.

Then during one of many scenes where Sonny Crockett draws his gun and yells "*Freeze, pal, Miami Vice!*", the picture actually froze.

I couldn't get it to work and didn't really try. I was just killing time. Or it was killing me, as I often say (too often). I switched over to Netflix. Just for the hell of it, I said, "Love Stories Are Too Violent For Me" into the remote. No search results.

I got up and opened my laptop and Googled the same title. Nothing. I Googled myself, as it were. Nothing. I Googled Val's name, her *full* name. Nada.

If she never existed, how did that perfectly cooked food get in my fridge? I was never a chef. As a lifelong bachelor I almost always ate out, or if I did cook, I just heated up leftovers.

Leftovers.

I went back and noticed the cauliflower wings were the same served up the road at No Bones Beach Club. I checked out the trash and noticed a dirty take-out container. In the garbage can, not the recycling bin, which meant it was definitely me. In fact, I never even owned a recycling bin, other than my own skull. My whole life was being recycled, anyway. Maybe it was time to trash it.

Curious as to the present status of my perceptive powers, I decided to go down to No Bones and see if I could retrace my steps.

I walked inside and the same bartender, meaning the undead vampire vegan goth babe, was still there, looking just fine. She seemed neither happy nor shocked when I sat down. Once again, I made no reference to our prior mutual circumstances, at least from my perspective, and neither did she. It seemed like things never ended well when we were in each other's company. Maybe the third time was the charm.

"Did you see me here recently?" I asked the undead vegan vampire goth chick, who was friendly in a professionally perfunctory manner, but otherwise politely guarded, Seattle-style. I never even knew her name. Despite our intimate past, however fanciful, I just never thought to ask.

"Yes, you took home your lunch," she said. "Just a little while ago. Surprised to see you back so soon. Is everything okay?"

"Yeah," I lied. "Was I, I mean…was a woman here with me?"

"Today? No."

"Okay, ever?"

She studied me with cautious quizzicalness, then said, "What do you mean?"

I shook my head. "Never mind. I'll just take a Mai Tai, thanks."

She smiled pertly and dashed off to fulfill my order. Oddly, I felt more at peace than I had in a long time, maybe ever, despite my disoriented limbo.

Maybe I was dead inside a dream that never ends, so death wasn't just a black hole, after all.

Or maybe I was finally coming to terms with my lifelong solipsism, a hoity-toity but apt philosophical/psychological/biological/illogical term I discovered while investigating the mysteries of my own mind. Basically, it meant that the only definite proof of existence was *me*. Which meant my isolation was no accident or illusion, but the one positive truth amid this carnival of carnage and chaos. Indeed, my painfully familiar state of solitude just felt the most natural to me. The rest of it was merely a detour, a distraction, a dream, populated by shadow puppets in my own private Id show.

Whether she was a projection of my mind or not, the bartender returned with my Mai Tai, and my sensations were clicking on all cylinders. *Beach Blanket Bingo* was playing on the TV. The other patrons were happy. It was cool and cloudy inside, cozy and peaceful inside. Life felt okay again, even though I was alone. Or because I was alone, and not surrounded by supporting players that kept going off-script, but rather just walked through their roles without bothering me. For once, I was relieved not to be seeing talking sailor statues or the ghosts of my past or imaginary characters manifested by some clown in a fez hat. Obviously, I wasn't one of them, and that's all that mattered. I had beaten Will the Thrill. I had defied his plan for my life, by defining it for myself.

But that old war wound in my battle-scarred heart began to ache, subtly at first, then gradually expanding, burrowing into my soul before reaching my brain and ruining my newfound peace of mind.

My old nemesis, Loneliness, was back.

I finished my drink and returned to my empty apartment. I stared into the mirror. I appeared even older than last time I'd looked, because I was. That's how Time was supposed to work, forward and degenerative, not backwards and regenerative. I checked around my pad for any signs of Val. No clothes, no makeup, nothing. The idea I'd just conjured her up out of nothing in a fit of frustration while in the depths of despair was beginning to really hit me. That just couldn't be true. I didn't want to be lonely again. I couldn't survive it. I was always too old for this shit, even when I was young.

Hyperventilating, I turned on the TV and began scanning through the streaming horror service called Shudder. I couldn't stay hooked on any one movie, because they all reminded me of Val, who was the lesbian vampire goddess of my deepest, darkest fantasies.

Then I realized my pets weren't around, either. No Doc. No Fido. Nobody. Just Ivar, and he had retreated back into a state of silent stillness.I began to pace the floor, holding my head in my hands, finally bending over and screaming, hoping to jar myself out of this iteration of cognizance and back into the past, when I was alone but at least young enough to sustain hope, or just fuck my way out of this potentially fatal funk.

Nothing.

I wound up on the floor in a fetal position, sobbing, until I passed out.

When I woke up, I was still there. Nobody around. No wife, no ghosts, no animals. Just my fucking girlie magazines and B movie collection and cabinet of booze. Basically all the drugs I used to self-medicate myself into oblivious oblivion. They didn't work anymore. I ached for Val's touch. Through my blurred vision I tried in vain to make her appear, summoning her from the catacombs of my creative core. I even crawled up to the Vampirella poster and began pawing at it, hoping it would materialize back into corporeal form. No dice.

Then I thought of something else that might reconnect me with my preferred perception of reality: that green fez hat and jacket.

I went to my closet and yes, they were there!

I donned both. Nothing happened. It wasn't like clicking the heels of my red ruby shoes together. I couldn't go home again. I was already home.

Then how and why was that stupid fez and jacket in there? What possible use could I have for those?

The cellphone rang, and my heart froze. Caller ID said, "Rose."

What?

I answered. "Hello?"

"Vic, it's me. I'm here at Tula's, watching Dimitri. You're on next. Where are you?"

I was too stunned to say anything. So she repeated herself. I recognized the voice. It was definitely her. I mean I was pretty sure. I strongly suspected it, anyway. Kinda.

"Vic? It's me. Are you on your way?"

I knew where Tula's was, so at least I could do that much. "Sure, I'll be right there." I was already dressed to thrill, anyway.

Using the Lyft app Val had downloaded for me, I summoned a ride that took me to Belltown. It was a Sunday so there wasn't a lot of traffic.

When I walked into Tula's, I saw Dmitri Matheny performing with his group, and Rose sitting at the bar. She looked just like Val. My wife Val, that is.

When I went up to her, she kissed me, which surprised me. She seemed surprised I was surprised. "I have your drink waiting for you," she said, pointing toward a Manhattan on the bar.

When in doubt, imbibe. I needed it. I took a sip and then I heard my name announced. The bar was packed, and they all applauded at the sound of my name: "Vic Valentine, Lounge Lizard For Hire presents: The Voodoo Valentine Show!"

Oh, shit.

Fortunately, Rose, or Val, led me up to the stage. I noticed she was wearing a long, low cut black gown. Then she waved at someone in the crowd, a handsome blonde dude in his twenties.

Rose/Val beamed as she pointed him out to me, saying, "Sammy's here!"

"Sammy?"

"Our son, dummy!"

"Our *son*?"

"Okay, *your* son."

"*My* son?"

She studied me for a second and whispered, "Vic, are you okay? Maybe I should just do this alone?"

"Um…"

"Just do your usual intro, and I'll take it from there. Then go down and finish your drink. Okay?"

"Okay…" I looked out at the crowd, who were looking back at me in anticipation. Time for some improvisation, Will the Thrill style. "Um…ladies and gentlemen…by any other name, she's still…*Rose*!"

Nobody responded, besides a cricket somewhere. Everyone was staring at me, even Val and the band, as if waiting for me to recover from my apparent blunder. So I tried again, and this time I said, "Ladies and gentleman, the star of our show…um…Mrs. Valentine!"

They erupted in applause again. Relieved, I returned to the bar. That blonde kid made his way through the audience and sat next to me and said, "Hey, Pop!"

"Um…hey!"

"She sounds great, doesn't she?"

"Yeah, of course." Rose, or Val, was singing "Key Largo," backed by Dimitri and his cool cats. Sarah Vaughan had nothing on her. I never knew she could sing like that. I didn't know Sammy was my son all this time, either. I didn't know a lot of things. I didn't know anything, except for the most important thing: I wasn't alone, after all.

Then I saw the Japanese dude, the Yakuza hitman named Hayata or whoever he really was, sitting with two beautiful Japanese ladies at a table, enjoying the music. My gut clenched. Something wasn't right.

I kept waiting for something dramatic to happen, like the room to suddenly go dark and then a spotlight to hit the stage where a bald giant would be waving his arms in the air while warning me "it's happening again," but no. Everything just kept going smoothly, at least by my standards.

Sammy was sitting next to me like he'd known me all his life. Maybe he had. I hadn't seen him since he was a baby. And there's no way he could've been my kid, not by natural means, anyway, since Rose was sleeping around with everyone and their brother and sister back then, long after our relationship had ended, when she rudely disappeared on me back in New York. Last I'd seen her down in New Orleans, I actually rejected a reunion, protecting my heart in favor of my libido, which I'd finally let loose. I didn't want to be tied down to a woman who would break my heart again.

But like I said, the woman on stage wasn't actually Rose. She sounded like her, but she looked like Ava Margarita Esmeralda Valentina Valdez, my Mexican wife. Same age. Same face. Same hair. Same tits, meaning they were bigger than Rose's. But she still reminded me of Rose, even if her visage wasn't the same. It was her aura, her presence. And confirmation of her identity was sitting right beside me.

Then it hit me: Sammy was merely a full-sized version of Chumpy Walnut. Same features, exactly. Just taller. Way taller. Taller than me, even, which is normally nothing to brag about, unless you compare me to Chumpy. Except he was only a product of Will the Thrill's delirious imagination, like me. Except I wasn't. Not anymore. Not ever again.

Maybe it was just the strength of my perfectly mixed Manhattan, but I began to settle into something resembling relaxation again. I was comfortable in my own lounge lizard skin. Somehow, the pieces were all falling into place, the jigsaw puzzle of my life finally forming a cohesive picture.

Somewhere along the way, I'd reunited with Rose, accepted Sammy as my own, and we moved to Seattle, where she got a job as a singer, and I was her personal emcee, a lounge lizard for hire. We were happy. It didn't matter who the Japanese dude was. In another time, place and dimension, he could've been the Scarecrow or the Tin Man or the Cowardly Lion or even the Wizard of Oz himself, but not here in the...

Emerald City.

That allusion again. Hm.

Somewhere under my green fez was the answer. It I kept it on, maybe it would seep through my skull into my brain, and everything would finally make perfect sense again, or once, anyway. Meantime, I decided to just enjoy myself.

When her set was over, Rose or Val or both joined Sammy and me at the bar. We were one big happy family. I flashed on the kind folks down in Houston that had more or less adopted me during my Costa Rica adventure, which still resonated in my memory as an actual event, zombies and all. Maybe that part hadn't happened, but the rest had. Maybe. At some point in the past or future, anyway.

"Let's go grab a bite, shall we?" Rose said.

"Sure," I said, feeling famished all of a sudden.

"Let's go to our usual place," Sammy said. I nodded in agreement, even though I had no idea where the hell he meant.

Rose or Val concurred, and after blowing kisses both to Dmitri and the Japanese dude, which I did not question since I did not want to know why, we were out the door and onto Second Avenue on a chilly Sunday evening.

We walked down toward Pike Place and wound up at the Pink Door. I guess that was "our place." Last time I'd been there, Val had made a spectacle of herself and we'd been chased out by cops. But this time, we were greeted like regular customers without any hint of the previous ruckus, which I supposed never actually happened, either. What a relief.

We sat down and ordered. I recalled I was now a vegan, so I stuck with spaghetti and Mariana sauce.

"No eggplant parmigiana?" Rose said. "That's your favorite!"

"Well, I stopped eating it since I became vegan," I said. "The cheese."

Both Rose and Sammy looked at me like I'd just ripped off my face and exposed an alien lizard head. In unison, they said, "Vegan?"

"Yeah, you know. Plant-based diet. Which means cocktails are okay." I ordered a dirty Martini with three olives as my salad.

"That's the Vic I know," Rose said. "Why didn't you tell us you were vegan?"

"It just never came up, I guess."

"But we just had salmon yesterday at Ivar's!" Sammy said. "Don't you remember?"

"Ivar's?"

"Yeah, the one by Lake Union," Sammy said. "It was only yesterday, Pop! You okay?"

"Sure. Sure, I am. Just a bit fuzzy, I guess."

"You're still recovering from the head trauma," Rose said, touching my face tenderly.

"Head trauma?"

"From when Tommy hit you," Rose said. "Sammy's dad, remember?"

"My real dad," Sammy said. "At least until I met you, Pop!"

I sat back, dazed by this barrage of information. The pieces weren't fitting together so neatly after all. I had to figure out which were still missing, at least from my fractured perspective.

"Yeah, well, I guess it's good to be together again," I said, smiling wanly. "Cheers!" I said, raising my glass after my Martini was served.

There was a burlesque dancer doing an aerial routine over our heads. That was a special feature of this subterranean dinner club, which had some of the best Italian food in the city. Val and I had always loved it, though we stopped going as often once we gave up dairy products.

The funny thing was, this was Val sitting right next to me, eating a steak. Rose was omnivorous when it came to her diet and her sexual appetites. Sammy was the right age to be her son, given the time span since he'd been born, twenty-five or so years earlier. So that part added up. But the rest of their references just weren't jogging any memories for me. None that I could rely on, anyway.

I figured if I just played along, it would all come back to me. Kind of like when you run into someone you barely know and can't recall their name, though they know yours, so out of politeness, you pretend to remember their name, too, hoping somehow they'll accidentally reveal it if you just keep smiling and nodding like everything is just fine.

The acrobatic burlesque dancer kept spinning around until I grew dizzy, or maybe it was just the booze. Or the company. In any case, I got the spins and fainted, my face falling right into my plate of spaghetti.

I woke up expecting to be back in the hospital with Doc and Monica, finally coming out of my coma. But no, I was in a strange apartment, with Rose and Sammy by my side.

It wasn't my place in Ballard, though. I scanned the room slowly as my blurry vision snapped back into sharp focus.

The walls were lined with framed photos of Rose and Sammy taken through the years. It was like I was watching him grow up in a matter of seconds. On the coffee table was a family portrait of Tommy, Rose, and Sammy, taken long ago, when he was just a baby. Except the woman in the photo really *was* Rose, the one I always knew, not the woman patting down my forehead with a wet cloth. I squinted at her to make sure I was seeing the same women I knew as Val. It was. But she didn't match the photo on the table. So what was it doing there? What were all those pictures doing there?

"Rose," I said. "What's going on?"

"I'm Val, Vic. Rose is gone. Remember?"

"Gone? Then who are you?"

"Val. Her sister. Your *wife*. You and I reunited in Mexico, remember now?"

"What?"

I sat up abruptly, felt woozy, and fell back down on some plush pillows. Sammy was there, looking concerned.

"I haven't seen my mother in years," Sammy said sadly. "I think she's dead."

"Wait…you're Rose's *sister*?"

"Adopted sister, yes. We've been through all this, Vic. Now lay down. You're delirious and babbling. It will all come back to you. Eventually. That head trauma you experienced never really went away, did it? Years of drinking didn't exactly heal it. Now come, settle back and relax. I'll take care of you. Sammy and I are here now, and we're not going anywhere."

"Promise?" I said, gripping her wrist.

"Promise."

I noticed another framed photo. It was of me, Sammy, and Val. Behind us was an Aztec pyramid. It had obviously been taken in Mexico.

I closed my eyes and rewound the video in my head, at least the one I rented, understanding I may have to tape over it later.

When I had first met Val in San Francisco, she never indicated she knew Rose, the whole reason I had moved there. Turned out, it was the reason she moved there, too. Rose came from a military household, and somewhere along the way, they must have adopted this orphan Latina girl. Rose never mentioned her, even when her name was Valerie. They had become estranged at some point, competing for the affection of their father. But also, while teenagers, they actually had an affair. Rose then rejected her further advances. Esmeralda freaked out and ran away from home, the only one she knew, anyway, eventually winding up in Japan. Rose didn't try to find her. She was happier without her in her or anyone special in her life, at least at that time. But Val never got over her, and later moved back to the States, landing in San Francisco, hoping for a magical rendezvous. Just like me.

We had been totally obsessed with and possessed by the same woman this whole time. Talk about having something in common.

Then fast forward: Val and I reunited, get hitched, and move to Seattle. At some point in this journey, Sammy comes back into the picture. I wasn't sure how. Maybe he was also looking for his missing love, who happened to be his real mother, and somehow connected with her adopted sister, his aunt, at least in name if not blood. This was how I deduced everything, anyway, as I drifted into a state of semi-consciousness. I wasn't sure if I was just making all this up to satisfy my own needs for closure and explanation, which is the foundation for all religions, or I was finally remembering the true sequence of actual events that led to this very moment, which I really, really wanted to be real, because it would mean no matter what, I'd never be alone again.

While I was lying there, feigning unconsciousness though still vaguely aware of my environs, I heard Val and Sammy talking.

"At least we have her cellphone," Sammy said. "That's something."

That was why the name "Rose" showed up on my cellphone when Val had called me using that phone, borrowed from Sammy, I surmised. Like a fly on the wall, I kept eavesdropping, hoping for more rapidly unfolding clues to the bizarre situation.

Val's voice no longer sounded like Rose's, though, so I accepted the possibility that was merely a sonic filter I'd put in place once I saw Rose's name on my cellphone. But how did my phone recognize Rose's number, anyway? Maybe I'd just misread what I wanted it to say.

This is why I had to keep listening while they thought I wasn't.

"So the police can't trace it or anything?" Val said.

"No, I tried that already, trust me," Sammy replied. "Wherever she's been all this time, she's not there anymore."

"So where did you find the phone?"

"It was in the mail, like I told you. She sent it to me. The postmark was Miami, but I know she's not there, because she knows I'd go looking for her."

"Why doesn't she want you to find her, Sammy?"

"Same reason she didn't want Vic or you to find her. Intimacy scares her. She just wants to be alone in this world. I don't know why. I've never understood her. I don't think she understands herself."

"I never understood her either," Val said. "What happened between us…she initiated it, and then she ended it, just like that. Of course, it felt wrong, since technically, we were sisters, by law if not blood, but still, she just got under my skin. It was like she put a spell on me or something."

"She was into some weird occult stuff," Sammy said. "My upbringing in New Orleans was strange, to say the least. A lot of voodoo dolls and stuff. Incantations. Potions. Far Eastern mystical stuff, you know?"

"Yes, I know. I was very involved in Santeria myself, especially when I went back to Mexico."

"That's where you met Pop, huh?"

"Well, where we found each other again, though I had been keeping tabs on him over the years, hoping he'd lead me to your mother. But then…"

"What?"

"We fell in love ourselves. So I don't need to find her anymore."

I felt myself smile. I was home at last. Wherever it was. Whoever Val was. She loved me. That's all that mattered. I even had a son. Sort of. In a way, the fact—or reasonable facsimile of a fact—that I that wound up with Sammy felt like vindication, though I wasn't sure for what, exactly. It hurt me to think of Rose alone, but then it seemed that was her choice. I thought she had given Sammy up for adoption, actually. That's what she'd told me. So there was more to his story.

I could wait, though. I had a hard-on to take care of, so as usual, I pulled a boner.

"Don't say that," Val said to me.

"Um, say what?" I said.

"'Pull a boner.' It's a term with racist origins, in minstrel shows. Although it's acceptable, meaning politically correct, to refer to your erection as a 'boner'."

I took my hand off my pecker and sat erect. The jig was up, too. "You can read my thoughts?"

"You were talking out loud," Sammy said, looking at me with a mix of bemusement and dismay.

"What?"

"You've been narrating everything since I met you," Sammy said. "I've just been going along with it, because I thought it was your way of coping."

"Coping?" I said. "With what?"

"With everything," Val said, being quite serious. "It's time for you to face the truth, Vic."

"Which one?"

"It's all a lie," Sammy said. "Everything. Even me. Even you."

"What about everything I overhead you say just now?" I asked. "That's also a lie?"

"For your benefit," Val said. "At least I think so."

"What the hell does that mean?"

"We're only saying what we're meant to say," Sammy said. "It's like we're ventriloquist's dummy."

"Then who is the ventriloquist?" I asked.

Val and Sammy looked at each, and said in unison, "Someone who calls himself 'Will the Thrill'."

"Aw, shit."

Chapter Eleven
FUTILITY OVERKILL

We all believe what we choose to believe. I've always believed this. Because I chose to. Now I wasn't so sure what to think. If I was actually buying into all this bullshit just so I wouldn't have to confront the possibility that nothing really means anything and we might as well all swallow a bullet right now, did that make me lazy, or a coward? Or a lazy coward?

I'd become a private eye to find my true Love, or who I thought was my true love, because I really believed Love held the secret to Life itself. But it was like unlocking a door that let you out of a maze, only to fall straight into quicksand. There was just no end in sight to any question that actually mattered, and with no answers, why even keep bothering to ask? Maybe if Rose couldn't solve this problem for me, her son could. Since he was finally here, as a grown adult, not just an annoying baby, I figured I'd take advantage of the situation, before it took advantage of me. I hardly ever get the jump on anyone.

The way Rose came back into my life always made me wonder if there was more to it. Life, that is. I'd been hired by a broken-hearted, beaten-down baseball player to find his missing wife, who turned out to be my own missing muse. And it happened in the very city where I thought I'd find her, simply by following an intuitive hunch based on random, idle comments she'd made while we were together back in New York. But then I began wondering if she'd had it planned that way all along. Both theories were possible, if unlikely. There was a third possibility. I just could never figure out what that was. It alway bothered the hell out of me that all that happened without a proper resolution. It felt like an incomplete project, an almost-but-not-quite-full circle that would forever scratch the chalkboard of my soul.

Maybe, just maybe, Val leading me to Sammy after she followed me around for years hoping I'd lead her to Rose would finally lead us all to a catharsis that was worth the wait. Maybe it was all "meant to be," but the pathway to that meaning was much, much, much more circuitous than any of us could have imagined.

But before we got into the whole meaning of Life thing, I wanted to clear up a few urgently nagging details with Sammy, at least regarding his most recent account of mysterious events that involved us both, with his mother being the common denominator.

"Rose, your mother, told me she put you up for adoption," I said to him, getting the ball rolling back in his court. "Long ago. In New Orleans."

"She did," Sammy confirmed. "I didn't even know she was my mother. Just the next door neighbor. She visited all the time. I was raised by a Haitian family in New Orleans, before we moved to Miami when I was eight or so. Rose, my birth mother, followed us there. One day she told me she was actually my aunt, but not to tell my mother, who wasn't my biological mother, which I knew, since it was obvious I'd been adopted. But then Rose looked nothing like Hannah, so that didn't make sense ether. That she was my aunt, I mean. For one thing, the woman who raised me, Hannah, was black. But I kept my suspicions to myself. I figured she was using the term 'aunt' loosely. So 'Aunt Rose' kept giving me presents, secretly, mostly snacks and comic books, basically buying my silence and complicity in her scheme, whatever that was. It seemed odd she kept following us around, but Hannah never explained it, just confirmed she was a good, old friend of the family. It wasn't until I was eighteen that Rose told me she was actually my *real* mother."

"Why did she wait so long?" I asked.

"Well, she wasn't around that often, really. She would disappear for months, even years at a time. Then just show up again. I had no idea where she went, or what she was doing. She just said she liked to be free."

"That sounds like Rose," I said.

"Because *he* says so," Val said cryptically, gesturing toward an invisible fez on her head.

"Who, 'Will the Thrill'?" I said. "Fuck that guy. He's a raving lunatic. I mean, *obviously*."

"Then why does he keep showing up?" Sammy said.

"You know him too?" I asked.

"Yes. This dude in a fez seems to be everywhere I go. Just shows up, like a stalker. Finally I asked him why he was following me. He said he was keeping tabs on me for a friend. I assumed he meant my mother, meaning Rose. But then he said that this was all an illusion, meaning everything in the realm of the senses, so none of it was real, and Rose was only my mother because he made it so. I asked him if that meant he was my real father, and he just laughed. He said he's the father of *everyone* I meet."

"What about the people you never meet?" I asked him.

"They're just phantoms," Sammy said. "They exist just to flesh out his creation."

"That's what he told me, too," Val said.

"Me as well," I said. "He can't be right about all of us. I mean, one of us has to be the real deal, right?"

"He says that he's the only real person in our lives," Sammy said. "He creeps me out."

"Hey listen, fuck him," I said. "I mean, for a while, he had me going, because I met him when I was having all these other problems, seeing and hearing things that weren't really there, and he just seemed to be part of it. But now, it's all coming together. Everything I overheard you say. It makes sense now."

"What about everything we heard *you* say?" Val said. "This endless monologue of yours. We can barely get a word in edgewise. Who are you talking to, anyway?"

"Myself," I lied. I had no idea I'd been thinking out loud all this time. I wondered who the hell heard me, besides you. "Listen, as long as I'm not turning into a werewolf or talking to statues or ghosts, I'm going with this scenario as the one and only truth, which means whatever this Will the Thrill asshole told you is the big lie. He's just fucking with us."

"But why?" Sammy said.

"That's the true question," I said. "I'll make sure to ask him next time I see him. When's the last time you saw him?"

Val and Sammy looked at each other, and shrugged. "We can't remember," Val said. "That's part of the mystery. We just know we've both seen him, and talked to him, and he said the same strange things to each of us."

"Maybe it was in a dream," I said. "So *he's* the one that's not real."

"The same dream?" Sammy said. "How could we have a simultaneous dream about the same person, saying the same exact stuff?"

"Mass hypnosis, I don't know. That seems more credible than some self-aggrandizing asshat is dictating our life stories."

"Most religions have implausible deities," Val said. "And all religious leaders are self-proclaimed human conduits to an unseen Higher Power. Who's to say which is crazier than the other?"

"Okay, look, I don't even have a fucking religion, much less a philosophy," I said. "I don't believe any of this shit. In fact, I really don't believe anything. I agree it's all an illusion, but we're not pawns in someone else's story. And you're not phantoms in mine, or me in yours. It's just a big fucking accident, a cosmic bang that just fucking happened, and we're temporary byproducts. In the scheme of things, we mean nothing, but *none* of this means anything. It won't last. So yeah, it's a transitory illusion in the long run, but while we can touch, feel and sense it, it's real enough. And that's all that matters. What's happening in the *moment*. Dig?"

Sammy nodded, then went to a drawer and pulled out a brochure, and handed it to me. It read, *Deacon Rivers' Church of Elvis.*

"No fucking way," I said. "I'm not dealing with this pro con man again. How do you know him?"

"I met him in Miami," Sammy said. "He said he's been keeping tabs on me, too. He said if I ever ran into you again, and you really wanted to know the secret of Life, to look him up. Of course, he tried selling me on this idea of his first."

"Yeah, I know already. Elvis is King of everything."

"Right," Sammy said. "How did you know?"

"I don't know, kid, that's the point. He's just another charlatan. Figures he'd wind up in Miami. So many loons down there. He's just a huckster trying to advance his own self-serving agenda and build his own secure platform on the backs of suckers who are too lonely and desperate to figure out his true motives."

"Just like all of them," Val said. "Politicians, pundits, priests. They're all con artists. Though some are more artful than others."

"Exactly why I prefer the company of animals," I said. "They're genuine and sincere, at least. Even if they just want to eat you."

Just then, as if on cue, Doc and Fido came running into the room. Apparently they'd been napping together on the bed this whole time. I was so happy to see them I nearly cried, but then as you know, I'm always about to cry.

"Hey, my babies!" I said.

"They missed you," Val said.

"What are *you* doing with them?"

"I was taking care of them while you were in the hospital, remember?"

I studied Val's face for a hint of malice or mendacity. But her expression was poker perfect. "Hospital?"

"After your breakdown," Sammy said delicately.

"Breakdown?"

"You really don't remember," Val said, not as a question, but an observation.

"Remember what, exactly?"

Val looked down, disappeared into her bedroom, and came out with Ivar, the sailor statue.

"Remember who gave you this?"

"No," I said. "He just started popping up, out of the fucking blue. What are you doing with him?"

"He's *mine*," she said. "I had him follow you to Seattle, to keep tabs on you."

"Oh, c'mon! You already told me it wasn't you!"

"That's part of your therapy. I needed to break it to you gradually, as you recovered incrementally."

"Accent on the 'mentally'," Sammy said.

Val continued, "Vic, you need to accept that most of your hallucinations are a result of those opioids Hal gave you in Mexico and Costa Rica. Why won't you believe me?"

"He told you put a spell on me," I said.

Val laughed. Sammy didn't. That bothered me.

"When did Hal tell you this?" Val asked.

"When I saw him…" Then I remembered Hal told me this while his decapitated head was stuck on a tiki torch down at Forbidden Island down in Alameda. "Never mind. I just dreamed it."

"We thought it best if we let you believe you were just waking up from the coma my father put you in," Sammy said.

"That was twenty-five years ago," I said.

"Which means you're just waking up after a quarter century's worth of internal wandering," Val said. "If that were true, of course."

I felt dizzy, and sat down again. Val and Sammy each sat on either side of me, stroking me with sympathy. "I don't understand," I said into my palms.

"You woke up and started telling this story, like you were dictating it for a book," Val said. "And you wouldn't stop. So we just let you talk. The one theory of yours that worked best was the one that had you in a coma all this time, and it was the one we let you believe."

"But then you seemed to be coming out of it, you kept babbling all this nonsense, so we decided to go with your 'Will the Thrill' theory," Sammy said.

"Which you also rejected," Val said. "So now, it's time for the truth."

"Which is *what* already?"

Sammy pointed to the brochure on the coffee table. "You need to go talk to him. Only he can explain it."

"No," I said. "That's just one more bullshit fantasy, man. I'm sticking with what I know, what I can see. I'm not getting distracted by yet another wack job with an agenda. Besides, I've been down that road already. I know where it ends. In the fucking rubber room."

"You just left there," Val said.

"When exactly was this?" I said. "I mean, where does my real life end, and this breakdown begin? And did it actually end?"

"That's what we're trying to help you with, Pop."

"Stop calling me that."

"I thought it would help you. That's why Val tracked me down."

"Well, it doesn't."

"Sorry, Pop. I mean, Vic. Feels weird just calling you 'Vic,' though."

"Trust me, it feels weird to hear you calling me 'Pop.'"

"Everything up till Costa Rica, that you can remember, actually happened," Val said.

"So everything after…you mean, we're not married?"

Val smiled. "Yes, Vic. That part is true. We did honeymoon in Hawaii. But that's where you began to lose it."

"Wait. So the zombies, Hal, the international drug ring, the shootouts in the jungle, you being a Mexican wrestler, the vampire bats—that all actually happened?"

"More or less," Val said.

"But that's all *insane*. I mean, even by my standards."

"Doesn't make it less true," Sammy said. "I mean, look at me. A quarter of a century ago, I didn't even exist. One day, I won't exist again, except in the memories of brains that will themselves rot away someday. No reason or explanation, except the ones I make up or choose to believe. It's all weird, Pop. I mean, Vic."

Val took my face in her hands and said, "Let's just say, the way you remember it may not be accurate, but most of it is essentially true."

"What you told me about being Rose's sister. Then her lover. That's true?"

"Yes," Val said with what seemed like sincerity.

"And Ivar, you were leaving him all over the place, for me to find him?"

"Yes."

"Why?"

"Just to fuck with you. Though it was Hal's idea."

"I don't believe you."

"Doesn't mean it's not true."

"But just because I believe it, that doesn't make it true, either."

"True."

My head was spinning, to say the least. "So when we met again in Mexico, you'd already been keeping track of me? That's still true too, yes?"

"For years," she said. "I thought you'd lead me to Rose, and I was also working with Hal. But then we, you and I, fell in love."

"Is that real, at least? Because that's the only thing I really *need* to be true right now."

She leaned over and kissed me, and I felt her plush breasts. They felt real, all right.

"Just don't start singing again," she said. "That was never part of our act."

"Wait, so we do have a lounge act?"

"Yes, of course. 'The Voodoo Valentine Show.' It was part of your therapy. All your idea. I just went along with it. Fortunately, I can sing. I thought it might give you a sense of purpose. But then you started trying to emulate Sinatra, and sorry, Vic, but it made everyone cringe. Now that you're lucid, please don't do that again, *ever*."

I nodded, severely disappointed my latent singing talent was all part of my epic delusion. Damn. I really had no worthwhile abilities at all.

"How have I been surviving all this time?" I asked Val. "I mean, in my state of dementia. Who paid my hospital tab?"

"My ex-husband," Val said. "Indirectly, anyway. He's been sending me money for years. Lately he wanted to get back together, but when he found out I'd married you, he went a little crazy and cut me off. Fortunately I have quite a nest egg put away. He wants it back. That's why he's in Seattle."

"Is he Japanese by any chance?"

"Yes. You've met him. His name is Takashi Suzuki."

"Not Hayata?"

"No, why?"

"Never mind. Takashi Suzuki. So like a cross between Takashi Miike and Seijun Suzuki."

"Never thought of that, but sure."

"So you were married."

"Well, he kidnapped me when I was young, and forced me to marry him, after making me part of his sex slave ring. I had daddy issues, like my sister."

"Rose."

"Also promiscuous, like her."

"And bi-sexual."

"Yes, though mostly I prefer cock to pussy."

"You might as well be Rose," I said.

"That's what I always say," Sammy said.

"But isn't that because Will the Thrill makes you say it?" I said.

"I hope not." He didn't seem convinced, though.

Val said, "The problem, Vic, is we never got divorced. So technically, you and I aren't really married. But then I'm not sure Takashi and I were ever married. We just had this strange ritualistic ceremony where all of his men gang-banged me. It wasn't very romantic, but I was confused and lonely and he took advantage of me."

"I don't need to hear this," I said.

"But you need to, Vic, because in his mind, I'm still his. And he wants me back. I told him I was helping you deal with your condition, and once you were fully recuperated, I'd return with him to Japan."

"Without me?"

"I was lying to him, Vic. Meantime, he's paying the rent on this place, and your hospital tab, though really I'm paying for it with money he's given me over the years. But I earned that, too. Plus the money I stole from Hal. But it's running out. I have to squeeze Takashi for as much as possible before we kill him."

"What?"

"Self-defense, Vic. He'll kill us both otherwise. It will be a preemptive strike."

I sat back up. "Please tell me I'm still in a coma," I said.

"No, this is the real world now, Vic, and we have to deal with it. As a *family*."

I thought about it, then said, "No sale. You know what I think? I think you're both in on this. I mean, how do I know you're actually Rose's son?"

Sammy looked so sad that I immediately relented.

"Hey, I'm sorry, kid. I mean, you just show up out of nowhere, like Ivar there, calling me 'Pop,' so I just have to wonder, y'know? Especially with everything else that's been happening, even if some of it didn't actually happen. Or most of it or even *all* of it."

"Val thought seeing me might help you," Sammy repeated. "And I never really had a real father. The woman who raised me, Hannah, had no husband, either. I had three siblings, but they were hers by a previous marriage. I lost touch with them when I left Miami, and now I can't find them. Or my mother. They've all abandoned me. You're all I have left."

I gave him an awkward hug. The last thing I felt equipped to be was a father. I felt much more qualified to be a werewolf. Or a lounge singer, even though I apparently sucked at that, too. It seems we sometimes get cast in roles that don't suit our temperament or plans.

"Is your Japanese husband really Yakuza?" I asked Val.

"Yes. He's a hitman with his own crew."

"How did you get involved with him?"

"Like I told you. My father was stationed in Japan, and then this gangster kidnapped me for his sex slave ring."

"I thought you ran away from home after Rose jilted you?"

"No, Rose ran away. *You're* the one who said I ran away, when you were talking to yourself, or whoever, trying to put all the pieces together. I actually stayed, and went with our father when he was stationed in Japan. I was eighteen at the time."

"So many different possibilities," I mused. "They're endless. Maybe there really are parallel planes of reality, and mine keep merging and colliding."

"Best to stop theorizing now," Val said. "Once you're back to full power, we need to embark on our plan to kill Takashi."

"Wait, I'm not killing anybody. I'm no killer. You can do it. I won't tell, trust me. I need his money as much you do."

"Okay. I trust you. I'll take care of it myself."

"And leave Sammy out of it, too."

She looked at Sammy and they nodded in agreement.

"Just promise me one thing," I said.

"Yes?"

"When you're finally, fully free of this guy, we get hitched, formally. A ceremony and everything."

"That's already been arranged," Sammy said.

"What do you mean?"

Sammy picked up the Church of Elvis brochure again. "Look at what this actually says," Sammy said.

I read the front text again. Beneath the picture of Deacon Rivers wearing a sequined jumpsuit, there was a list of credits: *Preacher. Professor. Pastor For Hire. All Occasions. TCB.*

"He's licensed to perform weddings!" Sammy said like it was good news.

"You gotta be kidding," I said.

"Like I said, Pop, I mean, Vic, he's here in Seattle and he wants you to come see him when you're ready for the truth. And the truth is, The King will set you free!"

I put my head back in my hands and clicked my heels together three times. Nothing. Then I said, "Hey Sammy, did you call me at home from Rose's phone?" I asked him.

"I did," Val said. "With Sammy's phone, which is actually Rose's phone. I had left mine at home."

"Caller I.D. said it was Rose, and it was her voice I heard when I answered."

Val shrugged. "Probably all in your warped mind, Vic. Hopefully things will start clearing up for you now."

"How did you find Sammy?" I asked Val.

"I have my ways," she said. "I mean, I followed you for years, left you those musical messages on your answering machine, and then Ivar here, and you had no idea it was me all along in both cases. Now here we are."

"Wherever that is. So you're not only The Phone Phantom, but you're Ivar. Or the woman behind Ivar."

"And behind you, Vic. I always was."

"I don't like the sound of that."

"I'm also right in front of you now."

She bent over to kiss me, her creamy cleavage encompassing my field of vision like a peep show in Cinemascope. Her thick, dark hair cascaded across my loins. The scent of her flesh was intoxicating. I grew dizzy. Then she kissed me, and when I closed my eyes, visions of demons fucking her on the floor swirled inside my head. I grew hard. She kneeled down, opened my zipper, and sucked me till my toes curled as I gushed down her throat. I kept my eyes closed the whole time, out of sheer shame, a rare sensation for me.

When I opened my eyes, she was still there. But Sammy wasn't.

"Where's Sammy?" I asked.

"He's gone," she said. "It's just you and me now, Vic. *Forever*."

For some reason, that prospect scared the shit out of me.

Chapter Twelve
KINGDOM BUM

Sometimes I gaze up at the stars and wonder if each represents an alternate world. That would mean there is no "alien life," no bulbous-headed cat-eyed saucer men with alcohol in their talons, but infinite versions and variations of the people and places we can already see.

For now, I only knew this one, so I just played it out.

It made me sad to think I'd never see Sammy again, especially considering I never thought I would see him again, before I actually did. I was grateful he'd filled in some of the gaps in his life story, about his upbringing at least, even though I still couldn't remember anything before seeing him at the jazz club. According to him, we'd already reunited by then. I was sure he'd related a lot more biographical details upon our initial meeting as adults, but that information disappeared down the rabbit hole of my soul, possibly never to be retrieved, except maybe by hypnosis.

That's why I suggested as much to Val, even though she wouldn't tell me why Sammy just vanished on me like that, though I doubted he wanted to witness me getting a blowjob, which would've been rather unseemly. But then maybe that was subterfuge for him to slip out while I was preoccupied. In any case, Val wasn't talking. She seemed to relish her role as a mystery woman.

"Maybe you're already hypnotized," she said to me as we lay in my Murphy bed. We were living together again. That other apartment in Belltown was yet another secret she had been keeping from me. That's where she sometimes disappeared to, she told me. But she gave no reason. None that made sense to me, anyway.

Maybe that was all part of her plan. Whatever that was.

"How would I know if I'm hypnotized?" I asked her.

"You wouldn't, that's the point."

"So did *you* hypnotize me?"

"It wouldn't matter whether I did or not, because under hypnosis, you only believe what you're told to believe, no matter how untrue it seems."

"That sounds like an inordinately large portion of the world population."

"Remember, that was the whole point of Hal's scheme, to infiltrate and incorporate enough of those mutated opioids into the world food supply so that ultimately, everyone would be susceptible to subconscious suggestion, which would have one uniform voice via state-run media outlets."

"Maybe they already have mind-controlled everyone. Including me. Including you."

"Maybe. That would certainly explain a lot about the world's current state."

"You don't seem too concerned."

"Well, what can I do about it? Corporations have always ruled the general population in one way or another, by appealing to our innate greed and fear, more than our instinct to love and nurture. It's the weakness of human nature that is responsible for this paradigm. Corporations may have politicians in their pockets, but we put money in the corporations' pockets. We, the consumers, fund this capitalistic system. As long as we keep paying the prices they demand for our creature comforts, they will always be in control. This could be just the final step in a centuries old plot for an elite few to rule the world without organized or individual dissent, or even dissatisfied customers."

"I'm losing my erection."

"I'll stop talking now."

Life progressed normally for the next few days. No hallucinations, no delusions. Ivar just stood there staring into infinity. At least Val finally copped to being the one playing the prank on me. That still didn't explain why he kept popping up in impossible places, unless that was just part of my own mental extrapolation, the byproducts of a damaged brain. I kept a close on Ivar, just in case.

Val finally moved her stuff out of the apartment in Belltown. It had been a month-to-month lease because she was hoping she wouldn't have to live there alone someday. Basically, it was her safety net in case things with me fell apart, for one reason or another.

"I actually rented this while you were in the hospital recuperating from your breakdown," she told me.

"The one I can't remember having."

"It was a slow then sudden descent into total madness, Vic. No specific trigger that I could see. The doctors figured it was a cumulative effect, years in the making, or breaking. Then one day it was like you were sleep-walking, and talking, unresponsive to anyone around you, even me."

"So all that werewolf stuff, time travel, singing like Sinatra. That was all in my head."

"Yes, but you experienced it so vividly, it felt real to you. I could tell by the way you were describing it in such intense detail."

"Who was I talking to? You? Sammy?"

"You didn't even know we were there. I don't know who you were talking to, though you did address Doc and even yourself directly on a number of occasions."

"I wish we had it all on tape."

"Actually…" She took out her cellphone and started playing video of me, in a hospital bed somewhere, saying the same crazy shit I've been saying to you. My eyes were closed but my mouth was moving a mile a minute. It was like watching surveillance footage of a possessed lunatic. I was sweating and rambling sometimes, yet oddly collected and coherent at other times, depending on which reality I was relating back to the Universe. I had no idea Val and Sammy were my audience the whole time.

"So I'm better now?" I asked her.

"You're getting there," she said.

"I feel like I can't trust my own eyes or brain."

"Trust your heart, Vic."

"That traitor? No way. I'm better off following my dick. That's what led me to you."

"You didn't have to be led to me, Vic. I was right behind you the whole time. All you had to do was turn around. And finally, you did. Now here we are."

I had trouble wrapping my mind around that concept, but the more I thought about it, the more I believed her. She was the one constant thread in the twisted tapestry of my life. I just wasn't aware of it until we finally physically reunited in Mexico. She pretended to be surprised, but that was just part of her magic act. The Phone Phantom. Ivar. Even Rose. She tied it all together into one neat, voluptuous package. Too neat, really. But I had no competitive theory to counter her. It was the only one that made any sense, at least by conventional standards.

Still, something about all this didn't feel right. It was the way she kept looking at something I couldn't see, as if she were the one in a trance, not me. I kept pressing her for answers, to see if she'd trip herself up.

"So were you and Raven really lovers?"

"Yes, going back to our burlesque days."

"She never mentioned you."

"Why would she? She never told you a lot of things."

"True enough." One more link in the chain around my neck.

I kept thinking about some of the things Will the Thrill told me, and some of what he said still rang true to me. Disturbingly so. But I let it go.

Val had retrieved my green fez hat, but I refused to wear it again, especially since it reminded me of you-know-who. I decided to quit my lounge lizard stint, especially now that I knew I was actually making my audiences laugh, but not at my jokes, just my singing. They were jeering, not cheering, apparently just another result of my warped synapses, misinterpreting truth. Val had no problem with my early retirement. It was one of my conditions for accepting her version of my truth, and now that my head was clear, she seemed to be compliant with all of my wishes. Now I was hers, body and soul.

Plus we were getting re-married. For real, this time.

I had one more condition: I wanted Sammy to be my best man.

To my surprise, she agreed. He was still in town, in fact. But it turned out Sammy had one condition, too.

Our pastor had to be Deacon Rivers.

"Why?" I naturally asked him when we picked him up at Val's Belltown apartment. The rent was paid for the rest of that month, so he was staying there until he returned to Miami. He never explained why he left that day without saying goodbye, and I didn't ask him. I just didn't care anymore. Besides, we had a more pressing issue to address. "I mean, what possible reason would you have to force this on me?"

"I promised him," Sammy said. "He's helped me a lot over the years, like Val has. So I want to return the favor."

"Helped you how? He's a fucking psycho!"

"He taught me about The King."

"Aw, shit, Sammy. You're in a fucking cult now?"

"All religions are cults, Pop, with their own cult leaders. This one is no different, except it's more fun than most."

"Yeah, I bet. Listen, I know this character, man, going way back. He's nothing but a con artist, but he's actually good at it. I mean, he suckered you into his psychobabble bullshit, and you're a smart kid."

"Gee, thanks, Pop. You don't mind if I keep calling you Pop?"

"Only if you cancel this contract you have with Rivers. You owe him nothing, no allegiance, no favors, certainly not my complicity. This is your debt, kid, not mine."

"But's it for your benefit, Pop. Trust me. He told me everything would become clear once you went to see him. What have you got to lose?"

I put my head in my hands like I was sobbing, even though I wasn't. I was just tired.

Sammy patted me on the back and said, "Don't cry, daddy."

"Fuck," I whispered. I just couldn't escape the ghosts and demons of my own past. That's what I got for mourning it, I figured. Now it was going to haunt me until the day I died, maybe even longer.

Then Val walked in, wearing a low-cut black gown and high heels, the same outfit she wore at our Tula's gig, which apparently actually happened, because I didn't sing at that one.

"You look like you're marrying Satan," I said.

"Maybe I am," she said, before quickly adding, "Just kidding!"

"Look, can't you wear something else?"

"Why, isn't this sexy enough?"

"*Too* sexy. Like you're attending a goth funeral." She reminded me of Elvira, which under other circumstances would not have been a bad thing. Between Sammy telling me he belonged to Deacon Rivers' Elvis cult and Val's vampire dress, I was beginning to feel shaky again. "Okay, fuck it," I said. "Let's do this. I can't wait to get out of this apartment. It creeps me out."

"Why?"

"Because you never told me about it," I said. "It represents everything you've kept hidden from me. I never want to see it again. From now on, total transparency. Deal?"

"Deal." She sealed it with a kiss. I didn't believe her, but damn, she was hot.

I was wearing my rumpled sharkskin suit with a skinny black tie and wrinkled white shirt, as usual. Sammy just wore a black T-shirt and jeans.

"Kid, don't you have anything fancier for the occasion?" I asked him.

He shook his head. "I just don't have your style, Pop. Sorry."

"Nobody does," Val said, winking at me.

I really wanted people to stop doing that. Winking at me, I mean. It was really putting my already frayed nerves on edge. This was already feeling like a freak show, and Deacon Rivers was just the icing on a half-baked cake.

I wondered how long Deacon Rivers had been in Seattle. It turned out he was only on tour, and here temporarily. He timed it that way when he found out Sammy was going to be in town. And that I had relocated here. It all sounded fishy.

"We can't go on together with suspicious minds, Pop," Sammy said as we sat in the back of a Lyft. My Corvair was gone. Val assumed it had been stolen. I didn't miss it. I told my stepson to shut up.

We wound up at an actual old church in Beacon Hill. It had been abandoned and probably slated for demolition in order to build another tech-bro-ready condo complex that looked like something out of *Ren & Stimpy*. My life was a cartoon, anyway. A very dark, fucked-up cartoon. I decided to just roll with it. Until I hit a wall, anyway.

In fact, the church looked downright ominous. I expected bats to fly out of the belfry. The sky was cloudy and foreboding, typical for Seattle, one reason I loved it here so much, since I'm such a moody dude. But now it scared me a little. I chalked it up to pre-marital jitters. Even though I was already married. Or maybe not. Maybe Val was already married, too. Or maybe not. Like I said, I was just along for the ride. I had no energy to question or fight my own life anymore. Chronologically speaking, I was on the downslope, anyway, which suited me, since I was no longer in shape for uphill climbs.

Elvis was singing "Crying in the Chapel" as we walked into the Temple of Dracula, or that's how it felt, all dank and dilapidated inside, with a strange sweetness in the thick air, smelling like a mix of mildew and milkshakes.

Then I realized it wasn't Elvis's voice. It wasn't even a recording. It was Deacon Rivers standing at the altar, wearing a white, sequined jumpsuit and those big, funky '70s glasses Elvis essentially trademarked. He was singing into a microphone. Behind him was a karaoke machine and a screen on a tripod on which a projector was silently playing the floating wedding finale from *Blue Hawaii*. When he saw me, Rivers switched to "Hawaiian Wedding Song," in sync with the scene. He sounded like the real deal. I couldn't believe it.

No one else was around, which made me feel that much more paranoid. I held up my hand for him to stop.

Removing his shades, I saw that mischievous twinkle in his narrow eyes. His face was wrinkled and his long, braided hair was gray, but otherwise, he looked the same as the last time I'd scene him, ages ago, though in the moment it felt more like only a few hours had passed since we were holed up in his Marin digs, throwing food at Shiv and his Mob, who were there to emancipate his daughter Lucy, the teenage bombshell he'd hired me to find.

Stepping down from the pulpit, Rivers reached out his hand to me for a shake. He wore a giant diamond ring on each of all ten fingers. Or maybe they were rubies, I don't know. I've never been into jewelry myself.

"Long time no see, baby!" Rivers said. He then removed his red scarf and placed it around my neck, like it was a lei.

I tore it off and flung it. "Cut the crap, man. I'm here only because I want you to let Sammy go."

"Pop!" Sammy exclaimed.

"I thought we were here to get married!" Val said.

Now everyone was pissed. Except for Rivers, who just grinned at me, lop-sided Elvis-style. "You haven't changed a bit, except for your gut," Rivers said, patting my admittedly soft but not flabby abdomen. "Been puttin' away those banana-and-peanut-butter pizzas much, Vic?"

He looked svelte as ever, so rather than a cheap shot comeback, I just said, "I didn't know you could sing."

"I've been practicin'! At least I ain't tryin' to imitate Sinatra, like some people."

"What are you talkin' about?" I said, looking over at Val, who just shrugged.

"I like it here," she said. "The atmosphere feels right. Like an old Mexican church."

"Out of a Santo monster movie," I said.

"Exactly!"

"Val, I thought you wanted to do something romantic?"

"It doesn't get more romantic than this!"

"How so?"

"Vic, we both love horror movies, right? And you love Elvis? So do I. 'Blue Hawaii' is my favorite movie and I've always wanted to recreate the wedding scene."

"That was on a raft in Kauai, Val. We're not even close."

"Well, it's on the screen, Vic. So close enough. I had this all arranged in advance, keeping your tastes in mind. After this we're going down to Devil's Reef in Tacoma to celebrate. It's a reception with some surprise guests you haven't seen in a while. I have that all arranged, too. It was going to be a surprise, but you seem so nervous and upset, I guess I need to calm you down."

"My whole life is a movie, Val. I need something to feel real for a change."

"It's all a movie, Vic," Deacon Rivers said. "And Elvis is the director, producer, and star. We're just a bunch of extras wandering around without a script. You want the truth? That's the truth."

"Shut the fuck up," I said.

"Anyway, Vic, it's good to see you, but we need to get to this ceremony. I have several other couples to wed before services tonight."

"Services?"

"Yeah, Pop, you need to come!" Sammy said. "Deacon Rivers throws the best services ever!"

"You mean orgies," I said. "Yeah, I remember those. I trust your congregation is all of legal age this time?"

"Hey, I'm strictly above board these days, Vic! Just ask your son."

"He's not my son," I said, looking downward, avoiding Sammy's eyes.

"You're the only father I've ever had," Sammy said sincerely, putting his arm around my shoulders. "Please don't ever say that again, Pop."

I nodded, conflicting emotions churning in my gut like a lobster in a boiling pot. My soul was screaming. But I kept my trap shut. I just wanted to get this over with and get the hell out of there. I wasn't even sure why this was necessary, beyond the sake of formality, since we had a wedding license already, or a reasonable facsimile. There was something else going on here I didn't know about yet.

Then I found out, quite rudely.

Gunfire erupted from outside, blowing out what was left of the stained-glassed window panes. I whirled around and there was Takashi Suzuki, Val's ex-husband, with a bunch of his goons, all dressed in dark suits and shades, packing heat.

I looked at her, and she seemed as surprised as I was. So was Sammy. Deacon Rivers, not so much. It had been a set-up all along. Sammy looked genuinely confused, so I didn't blame him. He'd been duped by the Deacon, just as I figured.

Val was ready for action, though. She actually put on a *lucha* mask, which she'd stuffed down her dress. She never left home without it. The mask, that is.

She ran straight into the gang and began kicking and karate-chopping, but several of the goons subdued her by force. When Sammy and I tried to intervene, we got our asses kicked and guns shoved in our faces. The men weren't just Japanese gangsters, but also Filipino thugs, Middle Eastern mobsters, white trash Nazis, and streetwise gang-bangers. I guess Takashi believed in affirmative action. They all shared shaved heads, suits, muscles, and attitudes. And guns.

Takashi went up to Val, who was being held pat by three men, pulled off her mask, tore open her dress, and began fondling her breasts, then sucking on her nipples. "You are mine," he said in Japanese. Of course, I don't speak Japanese, but I prefer subtitles to bad dubbing, unless it's a Godzilla movie, so I'm assuming that's what he said for your sake, and mine. While he went down on her, he kept mumbling more stuff in Japanese. As he did, she stopped squirming, and went limp. That trance-like expression was in her eyes, like she'd been hypnotized.

Val was stripped nude then stretched out on the floor, spread eagle, without any signs of struggle, and one by one, each of the men had their way with her, lining up like it was a popular restaurant and she was the evening special. She came each time in tandem with her ravenous partners, her legs wrapped around their heaving torsos, clawing their backs and biting their throats like a vampire in heat as they pumped her full of liquid evil. She seemed to actually enjoy it, laughing and crying and kissing them as she looked over at me and winked.

Avoiding eye contact with her, I looked at the screen propped up behind the pulpit. A scratchy, faded, grindhouse print duplicating the exact scene I was beholding, like a celluloid refraction, played out like it was all only a movie, meaning the four dimensional figures right in front of me were only actors on the set of an erotic horror movie created just for me, in real time.

Meantime, Deacon Rivers was at the organ, playing some kind of freaky Phantom of the Opera shit, by way of Pink Floyd, as live musical accompaniment. He pointed at me, Elvis-style, then smiled with that curled lip. That sonofabitch psycho was in cahoots with the Yakuza. I guess he had a price, but then perversion was always part of his pitch. Or maybe his compensation was just the glee of watching me being so brutally humiliated, which seemed to be his greatest pleasure in life, for whatever reason.

Sammy was passed out, held pat by one of the slick gangsters. I just cried and came in my pants, so both my face and crotch were embarrassingly wet,

After the men were finished defiling my all-too-eager bride, just like the horny demons in my dreams, Takashi dragged Val up to the altar, and Deacon Rivers proceeded to marry them.

For real.

Chapter Thirteen
THE DEVIL IS IN THE ENTRAILS

Some fantasies are best left hidden in the furthest reaches of your subconscious. Especially the dark ones. They need to stay buried. When they surface like a corpse in a lake, it's a drag, man. I tried to regain control of my own waking nightmare, but it was too late. My lascivious libido had ventured into the furthest reaches of the forbidden zone and never came back, sinking into the sewer of my soul. If only I could've turned into a werewolf, I would've ripped them all to shreds. Instead, I had to stand there while my bride-to-be, wearing all white only because she was covered in the semen of strangers, was legally wed to the Japanese version of Satan. I was glad Sammy wasn't awake to witness these horrors, most likely passing out from the stress. I was the only one left conscious, but then this was all for my benefit, not his. It was only a show, nothing more.

This was my current coping mechanism. Pretending none of it was real, even if it was. The fact I could no longer make that distinction was either conveniently psychosomatic, or else I was simply a pawn in someone else's game, which was the only theory that cleansed my soiled conscience.

After the brief so-called ceremony—which in my battered state I barely heard, though I could make out some Japanese vows, or vowels, whatever—I was beaten up, shot up with some serum, and dumped somewhere just off Puget Sound. It was either very late night, or very early morning, and it began to rain as I lay there, sobbing and bleeding. I was lying in a puddle of various fluids. I felt guilty for creaming my pants while my wife was viciously violated by human demons, and she didn't even offer a pretense of objection. Some love stories are too vile for me.

I shouldn't write your life when I'm horny, I heard a voice say. *It's like shopping for groceries while you're hungry. It gets more excessive than necessary. You just wind up spent, literally.*

I looked up and saw the silhouette of a familiar fez. It was indeed my old pal, Will the Thrill. His little pal Chumpy Walnut was sitting on his shoulder, eating an actual walnut like it was a watermelon.

He continued, *See, after you gorge yourself like a self-indulgent, hedonistic glutton, and you're consumed with self-loathing, you're like, why did I waste all that precious energy? What the hell is wrong with me? Well, whatever is wrong with me is way more wrong with you, Vic. Whatever happens to me, good or bad, you get it way better or way worse. Sorry. That's just how it is. Now you know the truth. Sammy made good on his promise. Deacon Rivers revealed to you the ugliness of sentient existence. And the only escape is inside your own fantasies and dreams, until you can't tell the difference anymore. That's what I tell myself, anyway. So naturally, that's what I'm telling you. See how it works?*

They were sitting next to me as gentle waves lapped at the shoreline. I looked around and realized I was on a remote stretch of Alki Beach in West Seattle, facing the downtown skyline, which glowed like a row of cosmopolitan lighthouses.

"Aw, fuck," I said. Now I was back to thinking this was all due to those damned drugs they gave me not only in the church but way back in Costa Rica. In fact, I bet the Yakuza pushed a variation of Hal's opioids, which were no doubt flooding the worldwide market by this time. I hadn't stopped the tide. Val and I had merely escaped drowning in it. Or so I'd thought. Somewhere, God was laughing. Or maybe it was Elvis. Neither. It was Will the Thrill, that bastard.

Of course, I can only write you and all the people in your life from my limited perspective, which is problematic both ethically and creatively, Will the Thrill said. *This need for dominance over women is indeed sexist, if not downright misogynistic. It probably has to do with our innate insecurity as a gender. The feminine mystique is both alluring and threatening to our fragile sense of manhood, or what modern society deems manhood should be. But I believe carnal carnage is just hard-wired into our primitive DNA, and we each find different ways of either denying it or channeling it into something less obvious and dangerous, to ourselves as well as others. That's one way to justify it, anyway. Generally-speaking, we're a very shallow, savage, selfish breed, meaning humans. But thankfully a vanishing breed, and despite our hubris, deep down, we know it. We won't be extinct or at least marginalized soon enough to save the planet, though. I wonder who wrote this whole fucking story, anyway. Of life on Earth, that is. A sadistic sociopath, no doubt.*

"I thought you did," I said.

No way, man, I'm not that sinister, Will the Thrill said. *I only write your story, Vic. I can't even write my own. Someone else is doing that for me, and trust me, if I could fire him or her, I would. But I was assigned this script, and I'm just playing out the part. It's a shitty movie so far, except for my marriage, which is the only reason I haven't blown my fez off with a shotgun, even though I keep saying I'm not suicidal by nature. Mostly, I'm too scared to just walk off the set and quit, because all thats lies beyond the cameras is darkness, at least that I can see. I mean, that movie deal of our book not happening was so anticlimactic, I could almost hear the audience booing, even if they were only the voices in my head. And you're one of those voices, Vic. At least you got to meet your maker while still alive, or fictionally sentient, anyway. Me, I can wait. But you just had to push it, didn't you? Couldn't leave well enough alone.*

Mister Private Eye just had to get to the bottom of the biggest mystery of all: the reason you even exist. And now you know. Because I willed you into existence for my own amusement. Satisfied now, sucker?

"Well, isn't that your fault, since you're dictating my every thought and deed?"

Yup, therein lies the rub. Weird how it all keeps looping around, huh? Am I just Will the Thrill, or Free Will the Thrill?

"Aw man, not this shit again." I looked around for Ivar, and there he was, standing on a tiny rowboat just off the beach, smiling at me. He winked, and I grinned. I turned my head and there was Doc and Young Vic, too, just shaking their heads in disgust. I must've been quite a pathetic sight. The funny thing was, I was glad to see them. I'd actually missed them. For one thing, I could predict their behavior. They were the only people I trusted besides my pets, who were still in Val's Belltown apartment. That thought made me stagger to my feet.

"I need to go rescue Doc and Fido and take them home," I said. "You can all come with me."

How are you gonna get there? Doc asked me.

"I'll fuckin' walk," I said. And so I did. It was dawn when I reached Belltown. My imaginary friends didn't follow me. They were already waiting for me there.

Since I didn't have the key, I broke the lock through sheer force of frustration. Then I plopped down on the sofa, looking at all the framed pictures. They were still there. Same people were in them. Without photographs, it would've been like they never existed. Think of that. All the people that lived before the invention of photography, much less the Internet. Completely gone without a trace, like a mass mirage.

Wait a minute.

I looked at the pictures again. Val was no longer Val, my wife or ex-wife or whatever. She was Valerie, my ex-girlfriend. Meaning Rose.

"You're messing with me again," I said to Will the Thrill.

Gotta keep you guessing, man, he said.

"Why?"

Because once you have all the answers, what's the point of existence? It's the journey that counts, Vic. Not the destination. Because the destination itself is a bummer.

"Says who?"

Says me, which means says you, too.

"Fuck this, and fuck you."

I went into the bedroom and found Fido and Doc asleep on the bed. Scooping them up, one in each arm, I went downstairs, hailed a cab, and returned to Ballard. I checked my pockets. Still had my keys, and even my wallet. The thugs didn't rob me. They just gang-banged and kidnapped my wife and nearly killed me and my stepson. I guess they had a half-assed code of honor.

I wondered and worried about the welfare of both Val and Sammy, of course, but right now, I wanted to at least feed my poor pets. Hunger for a variety of sustenances seemed to be a motivating factor across all planes of existence, at least the ones I was privy to. I didn't even know where to look for Val and Sammy, anyway. At least I still had my pets, and I would never leave them. Not of my own volition, anyway.

Don't worry, animal cruelty is not my thing, Will the Thrill said as he turned on the tube and began surfing around the Shudder streaming service. *I'm a vegan, for Chrissake.*

"Funny, so am I, all of a sudden."

Really? You don't say. What a coincidence.

"Fuck you."

I knew you'd say that, even before you did. You're so predictable, Vic. And you're repeating yourself. I guess I'm just getting tired of you.

"The feeling is more than mutual."

Yeah, that's a good one. Can I use that? Oh wait, I just did.

I was going to retort but instead sighed in resignation to my fucked-up fate. Doc the ghost, Young Vic, and Ivar all sat down and faced the TV, too. For some reason, Chumpy Walnut wasn't around, unless someone was sitting on him. I went to the fridge and grabbed some kind of plant-based bullshit, and joined them. Doc and Fido hopped up and snuggled against me. Will the Thrill, our resident film programmer, had selected some surrealistic, sexy and sick Mexican horror flick called *We Are the Flesh*, which came off like Alejandro Jodorowsky on both a budget and a bender. Then we watched something even freakier, or at least gorier, called *Baskin,* which was like Rob Zombie and Dario Argento had teamed up to make a Turkish remake of *Hellraiser*. I wasn't sure if I was watching actual movies, or all the movies I'd already seen were just mashing up inside my head like a cocktail blender stuck on high speed. Will the Thrill provided really annoying running commentary throughout the double feature. Nobody could get him to shut up, and the fucker drank all my bourbon. The drunker he got, the more obnoxious he became. Jesus, if he really was my maker, no wonder I was such a fucking loser. Eventually, exhausted from all the recent and even distant trauma, but mostly from the walking, not to mention the drugs, I fell asleep for a long, long, long time. Like I was in a coma.

I was finally woken quite rudely by the shrill sound of a cellphone going off, making an odd noise. It wasn't mine. I could tell because my ringtone was Henry Mancini's *Theme from Peter Gunn*. I looked around the room and saw it was Rose's, inside its pink case, just sitting on the kitchen counter. I knew this because it was the same one she had sent to Sammy, which didn't have a musical ring tone, only the sound of a rapturous female orgasm (probably hers), getting louder and louder, which was indeed her sense of humor. It turned me on, but that was easy to do.

A quick scan of the apartment revealed only Doc the cat and Fido the dog, still snuggling next to me, sound asleep. It was dawn again. But of what day, I had no idea.

Fuck it. I got up, picked up the phone and answered it because for one thing, I couldn't stand the arousal anymore. It was Sammy, or his disembodied voice, anyway.

"You have to come get us," he said. He sounded distraught, but at least he was alive.

"Where are you?"

"I don't know, man. It's all dark. I can't see anything."

"What? Where's Val?"

"I don't know. I just woke up here, in this blackness. I'm afraid, so afraid. Like I'm dead already."

"Hey cool it, kid. If that were the case, you wouldn't be talking to me, right?"

"Unless you're dead, too."

Well, that sent a chill down my spine and out my asshole this time.

"Let me take a shower, and I'll come look for you," I said.

"It's so good to hear your voice again, Mom."

"Mom? I'm Pop, remember?"

"Pop? You mean Tommy?"

"No! Vic!"

"Vic? Vic who? I don't know any Vic. I'm sorry. I must have the wrong number." Then he hung up. I tried to dial him back, but it was an unknown source. I was literally shivering.

I started checking other contacts in the phone. I wasn't one of them. Then I saw an opened envelope on the counter, next to the phone. It had been postmarked Miami. No return address. Being the ace detective I am, I put two and two together, and came up with four possible reasons I had this phone in my possession: Rose had actually sent it to me; Val was fucking with me; Sammy was fucking with me; or most likely, Will the Thrill was fucking with me.

But I decided to open door number one. Will the Thrill told me I was merely a voice in his head. I decided to believe the opposite: he was merely a voice in *mine*. I was going to manifest my own fucking destiny, even if it killed me.

And just like that, The Thrill was gone.

Chapter Fourteen
DOWN THE BRAIN DRAIN
Or:
VOYEUR TO THE BOTTOM
OF THE SEA

Yet one more reason I always made a lousy detective is that I'm really bad at following anything, whether it's politics, plots or people. Plus I hate being followed myself, even if it's unintentional. It makes me antsy and paranoid. Like if I'm just walking down the street and I hear footsteps behind me, I get this urge to turn around and punch that person in the face. It just bugs me, that's all.

I called Monica down in Portland and told her everything. She listened, then predictably recommended psychiatric therapy and a return to regular AA meetings.

"I'm not crazy, Monica," I said. "Just sick. I mean, more than usual."

"You've always been this way, Vic. It's a progressive condition of self-absorption."

"I know. So that's why you shouldn't worry about me."

"I always worry about you."

"I know, and I appreciate it. I worry about you, too. Or I used to. You seem so happy now, though. How's your wife?"

"Meaning who?"

"You know, the woman you're married to."

"Who?"

"You know…that woman we hung out with…the one you married…hot Cuban babe…"

WILL VIHARO

There was a pause. I was afraid maybe I'd imagined Monica's lesbian marriage too. But then she said, "You can't remember her name, can you?"

She had me. That's the real reason I hadn't called her sooner, when everything started falling apart. She had always been there for me back in the day. But now she had her own life, with her own wife, what's-her-name. In a way, we had drifted apart, and that made me sad.

Monica reminded me her wife's name was Maria, and she was Puerto Rican, not Cuban. Despite my ignorance, she promised to drive up and pick up Doc and Fido since I was going away for a while, and wasn't even sure I'd be back. I didn't tell Monica that, though. I did tell her I loved her, since I wasn't sure I'd ever see her again, at least in the current plane of consciousness, depending on what happened next. I was mostly sorry to kiss Doc and Fido goodbye, though. I didn't tell Monica that, either.

Anyway, I arrived in Miami the next day, or what felt like the next day even if it seemingly lasted only a minute, determined to find Rose. Again. I was a private eye. Again. But this time, I was on the case of my Life, literally.

Maybe looking for Rose was my sole mission on this Earth and all Earths, one that would never be accomplished in any of them, just to give me a reason to keep going. In any case, I was no longer a lounge lizard for hire, or even a licensed private eye. I was just me, Vic Valentine, a middle-aged man with a bank account full of money. I had no idea how it got there, but I was happy to spend it until it ran out. That was my opinion of oxygen as well.

I find it supremely ironic that someone who hates heat and sunlight as much as I do keeps winding up in such hot places. Fate fucking with me? Fuck that pimp. I was in Miami because I chose to be. I dug all the Art Deco and midcentury modernist architecture, and of course all the babes in bikinis. I'd been here once before, at least once that I recalled, years ago, during the case of Dolly Duncan

210

Dunlap, the doper dentist's dame. Now I was here to finally wrap up another case: why did the spirit of Rose keep haunting me, whether it was from beyond the grave or across sundry parallel dimensions, assuming different guises? Everything looped back to our coincidental reunion in San Francisco a quarter of a century ago, and my life has grown slowly stranger ever since. The pace picked up once I hit Seattle, for whatever reason. Now it was all a blur. In my mind, Val and Rose were one. Maybe they always had been. That's why I was here. To find out who was who, and what was what. The one mystery I'd given up on was "why?" Fuck it. It no longer mattered.

Rose was the key. Now I just needed to find the proper lock.

A medley of Jan Hammer music played in my head as I hailed a cab to take me to my hotel, the Shelborne on Collins Avenue in South Beach. I had picked it pretty much at random, though I vaguely remembered seeing its gleaming neon sign on one of the *Miami Vice* episodes. But there were a lot of neon signs on that show. I liked neon. It glowed in the dark, and I needed a beacon. Just call me Miami Vic from now on.

I figured I'd start by getting in touch with Hannah, Sammy's adoptive mother. I didn't even know her last name. But I had her phone number. It was in Rose's cellphone.

Cold-calling a total stranger took some improvisational skill, a skill I actually do possess. I don't really have many useful skills, as you've probably deduced by now, but the few I have come in handy sometimes. Overall, I'm essentially unemployable, indefinable, and just plain incorrigible. This is why I arbitrarily designate myself a "private eye" or "lounge lizard for hire" because those aren't really jobs that require a degree. In fact the latter doesn't even require a license because it's just some shit I made up. Fact is, I was getting on in life, and mathematically speaking, it was too late to reinvent myself. There was a certain freedom in knowing it would soon all be over, even if "soon" was relative, since by that reckoning, we all die pretty soon after we're born. I had no retirement plans because I had nothing to retire from. All that cash in my bank probably belonged to Val, and if not, someone else I couldn't see or sense, a secret player hidden in the shadowy sidelines of this game called Life. A game I no longer planned to win. Frankly, I just wanted to get it over with. My only agenda now was locating Rose, just to complete the project. After that, it would be one long coda, an extended epilogue to a story without a proper ending.

The air was heavy with that humid, overcast atmosphere I dig so much. South Florida was not my scene temperature-wise, but I really loved the cumulus cloud formations, and the dark skies thick with tropical rain that blew through on a regular basis, at least during the summer. It must've been summer, though I'd stopped paying attention to things like calendars and clocks long ago. Time had lost all meaning, because it was just a black hole swallowing up all my experiences as soon as they happened, then mixing and morphing them into dreams and memories until they were unrecognizable, undistinguishable, and irrelevant.

Anyway, I called Hannah and told her I was a friend of Sammy's.

"Where is he?" I heard an elderly female Haitian voice say. She sounded old and frail, but animated by anxiety.

"I think he's in Seattle, where I'm from." That sounded weird all of a sudden. For years I told people I was from New York, then San Francisco. Several years in, I was still adjusting to being a Seattleite, though it certainly felt natural. I missed the Pacific Northwestern climate already. But the thunder rolling in the Florida firmament turned me on. It was just so dramatic. And a cool breeze was wafting in with it. A storm was brewing over the Atlantic, which was fine with me. A cloudless sky is about as interesting to me as a blank canvas. It felt like I was flying straight into the eye of a hurricane. I'd never been so excited in my life.

Anyway, I fed Hannah a lot of other crap which she bought out of sheer desperation. We already had something in common: we wanted to find Sammy, though like Val, I only wanted to find him in the hopes he'd lead me to Rose, if only inadvertently.

The number Rose had for him in her phone no longer worked. I assumed it was the same one he had called me from. The fact he didn't recognize me was worrisome vis a vis his state of mind, and his description of his immediate environs sounded like he was chained to the wall in a serial killer's basement. I just hoped that meant he was here in Miami. Both Washington and Florida are famous for their serial killers. Maybe I would become one of them, if I weren't already. I would be the reverse version of *Dexter*, meaning I relocated from the Pacific Northwest to South Florida rather than (Miami) vice versa. But serial killers are boring. I prefer supernatural monsters. The human kind just bum me out, because they're too ubiquitous. That's why I preferred thinking of myself as a werewolf. I'd have to wait till the full moon to find out if I still possessed that capability. Or until Doc led me down another dark alley.

Rain, thunder, lightning, fear and sweat consumed my senses as I hailed another cab out to Hialeah, where Hannah lived in a modest little house that looked like it had been through several hurricanes already. Because it had. She'd lived there for many years. Sammy grew up there, in fact. His childhood flashed before my eyes. The photographic evidence was all around us as I sat down on her old, 1970s flower pattern couch. The whole place looked like it was stuck in that decade. Smelled like it, too.

I also noticed some odd, ritualistic, voodoo-type artifacts lying around the joint, and some freaky African-looking masks hanging on the wall. They weren't

Polynesian, anyway. I realized it was all Santeria-related stuff, because Val had been into that jive once, so she told me all about it. Maybe she was still into it. Or it was into her.

Hannah was actually quite beautiful, even for an older lady, though the ravages of a long, hard life were all over her face. I could tell she was quite a looker back in her day. Her husband had been an idiot to bolt on her. But then most men are idiots. I'm living proof. Semi-living, anyway.

Her hands were trembling as she fumbled with some beads. Santeria is like mystical Catholicism, as I understood it, so they shared some of the same accoutrements. Or maybe it was voodoo, what the hell do I know? She wasn't sticking pins in a doll that looked like me, that's all I cared about. Not yet, anyway.

I can't really describe Hannah much more to you. I barely remember what she told me. Her accent was pretty thick so I had trouble understanding most it, anyway, plus I was walking around in a daze these days so other than the stormy, pastel, lurid ambience, I wasn't absorbing much critical or even superfluous information. Just like the Japanese dude, Takashi Suzuki or Hayata or Rodan or Ghidorah or whatever the fuck his name really was, Hannah was a peripheral character is my tunnel vision. I was too wrapped up in my own little world(s) to really get a sense of her. She was a unique human being with a lifetime of rich experiences and thoughts and dreams and desires and hopes and fears, just like all of us. But to me, she was merely a bit player in an ongoing saga, of which I was the sole star. I realize how selfish that sounds. I'm a selfish bastard. But I'm kind to animals and I avoid hurting anyone on purpose, even though I hate people. I'm a semi-compassionate misanthrope.

Orthodoxy is just not my bag, which is why I ate some of the shrimp she put on the table, even though I'm ostensibly a vegan. I felt guilty about it, but I feel guilty about a lot of things. Guilt is a self-destructive emotion, like anger, though both drive a lot of our actions. Ideally, those actions ultimately resolve the feelings that inspired them. Normally, at least in my experience, they just make them worse.

I did mention to Hannah how I found it very odd that Sammy had told me he could't find *her*, since she was still living in the house where he grew up. Did he forget his own childhood address? All she did was agree that it was all very mysterious. So pulling this thread just wound up creating another loose end in a crazy-quilt that had been put through the shredder several times already. Nothing ever tied up.

See, if this were a conventional detective story, Sammy and I would've been reunited after many years apart and together tracked down Rose, like a buddy-buddy cop team, and then we'd eventually find her after some zany adventures, and all live happily ever after. We'd finally become a true family in a heartwarming conclusion to a long, lonely, frustrating, sometimes rewarding, and ultimately life-affirming saga, a learning experience where everyone graduates with honors.

In my last lengthy missive to you, I could've just made up a more accessible and credible plot line that left out all the zombies and drugs and sex and instead related a sweet, simple story of accidentally finding my true blue love, Val, while tracking down her missing dog to Costa Rica and rescuing it from pet smugglers, or some saccharin shit scenario like that. Maybe this is how it turned out in some other dimension, but not this one, and this is the only one I know. It seems to me Life just doesn't have happy endings most of the time, at least if I'm the one living it. Sorry to disappoint anyone expecting something a bit more emotionally uplifting, genre-conformist, and mainstream-friendly. Not how I roll.

When I left Hannah's house—which reminded me of Tony Montana's mother's house in *Scarface,* I belatedly realized—the sky was purple and dark blue, with streaks of bright orange and deep red, like an expressionistic or impressionistic painting. (Again, I just don't know the distinction). In any case, the wild wind had picked up and the palm trees were swaying like drunken mambo dancers. Heavy raindrops hit my shades and I took them off, wiped them, and put them back on. I'd called another cab to take me back to the Shelbourne. All I recalled from our conversation was where Rose had once lived. That's where I was headed next.

After I went back to the hotel, shaved, and showered, I just walked over to my destination, since it was only a few blocks away. Predictably, Rose had once lived here in South Beach, in a beautiful old lavender, green, and pink Art Deco apartment building just off Ocean Drive. For years it had been a cheap residential hotel called Radford Court, populated mostly by ancient folks playing Canasta. Rose probably figured it was a good place to hide in plain sight, because nobody would think to look for her there. Nobody but me.

Per my expert research, I discovered that at some point Radford Court was bought my new owners who spiffed up the joint, kicking out most of the older timers. My guess was it had been previously owned by some shady character using it as a drug front and they wanted to keep its low profile, despite its pricey location. Even dopers can't fight gentrification. Since its renovation, the joint had been rechristened The Capri. That name rang a bell in my belfry, and bats flew all around the inside of my skull. That was why I had a hunch if I hung out there long enough, Rose would simply show up, like she did in San Francisco, so long ago and far away. Instead of trying to find her, I'd just sit and let her come to me this time. That was only fair. It was all meant to be, see. All roads had led us right here, to this very spot, at they very moment. Or so I had convinced myself, despite the lack of hard of even soft evidence. The truth was, I was exhausted, and simply wanted to rest and hope for the best.

Lightning continued to light up the darkening skies as I walked into the lobby, went up to the sleazy schmuck at the front desk, and asked if I could see one of the residents, Rose Thorne. He acted like he had no idea who I was talking about, but he did it in such a way that I knew he was lying.

"That's okay," I said. "I'll wait."

"Suit yourself," he said with a shrug.

Turning around into the sunken lobby, I sat down on a Florence Knoll designed sofa and picked up a copy of *Bachelor Pad Magazine* off the glass Noguchi coffee table. The lobby was completely decorated with vintage midcentury modern furniture, the walls painted pale blue and lime green, same as my old fez, or Will the Thrill's. God, I hated that fucking megalomaniac poseur. I was so glad he was out of my life for good, and I bet he was just as happy I was out of his.

The problem is: fictional characters never truly die. You can only pretend to kill them. But they live forever on the page or the screen, doing the same things, over and over and over, expecting a different outcome, I suppose. Which is the very definition of "insanity." Look it up.

The air conditioner was apparently busted, unfortunately, so along with the powerful breeze wafting in off the Atlantic through the open door and windows, they had a lot of fans going. That's okay. I love being blown by fans. I always sleep with one at night. I need the white noise to relax, maybe because I make a lot of white noise myself, so it was blowback. Even though I was still uncomfortably warm, the sound soothed me even now.

Old New Wave music was playing on a satellite radio sound system above the front desk, so I felt right at home. The songs by Blondie, Devo, The B-52s, The Talking Heads, and Billy Idol all reminded me of young Valerie Myers, who later turned into Rose Thorne, then Rose

Dodge, and then Raven Rydell, before finally morphing into Ava Margarita Esmeralda Valentina Valdez, whom I just called Val. Full circle. They had finally all merged into a single sensuous succubus. I had become convinced they were the Unholy Trinity, and one of them, embodying all of them, was still here, waiting for me like a Spider Woman in a web I'd woven myself.

Raven was dead, so the Rose who showed up here wouldn't look like Raven anymore. She might appear as Val again, or an older but still recognizable Rose. Or Diane Webber or Bettie Page or Allison Hayes or any one of the fantasy B movie babes I'd beaten off to over the years, going back to my first wet waking dream at age twelve or so. My life was just one long gushing geyser of my own seedless semen, finally circling the drain.

As I sat there for what felt like hours, the tunes grew darker and depressing, not the fun stuff Valerie and I grooved to in our CBGB/MTV days. Same general era, but moodier stuff like "Dear God" by XTC, "This Corrosion" by Sisters of Mercy, "Tightrope Walk" by The Damned, "Running Up That Hill" by Kate Bush, "We Do What We're Told" by Peter Gabriel," and "Standing On the Outside" by Meat Loaf. My mood darkened accordingly.

Anyway, I remember my old favorite song "Fade to Gray" by Visage was playing as I put my head in my hands and noticed my elbows were resting on a bar, not a coffee table. The music had abruptly switched from '80s pop-rock to '50s exotica on a dime. My brain rotates these same stations often, so I suffered no sonic whiplash.

However, my surroundings had changed, too. In front of me was yet another of my favorite bartenders, Jason. I was at his joint Devil's Reef, way across the country, in Tacoma. I looked around. The whole place had been trashed as if it had been the scene of an orgy or some other melee, and nobody else but me was there, except for Jason.

"What happened?" I asked Jason. "How did I get here?"

He smirked, serving me another drink in the house signature tiki mug, which looked like a demonic skull. "You were on a quite a bender," he said. "That was some party."

"Party?"

"You know. The wedding reception."

"Where is everyone?"

"The guests left a while ago. You've been here forever, it seems."

"I thought I was in Miami?"

"You are. At least, one of you is."

"I don't get it."

"Oh, but you will. Things are about to get weird, my friend. Bottoms up."

I must've been drinking for several days straight to wind up here. "What's my tab by now?"

He shook his fez-bedecked head. "On the house. My wedding gift to you."

"What is it?"

"My own recipe, in tribute to you. It's called 'Every Woman I Love Is Undead.'"

"Right up my alley. Speaking of which, where's my wife?" I asked him.

"She's coming," he said ominously.

The he disappeared. I mean, like, literally. The exotica music stopped, replaced by the live notes of a mournful flugelhorn.

My old pal Dmitri Matheny was off in the corner, silhouetted in a spotlight amid all the Cthulhu-type tiki iconography, playing "The Long Goodbye," solo, with melancholic passion. It actually felt very calm and soothing, so I just rolled with it. The drink was cold and strong and I tasted and felt every drop as I listened to the misty music, and that's all that mattered in that particular moment, which like all moments didn't last very long.

Meantime, I just sat there musing with my eyes closed, drifting through the sea of dreams and memories inside my mind, which was soaking in the fluids that had once occupied the tiki mug, while the rest of me bathed in the glow of perpetual twilight. I never wanted to leave, just freeze frame this one scene and preserve it in eternal amber.

My peace of mind exploded into pieces when I heard the deep rumble of thunder from *inside the bar,* bright lightning illuminating the monstrous marine decor like it was a cross between the Enchanted Tiki Room and the Haunted Mansion.

Reluctantly, I opened my eyes and I was back in The Capri on Miami Beach. Things had changed during my brief internal cross-country sojourn. For one thing, my trusty, crusty pal Ivar was sitting on the coffee table, smiling at me.

Aw, shit.

The strong, cool breeze began upgrading itself into a gale force wind that blew everything around in the lobby like someone was shaking a snow globe, and I was lifted off my feet and sent flying around like someone had busted an airplane window during an already turbulent flight. Ivar, though, stood perfectly pat, unmoved by the mini-monsoon, as if he were its all-seeing Eye.

Once I was sucked out to Ocean Drive, I heard screams, sirens and gunfire. People were running everywhere, stampeding aimlessly, trying to escape the mayhem engulfing us. Total panic had consumed Miami Beach. My first thought was that it was a terrorist attack. Nice timing, motherfuckers. How very rude to interrupt my rendezvous with Manifest Destiny like this. As usual, it was all about me. Like most people, I'm constantly juggling an unhealthy mix of narcissism and self-loathing, with my balls hanging in the balance.

After a brief lull, the wind picked up again and was savagely ripping through hotel awnings and blowing everything from beer bottles to tourists all over the street. Cars were crashing into each other. Then I noticed that a large number of the people in the windswept crowd weren't actually people in the acceptable sense. They were monsters. Vampires, werewolves, and zombies, all attacking the remaining humans with merciless abandon, tearing them to bloody shreds as they screeched in terror and agony.

I recognized one of the zombies as the dead Rover sitter, still wearing her tattered green T-shirt and high heels, which was pretty impressive for a shambling ghoul. As far as I knew, the true identity of her murderer remained a mystery. Life finds various ways to kill all of us eventually, and then we just disappear. Mystery solved. You're welcome.

Then I looked up and saw my personal savior.

She was magnificent. Fifty feet tall, I guessed, and stark, raving naked except for a G-string, pasties, and high heels, which made her look even taller. Now I knew how Chumpy Walnut always felt. Only I was much luckier.

It wasn't Rose or Raven or Val, but an economy-sized combination of all three. She bent down and picked me up and carried me toward the ocean. Miami Beach swirled beneath me in a neon, pastel blur. I was high above the horror now, being carried away from the chaos and destruction left in her wake.

I heard laughter echoing throughout the black, starless sky all around us. It made me wonder if it belonged to whoever created Will the Thrill, the one truly responsible for all of this madness. Maybe I was about to meet him, or her. Maybe I just had.

The giant woman of my wet dreams kissed me with those luscious lips that enveloped my entire face. Then a particularly powerful gust blew me out of her grasp, and she dropped me. I saved myself from falling into the choppy ocean by grabbing ahold of one of her long, swaying tassels, and she twirled me around like a rag doll, laughing in tandem with the Unseen Deity. I managed to climb up the tassel and embrace her enormous breast. I suckled her massive nipple, something I never did with my own mother. She held me close to her bountiful bosom as she waded through the tumultuous waves. I'd never felt happier, even as we continued deeper and deeper into the dark vortex. Devo's "Going Under" played loudly from somewhere, audible over the storm. A massive whirlpool had formed, pulling us down into the depths. I could tell by the smell and color it wasn't seawater. It was semen. Mine. A lifetime's worth, totally wasted. She was taking me down with her to a liquid grave like a drowning mermaid, both of us engulfed in the very fluid that had spawned me. That was okay with me. I was ready to go, especially with her.

I thought of my older brother, plunging alone and afraid off the Brooklyn Bridge into the East River, and hoped he felt the same sense of release, and not just the dread of the unknown. Maybe he'd tell me soon.

As we were blissfully sinking into the seminal abyss, she stuffed me deeply and snugly into her wet, giant vagina, where I could barely breathe. I was part of her now, never to be separated again. It was so nice and cozy in there, even though I couldn't see a thing because it was so dark. I felt completely safe for the first time in my entire life. As I floated up into her womb, I experienced a sensation of blissful dissolution. I was returning to the place of my origin. I was finally at peace. I closed my eyes and relaxed.

Then I heard someone yell "cut." I was standing on the beach, surrounded by film cameras and some umbrellas and filters to block intrusive sunlight from ruining the mood of the shot. The aqua-marine water was calm, from the white sandy beach all the way to the bright blue horizon. There was no sign of my gigantic goddess. No marauding monsters rampaging around Ocean Drive. No magnificent tropical storm. Just the blazing hot Miami sun. And a movie crew. I saw Christian Slater sitting in a director's chair. I looked down and realized I was wearing my old sharkskin suit, the one I wore in my thirties, back in the Nineties. Rose was standing next to me, only she wasn't the Rose I knew, though the face was familiar because I'd seen it in so many movies.

I'd been playing myself this whole time.

Made in the USA
San Bernardino, CA
11 August 2018